Jonah's Redemption: The Complete Series

An Amish Romance

SYLVIA PRICE

ISBN: 979-8-6681-8269-5

CONTENTS

CONTENTS

CONTENTS

BOOK 5

BOOK 1

CHAPTER 1

When Mary Lou awoke, the birds were chirping, and the sun was just starting to rise. She had gone to bed early because she knew that she was going to have trouble sleeping. Today was not any ordinary today. Today, instead of rising to help her mother with the morning chores and preparing breakfast for her brothers and father, she had a different task. She had packed a trunk with her few belongings, and as soon as her father was done with the morning chores, he was going to hitch up the cart and take her to the city.

Mary Lou had turned 18 that winter, and she had decided that she wanted to go on *rumspringa*. *Rumspringa* was taken by young people as they reached adulthood within the community, in order to determine whether the Amish way of life was what they wanted for the rest of their lives. There were different ways to do *rumspringa*, from simply having English friends to getting a job in the city. Mary Lou had decided that she would work in the city for a year, and if at the end of the year, she were still certain of her choice to stay Amish, she would return to her community.

Mary Lou had found a job as a seamstress, something at which she excelled with her own clothes. She was given a small apartment above the shop. To everyone who knew her, it was a surprise, because she was one of the most devout young women in the entire Amish community. She read her Bible daily, memorized scripture, and prayed even as she completed her chores. No one could imagine her separating herself from the community even for a moment.

Mary Lou was reasonably certain that she was going to return to the community. She loved everything about the Amish lifestyle; from the people, the simplicity, the grace of God evident through every tradition and custom, to the silence in which she could hear God's still, small voice in every moment. The city, however, was big, and loud, and filled with distractions. Nevertheless, she felt as though she would miss an opportunity if she didn't at least experience *rumspringa*. She was certain that it would bring her closer to God, and so she had informed her parents that she wanted to try.

It seemed like a brave decision to be met with when the day to move out finally arrived. On that morning, though, Mary Lou was a bundle of nerves. A year was a long time, and while work would keep her busy, she wasn't sure what she was going to do with the rest of her time. Free time amongst the Amish is scarce. What would she do? With no family with whom she might speak, she was at pains to imagine how she would fill her time with work so as not to be tempted by the devil from idle hands.

It was going to be a hard year, but Mary Lou tried to see it as a challenge. The Lord was inviting her to grow closer to Him. She would test her theory that she could maintain her faith in God anywhere because God was everywhere with her, although she kept this to herself.

Mary Lou rose and splashed water on her face from the washbasin before putting on the one dress that she had not packed. It was her warmest dress that she had sewn last year, chosen because she could still see the frost gripping to her bedroom window as though it were trying desperately to come in from the cold. She made her way downstairs for her usual breakfast routine with her mother, only to be surprised that breakfast was already made.

"*Maem*," Mary Lou said. "I was prepared to assist you."

"Today is special," her mother said. "I wanted you to rest."

"Idle hands make the devil's work," Mary Lou reminded her, but she sat down to eat, nonetheless. When she heard her father outside, she realized that she had slept in. He was back from the barn and setting up the cart. "Thank you, though. I shall miss you very much."

"I shall miss you, too," her mother said. "Please write often. And remember that you can always come home for a visit. Just find a phone and call John at the general store. We will come and pick you up."

"I appreciate that," Mary Lou smiled at her mother. "But I am also sure I will be fine. At least, I will be fine for a little while. It will bring me closer to the Lord."

"I know it will," her mother said. "Now, eat up. You want to make sure that you have a full stomach before you begin your journey."

"It's not that far," Mary Lou teased. She dug into the homemade oatmeal to satiate her appetite and settle the butterflies in her tummy. Her adventure excited her and stressed her. Food was her greatest comfort.

"It's not that far," repeated her mother, "but it is a different world."

"Aye, that it is," Mary Lou agreed.

Once Mary Lou was finished with breakfast, she found her siblings to say goodbye. It seemed surreal that after much planning, the day was finally here. She made sure she had everything that she wanted in her trunk before her father helped her carry it down the stairs and loaded it into the cart.

"Now, if you need anything…"

"I know! *Maem* already told me," Mary Lou said with a smile. "She said if I needed anything, then I could call the general store and you would come get me."

"I will," her father said. "It is not that I don't support your *rumspringa*, Mary Lou, or your reasons. I will worry about you every day until your return, though."

3

"I appreciate it, *Daed*," Mary Lou said tenderly, hoping to comfort her father and to stop herself from crying. "And I know everything will be well. I will come out of this with a new appreciation for sewing and a new love for the Lord."

"That is not always the outcome of *rumspringa*," her father opined. Mary Lou nodded knowingly. The English life, with its leisure and conveniences, was tempting. She reminded herself to be always on her guard.

"Well, it will be the outcome of mine," she assured him. "I promise."

As they drew nearer to the city, its sounds increased exponentially. It was noise like Mary Lou had never heard before, like infants screaming for their mothers' milk in an empty church as a carpenter hammered together a pew in a thunderstorm. It was a wonder how anyone could understand anything. The babbles and honks, the cheers and cries, the anger and the violent motions were as deafening as they were blinding. Mary Lou closed one eye as she flinched from the initial shock. It seemed like everyone who lived in the town was out and about with their dog and nagging mother.

"Here we are," her father exclaimed, at last. He pulled the cart up in front of the seamstress shop. Mary Lou got out and looked about. She stood on a sidewalk, though she did not know what it was, and looked down at the black road under the horses' hooves.

The gray seamstress shop had bold, white lettering across its dirty window telling the world what it was. Its glass door was decorated with the shop's hours of operation and a sign advertising the dates for a Chinese dance show. Mary Lou noticed a lovely lady flying through the air in what she could only describe as her legs telling the other dancers beneath her that it was a quarter to three. Mary Lou had never seen such a costume—a dress the color of jade and sleeves like the waves of the ocean—nor such a posture in a lady before. Another sign beneath the door's handle showed a pine tree with an angel at its top and lights all around it. The writing was too small to read. The whole façade of the shop could be quaint if it were equipped with a green awning and some window dressing like the lovely three-piece suit in the shop next door, or the purses in the next shop window.

Conscious that they were the center of attention to the multitude of passersby, Mary Lou decided to act. "I'll go into the shop and get the key. They said it would be waiting for me if Deliah wasn't there."

"I'll wait here," her father said. People stared at him from their car windows as he blocked a lane. Mary Lou ignored it all and headed into the shop. Sure enough, there was a key waiting for her at the front desk. Her new boss, Deliah, was off that day, but one of the girls who would be her colleague greeted her and instructed her to be at work at 8 a.m. the next morning. Mary Lou agreed, and then went back out to her father.

"Shall we?" Mary Lou said, as she unlocked the door beside the shop. Her little apartment was at the top of the stairs. Her father carried her trunk briskly up to the landing while Mary Lou struggled with the lock to the apartment door.

"Wow," Mary Lou said, as she looked around. It was furnished with furniture from all corners of the earth. None of the colors matched, the ottoman was a dysentery brown while the easy chair was beige with spots of tea stains, and the coffee table was filthy white. Her kitchen table was round with two chairs, a blue plastic patio one and a mahogany brown one. Her utensils included a plastic spoon, a serrated steak knife, two butter knives, four silver forks, and three chopsticks. A bright red refrigerator stood humming in the corner next to the sink, while the black electric stove and oven bookended the counter. She opened the door to a black contraption with *Samsung* written across the top, to find that it had a fitted, round plate at the bottom. She could only imagine what it was for. She marveled at the light turning on and off as she opened and closed the door.

In the bedroom, her father raised an eyebrow as he shook the bed frame with his hand.

"Make sure that you test this out before spending a full night on it," he said. "I'm not sure who made this, but it seems unstable."

"I'll be okay, *Daed*," Mary Lou said to him. "Really, I will be. I think it's lovely."

"It's certainly different," her father replied. He moved toward the washroom to see if the plumbing worked. There were brown stains on the white porcelain of the tub and sink. The clownfish shower curtain had mold on its bottom corners. The toilet bowl had a seat but no lid, and the toilet paper was missing.

"Yes, it is. And I think it will be delightful," she declared stoically.

"Well then…" her father retorted, unconvinced, "is there anything else you need?"

"That's all," she replied. "You still have your evening chores to do, so I don't want to keep you."

"What will you do for the rest of the day?" he asked.

"Figure out how some of this works," she let out with laughter. She wasn't used to living with electricity. Many of the Amish found that modern conveniences distracted them from the things of God. Having seen through her living room window the plethora of pedestrians staring blankly into the bright devices in their palms, Mary Lou wasn't surprised. *Rumspringa* would be the only time in her life when she would have electricity, unless she decided to work outside of the community. She had a vague idea of how it all worked. Her sense of adventure would allow her to figure it all out through trial and error. "I will write to you soon. Thank you for bringing me here, *Daed*."

"You take care of yourself, Mary Lou," her father said, as he embraced her. "And write home if you need anything at all."

"I will," she assured him.

Mary Lou waved to her father as he mounted the cart and coaxed the horses to move. It was only then that she realized that she had no food. She hadn't quite thought ahead to her next meal and felt daunted by finding a shop on top of discovering how to cook with electricity. *Welcome to rumspringa*, she thought.

It was unlikely that there would be a market in the middle of the week in the city. Mary Lou needed to know where the English got their food. She took her keys and a woven bag from her trunk, and then headed downstairs. She planned to ask her new colleagues where there was a food shop, and hopefully find out if there was a market at least once a week. Shopping at a local market would make her feel at home. She knew that her own community had a market in the city once a month, but for the most part, their goods were sold a bit closer to home. Her heart skipped at the thought of discovering English ways.

The seamstress shop was busy when Mary Lou walked in, so she waited at the front as a few women dropped off and picked up their orders with the seamstresses. She knew that it was one of the only shops in town that still did hand stitching, which is why she had applied.

Mary Lou had no idea how to use a sewing machine or even an electric iron. This environment would suit her, and she could see that there was plenty of work to keep her busy.

The shop bell rang, and a man walked in carrying several boxes. "Pardon me."

Mary Lou moved to the side.

"Jonah, can you just put that in the corner?" someone called to him. "We'll deal with it once we close."

"There's not a lot of room up here," Jonah responded. Curious to see the man, Mary Lou looked up at him. The name *Jonah* wasn't a typical English one. She knew that there were a few Amish men who worked in the city, but this Jonah was dressed as an English man.

When he caught sight of her, however, his eyes widened. Mary Lou assumed he was reacting to the fact that she was dressed in Amish attire, with a white cap on her head, a long-sleeved dress with a high neckline, thick woolen stockings, and comfortable boots.

"There's room here," she said, as she found another place to stand. "I won't be here long; I've only a question to ask."

He shook his head and put the boxes down. "Sure, that's fine. Everyone is going to trip over it, but that's fine."

"Oh," she said, taken aback by his attitude. "Those boxes look sturdy. I'm sure it will be okay."

"Sure," he said. "You Amish know best, don't you?"

"No, I...," she said, but he shook his head and held up his hand as though to silence her.

"Whatever." He turned and called into the shop, "I'll send you the invoice," and then was gone.

Mary Lou stood stunned. Had she said something wrong? Was it not her place to suggest where he might place the boxes? She was certain that her tone had been pleasant.

"Don't mind Jonah," a lady in the shop said, looking at her from atop her glasses. The thick, dark frames were perched perfectly at the tip of her nose. Her auburn hair and pale skin softened her countenance, but her blue eyes betrayed sternness, perhaps even severity. Mary Lou wondered if she had a temper. She was sat upon a stool before a table, hemming a pair of beige trousers. She held a sewing needle in one hand and a spool of thread in the other. "He's always like that. He's harmless."

"That's all right," Mary Lou exclaimed nervously with a wave of her hand. "I try not to judge others because we are all guilty of sin every day."

"Sure," the girl said bluntly. "I'm Jessica, by the way."

"Mary Lou," she said, even though she was sure the girl already knew that. "I was just looking for somewhere to purchase or pick food?"

"Like...a restaurant?" Jessica asked.

"No," Mary Lou said. "A market, perhaps, or a grocer?"

"Oh, like that," Jessica said. "Sure. I'll mark it on one of those tourist maps that we keep handy. Hold on."

"Wonderful," Mary Lou said. She had never set foot in an English-style grocery store, so she was both excited and nervous.

While Jessica was drawing the map, her mind drifted back to Jonah. Who was he, and why was he so abrupt with her? He was young, perhaps a little older than she was, and she couldn't imagine what would have happened to make him so bitter at such a young age. She hoped that he was simply having a bad day, but there was something about his eyes that made her think it was worse than that. She didn't know why, but she hoped that she saw him again, if only to pray for him.

CHAPTER 2

Mary Lou rose with the sun, eager to start her first day of work. She didn't know exactly what she was going to be doing, but she did not want to be late. She decided to make herself a simple breakfast of oatmeal with milk, purchased at the English grocer the previous evening. Upon struggling with the electric range for 20 minutes before she could warm her food, she appreciated the wisdom of her choice. Anything more complex and she would have been late. It seemed to her as though electricity made things more difficult.

Dressed and ready to go with 15 minutes to spare, Mary Lou decided that it was too early to head down. It would be luxurious to pack her lunch using a premade sandwich she'd purchased from the store, and it would kill some time. With her scarf around her neck and her coat bundled, she headed next door for work.

Mary Lou pushed open the door, and Deliah, the woman with whom she interviewed, was there waiting. She was a slender woman, whose eyes seemed to disappear into her cheeks whenever she smiled, which accentuated her doorknob-like chin. She had straight, shoulder-length black hair like a Chinese woman, but her features seemed muddled to Mary Lou. She crossed her slender fingers below her belt line and tilted her head when she looked happily at the Amish girl. She wore a bright red woolen shirt with a neckline too low for a conservative girl like Mary Lou and too high for any English man to notice. Her jeans seemed to caress her thighs and calves before slipping nicely into black, laced, thick-heeled boots that could not possibly keep her feet warm in the winter.

"Mary Lou!" she said. "How lovely to see you."

"Good morning," Mary Lou said, with a smile.

"You got all settled in last night?"

"I did," Mary Lou replied. "And I am happy to report that I managed to cook myself breakfast without burning down the apartment."

"Well, that's the important thing, then," Deliah said. "Come and meet Jessica."

"Yes, we met yesterday," Jessica said, as she looked up from her work. She was fixing someone's ripped wedding dress. Her stitches were so small as to be nearly invisible. Mary Lou wanted to compliment her, but the conversation quickly shifted. "The poor girl had a run-in with Jonah at his usual."

"Ah," Deliah said. "I apologize for that. I don't know what he did, but I assume he was a jerk."

"No, it was fine," Mary Lou said right away, not wanting to cause trouble on her first day. "I was standing in his way."

"You weren't," Jessica said sternly. "Jonah just had a fit because he saw that you were Amish."

"Oh," Mary Lou replied, and hung her head. "Well, I mean...I am used to people reacting in surprise..." her voice trailed off as she wondered what this meant. Jessica finished her stitch before she continued.

"Oh, it's not like that," Jessica informed her. "He used to be Amish and now he's not."

Mary Lou was surprised. She held her breath.

"Really?" she finally let out. "I mean, I assumed with a name like Jonah that he might be."

"Yeah, there's some complicated story behind it," Jessica shrugged. "All we know is he was thrown out."

"He was shunned?" Mary Lou gasped. She didn't know

anyone who had been shunned from the community. To be shunned from the community at a young age meant that he must have done something unforgivable. She was curious, but the Amish were not to gossip. She was unsure of what to say next.

"Don't know," Jessica said, "but, he's grumpy to everyone, and especially anyone Amish. Like I said, though, his bark is worse than his bite. I wouldn't worry about him. He delivers for our top supplier, and the products are awesome, so we tolerate him."

Mary Lou turned away to ponder the news. It seemed no mere coincidence. Why had God placed her in a shop that had regular contact with someone who had been shunned? How could she discover her purpose? Usually, she'd walk through the woods to pray, but the city was poorer for trees. Perhaps He would speak to her as she read scripture in the morning; she would have to improve her time at making breakfast with electricity if she were to have enough time. What could he have done? What could she do to earn his trust?

"Why don't you sit beside Jessica, for the first day?" Deliah suggested, shaking Mary Lou out of her trance and bringing the Amish girl back to the task at hand. "She can give you a rundown of the day-to-day operations, and then tomorrow, you can start on your own projects."

"That sounds wonderful," Mary Lou smiled. "I am looking forward to working on something that isn't my sisters' dresses that I have mended a hundred times."

Jessica laughed and pointed to a stool behind her, as if telling her to fetch it. She made space beside her so that the two might fit at the table. Mary Lou sat down beside her and was sure to compliment Jessica on her handiwork with the wedding dress.

It didn't take long for Mary Lou to understand the way things worked in the shop. They stitched everything by hand, and all the orders were pinned to the dresses to remove all guesswork as to pricing and deliverables. When she focused on her work, she felt like she was back at home, sitting around a quilting circle like she used to with other members of her community. But once she lifted her gaze, it was easy to see that she was not at home. The girls listened to music with small pods in their ears; there was little by way of conversation except for the occasional bark to be handed something or a call for help, and everyone worked alone. Still, the days went by quickly, and Mary Lou was soon lost in her work, forgetting that she had a purpose to discover regarding Jonah.

Mary Lou was slowly getting used to electricity, but Deliah felt it would be too much to train her with electronics. Thus, the computer and the credit machine were happily off-limits to the girl. Still, she could not see how they were more efficient than handling cash like she was used to at the general store.

"Would it not be faster to do things by hand?" Mary Lou asked when the payment system went down for the third time in two days.

Deliah snorted as she fiddled with it. "I don't think so," she said. "But if this thing keeps doing this, I am going to return it and switch merchants. This is ridiculous."

"Switch merchants?" Mary Lou asked, confused.

Deliah huffed, though she did not lose patience. Mary Lou's innocence endeared her. "Payment merchants," she clarified, although Mary Lou was none the wiser. She smiled and nodded just the same. The English world was confusing and overwhelming. Oh, that she could walk in nature and hear the birds chirp. Would that bubbling water echo in the city's concrete canyons? But, alas! She had no idea how to access nature in the city. Everything seemed to be gray: the buildings, their décor and accents, the day that seemed constantly overcast by the towers' shadows, and the night, too brightly lit to allow the stars to shine overhead.

Mary Lou arose once she finished her work and thanked Deliah for the day. The latter inspected her work. "You did a wonderful job," Deliah said, impressed. "You have a natural talent for this."

"Thank you," Mary Lou said. "Are you sure that you don't need me to stay later? There's a big order tomorrow."

"No, no it's fine," Deliah said in a reprimanding tone, though it had not been her intent. She softened her gaze as she looked away from the finished piece. "Go off and enjoy your evening. Is there anything you need? A restaurant recommendation or something?"

"Actually, I was wondering if there was somewhere I could walk in nature? A trail or a forest, maybe?"

Deliah thought for a bit. "Would a park do?"

"Sure," Mary Lou said, although she had no idea whether it would or not. She had never been to a park before. Deliah pointed one out on the map that was within walking distance. Mary Lou thanked her and left. It didn't seem like it was too far to walk, so she decided to head there immediately. She wasn't quite hungry for supper, and she didn't feel like wrestling with her stove.

Mary Lou ventured away from the store in the opposite direction of the grocer. This bit of exploration sparked a sense of adventure in her, though she giggled at the thought. There was nothing over which to climb, nothing on which to swing, the spruce's perfume was missing, and there seemed to be no wild animals to coax or birds to imitate. Instead, she was deafened by honks, asphyxiated by diesel fumes, and disoriented by the lack of landmarks. Deliah had told her the street names, and now, the irony caught up to her: a left onto Cardinal Avenue, then another onto Swallow Lane, and she could enter the park on Oak Drive. She hoped to find it soon because it was impossible to concentrate while in the city due to the chaos, the noise, and everyone's heads bent over their palms. *It's a wonder no one is killed*, she thought. She feared she might be injured by another pedestrian more than by an automobile.

Mary Lou breathed a sigh of relief when she finally saw the park. There were trees, a fountain, some gardens, and places to sit, which was good enough for her. She crossed the street carefully and managed to find a bench. She sat down at first, and then leaned over onto it, exhausted more from how hard she had concentrated than from any exertion. She was close to the street, but sounds were not as pronounced. There, she could look up at the trees, down at the flowers, and find a moment of peace.

The city was not for her. Mary Lou liked the job, and the English women she worked with were interesting, albeit distant. However, she was sure she wasn't going to last the year. She was Amish at heart. She sought silence to be close to God.

"You shouldn't be out here."

Mary Lou sat up in surprise. Standing before her was Jonah. He looked like any other Englishman, dressed in a down winter coat, his hands in his jean's pocket, and a baseball cap on his head. He was looking at Mary Lou like she had made a grave mistake. She didn't know what to say.

"Why not?" she asked at last. "Is this bench reserved by someone else?"

"No," he said, shaking his head, incredulous at her innocence. "This just isn't a very safe place for a girl to be alone."

Mary Lou was confused.

"But…my employer, Deliah, told me I could come here."

"I didn't say that you weren't allowed to be here," Jonah managed, trying miserably to hide his impatience. "All I said was that it wasn't a very safe place for a woman to be alone."

"Oh," Mary Lou said. She looked around and didn't see anything out of place, but perhaps Jonah knew more about the area than she did. "Why not?"

He sighed.

"Look, I'm just telling you, okay? It's not a place to commune with nature or pray or anything like that."

"Do you know a place that is good for that? I just wanted a moment's peace."

"You won't find peace in the city," he said. "You can't hear yourself think here."

"I've noticed," she said, leaning back in despair. "That's why I was hoping for somewhere with nature, just to think."

"Are you kidding?" he shook his head. "That's the best part of this place. You can't be alone with your thoughts."

She paused at that, and then took a deep breath.

"So, you're Amish too?" she asked, and his eyes narrowed.

"Who told you that?"

"The girls at the shop told me," she replied, innocently.

"Yeah, what else did they tell you?" he asked.

She wanted to say that there was nothing else, but Mary Lou had never been a good liar. "They told me that you were…"

"That I was shunned?" his smirk was not friendly. "You shouldn't even be talking to me. It's breaking all the rules."

"Oh," Mary Lou said. "Well…I'm on *rumspringa*."

He looked at her for a moment and then laughed.

"Of course," he said. "The rebellious *rumspringa*, where you break all the rules. Which rules have you broken so far?"

"Oh," she said. "I've used an oven and an electric kettle."

"Dangerous," he replied. "Look, let me tell you something about the English world. It's loud and it's busy, and there's no place for rules or religion."

Her back stiffened as if to defend herself. "I don't believe that," she declared. "I think there's a place for them. You just have to find it."

"You've been here what, three seconds?" he asked her. "Take my word for it, and don't spend time here if you don't want to break any rules. You might as well go home, back to where people tell you what to do and what to think."

"That's not…," she started, but he shook his head and raised his hand, signaling her to stop.

"See you around," he said as he headed down the path. Mary Lou was left alone, sitting on the bench. Others may have been offended by his words, but she was curious. Who was this Jonah, and what had happened to hurt him so much that he had to act this way?

CHAPTER 3

Another week passed before Mary Lou saw Jonah again. It was on a day when she had volunteered to come into the shop early to get a big order done, and, for once, Deliah had accepted. Mary Lou rose earlier than the other girls did, so she took advantage of the opportunity to be at work alone, in the silence. She liked her colleagues well enough, but they could be distracting. Mary Lou was glad that her new boss trusted her and could see that she was a hard worker who was dedicated to their service. So long as the work was done, Deliah told her, she could come in whenever she wanted.

The shop bell above the door rang just as Mary Lou had finished tailoring a pair of pants. She would have told whoever it was that they were not yet open, but the sight of Jonah took her breath away. When she saw him, she was enjoyably terrified— happy to see him yet afraid of his usual attitude. Would she be able to change his mood? Could she get him to be happy to see her, to look at her as a woman rather than as Amish?

He, on the other hand, was surprised to find her, alone.

"Hello," she said more feebly than she had wanted.

"Did they all flake out today?" he asked her indignantly.

"No," she reassured him with a smile, relieved that he was not rude to her. "I just enjoy coming in early and getting a few things done before anyone else is in. Almost as quiet as the park." She paused as he put the packages down to find another pair of trousers to mend, then continued, "How is your morning?"

Jonah could not look her in the eyes. He lowered his gaze to smirk, then shook his head in disbelief. "You're an odd one," he said. "I told you off in the park, and yet here you are, acting like nothing happened."

Mary Lou gave him a moment. As he turned towards the door, she shrugged and exclaimed, "That's all right. I think everyone has bad days once in a while."

"It's my normal," he said, still unable to face her. "What is your name?"

"Mary Lou," she said. "Sorry, I thought you knew that."

"A good Amish name," he said. "I should have guessed."

"So is Jonah," she replied.

"Yeah, I should change it," he said, looking up as if to ask the heavens for suggestions.

She raised an eyebrow. "Why? Even if you are shunned, you're still the same person." She said it with such conviction that he had to turn to look at her just to see if she was serious.

"What do you mean, *even if I'm shunned*?" he asked. "I am."

"I know," she replied. "But, you're still the same person from before you were shunned."

Jonah sighed at her delusion. It had been a long time since he'd been himself, since he'd felt like himself. Leaving a community doesn't necessarily mean joining another, nor does it kill the yearning for things past. The city had been a terrible place to find redemption.

"I don't feel like the same person," he said.

She put down her sewing to look him in the eye. "I understand that," she replied. "It must be quite a shift."

"I'll say," he scoffed. "Are you still into breaking the rules?" The Amish speaking to those they shunned is forbidden.

"Sure." She never broke her gaze. God had sent her on

rumspringa to meet this young man and to return him to the faith. Her conviction drew her to him. She would fully embrace *rumspringa* and do anything God wanted her to do so that Jonah's soul might be saved. *Oh God! Open my heart, open my mind, and open my eyes that I might see Your will*, she prayed silently.

"We should get coffee sometime," he said. "I don't want you wandering in that park, but if you're dead set on finding places that are quiet to think, I can show you a few others that are safer."

She was surprised at the offer. "Thank you. That'd be lovely. Except, I don't drink coffee."

"Ah, so you don't want to break too many rules," he said, proud of himself that he had discovered a weakness in her faith. "Well, there's herbal tea. And there's water. You do drink water?"

"I do," she said, with a smile. "That'd be lovely, thank you." Her calm demeanor and sweet tone melted his hard heart. He ceased to tease her.

"What time do you finish today?" he asked with a softened tone. "Seeing as you're here at the crack of dawn."

"I think I should be finished everything by about 2 p.m.," she answered. "But if you don't want to do it today, I completely understand."

"No, that's fine," he said, feeling a sense of urgency to seal the deal, presently. "I'll see you then."

Jessica came in just as he left, and from the look on her face, Mary Lou could see that Jessica caught the tail end of their conversation.

"You'll see him when?" she asked excitedly. Mary Lou blushed. She didn't know why she was blushing, because it wasn't as if they were doing anything wrong. According to Amish tradition, she shouldn't be walking without an escort, plus they weren't going anywhere alone. Yet she blushed all the more. Jessica stared at her wide-eyed.

"Jonah just offered to show me some quiet places in the city," she finally managed, unable to look her in the eye. "Because he said the park was a bit dangerous."

"The park is dangerous?" Jessica quirked her eyebrows in surprise. "I mean, sure, it can be sketchy after dark, but I don't think it's dangerous. Just don't talk to anyone."

"It's so different," Mary Lou said. "I'm used to knowing and talking to everyone. Now, when I go outside, there's not one person I recognize."

"That's what I love about the city," Jessica said. "There's always a chance to meet someone new. The most unlikely people ask you out on a date."

"I…" Mary Lou's mouth fell open. "Oh no, I'm not being courted by Jonah!"

"Courting?" Jessica grinned. "Such an old-fashioned word. We just call it grabbing a coffee, or a date."

"The Amish don't date," Mary Lou said. "We court with the intention of marriage."

"When?" Jessica blurted out in astonishment. "Like now, when you're 18? That's so young!"

Mary Lou shrugged with a smile. "I guess it's a different world," she said.

"Yeah," Jessica said. "I guess it is. Anyway, whatever you're going to do, good for you."

"It's just a walk," Mary Lou said, but now she was starting to worry. Jonah seemed like he had been in the English world for quite a while. What if it were a date? That certainly was breaking the rules. Still, she had to do God's work.

Jonah arrived promptly at 2 p.m. Mary Lou bid farewell to her colleagues as they giggled. He returned their silliness with an inquisitive look, though no one for a minute thought he cared about what they would answer.

Jonah held the door for her as they headed out into the brisk afternoon air. "Did I miss a joke?" he asked. Mary Lou turned her face towards the sun, basking in the light. She missed the outdoors.

"No," she said. "They thought that we were courting."

"Oh," he said. "English girls think everything is a date. You ask them for a Kleenex, and it's a date. You hold the door for them, and you are courting them." He looked back over his shoulder into the shop to see the girls still giggling as they stared at them both. The sight of Mary Lou smiling as she enjoyed the sun was being misconstrued. Embarrassed, he hurried her along.

"Surely not," Mary Lou said with a smile as they walked. "But then, they don't get married until they are nearly 30. Jessica was telling me how her sister was 32 and still not married, and she acted as if it were completely normal."

"It really is a different world out here," Jonah said to her. "It's not…they don't court with the intention of marriage. They court with the intention of just passing time."

"Wow!" Mary Lou exclaimed in disbelief. Jonah hustled into the café to get them each a cup of tea. Mary Lou thanked him profusely, and they continued to walk.

"It reminds me of home," he said, after a few moments. "All loose-leaf tea, dried in the sun on the window of the shop."

"It is wonderful," she said, as she took a sip. "Where is your community?"

"It was to the west," he said. "About three hours from here."

"And you've never been back since?" she asked.

"That would be breaking the rules," he replied smugly.

Mary Lou desperately wanted to ask him what he had done, and why he wouldn't consider trying to go back. She put those thoughts out of her mind and focused on their walk, instead. If she gave him time, he'd open up.

Jonah was true to his word about showing her quiet places where she could relax in nature. He showed her a stream behind a university campus that none of the students seemed to know about, as well as a greenhouse that was open to the public and yet rarely occupied. She could already feel herself relaxing. Jonah seemed to know all the secret spots to hide from the city's noise. He must be trying to return to his roots. You can take the boy out of the country, but you can't take the country out of the boy. He must be desperate to return, to be accepted, to be…forgiven?

"How did you find these places?" she asked as they left a second greenhouse filled with butterflies.

"When I first came here…" he picked his words carefully. "I thought I needed peace and quiet too."

"Oh," she said. "But now you don't?"

"Now, I prefer not to be alone with my thoughts," he replied. His countenance darkened, and the mood felt somber. It was the same gloom that she had witnessed in the park. She would have to be careful about her next sentence.

"Or alone with God?" she asked.

"God knows what happened," he replied. "I don't feel like there is anything else to be said."

"Oh no," she cried, incredulous at his words. "There is always a conversation to be had with God. There is always an opportunity to have Him speak to you, especially when you feel like you can't hear Him at all."

"You see, that's what they teach you, but the world isn't like that, Mary Lou. The world is far from connected to God or black and white. You don't just pray and get everything you deserve. You don't just hope and have it work out. Sometimes God tests you…and you have no idea why. And you spend a lot of time wondering why, and by the time you come back to reality, you realized that you failed the test."

Thoughts swirled in Mary Lou's mind. She opened her mouth to speak, yet her words seemed to want out all at once, pushing the air out from within her but choking the sound. She became so dizzy from the desire to speak that she reached out for his arm to keep her balance. Unaware of her inner turmoil but pleased that they were now arm-in-arm, Jonah smirked and shook his head.

"Not that someone like you would know anything about that," he said.

"About what?" she heard herself say, surprised that she had

managed to say anything at all.

"Being tested by God."

"Of course, I would," she defended herself.

"Would you now?" he asked with a raised brow. "Like what?"

Mary Lou wrestled with herself whether she wanted to tell him or not. He may laugh at her. But something in her heart—perhaps Holy Spirit himself—told her that he was not going to speak to her until she opened her heart first. "Do you want to know the reason I went on *rumspringa*?"

"Because you wanted a year of freedom, a year of peace without the straight-jacket that is your faith?" he asked crudely.

Mary Lou shook her head. "No," she said. "This time last year, if someone told me that I was going to take *rumspringa*, I would have laughed at them. I would have laughed if someone told me that I was going to do anything in a year because everyone thought I was going to die."

"What?" He stopped walking and turned to her. "What do you mean?"

"I got very sick," she said. "About a year and a half ago. I tried to push through, and then I tried to pray. I thought God was just testing me, and I was being lazy. But things started to get worse...and before I knew it, I was being rushed to the big city hospital. They told my parents that I would die within the month."

Jonah was mute.

"By that point," she continued, "I had been sick for so long, and I was in so much pain, I wanted to give up. They gave me the option, to give up rather than try to fight because my chances were so slim. I was ready to say yes...when God said to me, *Fight. For Me.* I knew the treatment would be painful, that things would get worse before they got better. I knew that I'd have to deal with the English world for a while, and there was a chance that it would be all for nothing...but God asked me to believe, so I did. I knew that He would be with me through the worst pain I had ever felt...but I fought, with Him. And here I am, able to tell the tale."

Sheepishly, Jonah looked at her and could only say, "Wow, I had no idea. You look strong and healthy."

"I am, now," she said. "After I got better, and the question of *rumspringa* came up, I had to take it. I almost lost my life, and if this was my only chance to see if the English world that saved my life was where I belonged, then I had to find out."

"You are strong," he said, fighting back tears. He nodded his head. "That is a good reason."

"So," she said to him, carefully. They had finished their tea and were standing outside by the second greenhouse. The wind was blowing softly, chilling them just enough to draw them closer for warmth whilst Mary Lou's story pulled them together for comfort. She felt a connection with Jonah then, but she wouldn't dare put her arms around him. Still, she needed to find out what ruled his soul. "What happened to you? What was your test?"

"You don't want to know," Jonah said.

"I do," Mary Lou said, as she met his eye. "I do."

"I killed my sister," he said, bluntly. "She's dead, and it's my fault."

CHAPTER 4

Mary Lou could not believe what she had heard. *This gentleman, so wracked in agony, had killed someone?* The man in front of her, with kind eyes, and a charming smile, even on his worst days, could not possibly be a murderer.

"I don't believe that," she said to him.

"Well, I did," Jonah responded, his voice flat and his eyes wet with emotion. "You can believe whatever you want, but that's the truth."

Mary Lou paused to gather her thoughts and plan the next course of action. "What happened? How long ago was this?" She figured this was the moment she'd been waiting for, when he would open up, though murder was not the subject she'd had in mind to discuss over tea.

It was obviously painful for Jonah to talk about, but there had been magic between them but a moment ago. If he didn't tell her now, he would never be able to.

"It was last year," Jonah said. "Probably around the time that you were sick." He paused, as though waiting to be prompted.

Mary Lou racked her mind for another question. "How did she die?" she finally asked, surprised at how long it took her to ask such an obvious follow-up.

"She drowned," Jonah said. He wouldn't look at her but instead turned pale to the point that Mary Lou feared that he might faint. "She was only six."

"I'm so sorry," was all Mary Lou could say. It did not sound like murder to her, but she feared provoking him. Gathering all of her courage, she said, "It doesn't sound like you killed her."

"But it was my fault," Jonah replied, as sorrow welled up within him. Only weeping would keep him from drowning, yet pride caused his face to strain as though it were a dike about to burst. "I was supposed to be watching her," he sniffled, his grief oscillating between rage and despair. Finally, hopelessness overcame him. His face relaxed. The dikes had held. He would not cry, though he took no pleasure in conquering the soft saline tide. When he resumed, his tone was deadpan. "I took her and her friend down by the river, to look for frogs. They loved to catch them and keep them as pets." He looked to Mary Lou, and, seeing her anticipation, he shot out, "I guess she slipped and fell." He hoped that that would be an end of it.

"What happened to her friend?" Mary Lou heard herself ask. She would have cursed herself if she weren't Amish, for she had wanted to let this man feel, to let him cry, to feel safe in his sorrow so that she might comfort him. She knew that this line of questioning would only give him an outlet back into his shell. *Trust yourself, and trust in Me*, the Lord reassured her in His still small voice.

"Her friend had slipped just a moment before her. I told my sister to stay still while I went to rescue her friend, Gabby. She had fallen face first, and there was blood everywhere. It looked like she had hit her head. I only looked away for a moment, to go and swoop Gabby out of the water. When I looked back…," his voice shook as he relived his terror, "Jennie was gone. It took them all day to find her, and by then, it was too late."

"Oh Jonah," Mary Lou said as her heart broke. "That wasn't your fault. You rescued Gabby. You weren't doing anything wrong."

"Really?" Jonah asked. "Because what it felt like to me was that I was being tested, and I chose the wrong girl. Gabby would have been fine. She was in a shallower part of the river. But Jennie was swept away by the current. I should have been watching her. She trusted me. My parents trusted me, and now…" The dikes broke. He looked back at Mary Lou with tears streaming down his face, his fists clenched in rage at his failure as a man.

"And your community shunned you?" Mary Lou asked, despite herself. She panicked at the thought that he was blaming himself and cutting himself off from God's life-giving presence. She wanted to scream at him for his logical fallacies and simultaneously pull him to her breast to stroke his hair and soothe him with her heartbeat, like an infant on his mother. Mary Lou's calm demeanor offset Jonah's stormy grief. He gathered himself, took a deep breath, and wiped away his tears.

"I don't know," he said. "Probably."

"What do you mean, 'you don't know'?" she asked. "They didn't shun you?"

"I never said my community shunned me," he answered. "I just said that I was shunned."

"You shunned yourself?" she inquired, putting the pieces together. He laughed, but she could see no humor in it.

"Sure, you could say that," he replied nonchalantly.

Jonah's nonplussed attitude irked her, yet Mary Lou was relieved that things weren't as bad as she had imagined. *This will be easy*, she thought. *Just a little coaxing and he'll come around, re-embrace his Amish faith, and be reunited with his community.* What else might *rumspringa* have in store for her, she wondered, getting ahead of herself. "Oh, Jonah," she said. "I'm sorry to hear that. You must feel lost without your community."

"I'm not," Jonah insisted. His tears were down to a mere trickle, yet they betrayed him. Mary Lou could ignore whatever he said next. "You see, I just work all the time, and I stay out of places where I can think. I don't bother with praying, or thinking, or even being alone with my thoughts. That's why you shouldn't be around me. I've been shunned."

"You shunned yourself," Mary Lou said, quietly. "And now your parents have lost two children, rather than one. I don't mean to be harsh, but I think they would like nothing more than to have you around again. Have you spoken to them since?"

"Of course not," Jonah responded. "How could I face them? I left as soon as they found her. I couldn't…" His voice trailed off. He wondered if what she said was true, if she was onto him. He wanted to run, but she touched him. Mary Lou fought the maternal urge to wrap him in her arms because would not be proper for an Amish woman to do so. Instead, she thought of something else to say.

"What can I do?" she asked at last. "I want to help you."

"There's no way to help," he scoffed. "She's gone."

"I know," she said, softly. "But you should know that Jennie is in heaven and at peace. The same God who comforts her there can comfort you here. I'm sure that neither one of them blames you."

"You don't know that," Jonah retorted in disgust. He fought desperately to close himself off from Mary Lou. He did not like to feel exposed. Being grumpy was his armor. If no one became close to him, he would not have to grieve another loss. "You haven't they seen the horrors of the world yet, Mary Lou. What's an innocent girl like you going to teach me about life, huh? You should end your *rumspringa* and go back to your community before this world ruins you."

Jonah's vitriol surprised him. Vulnerability both scared him and endeared him to her. He couldn't risk loving her, yet he yearned to. He didn't want to show his face to his parents ever again, yet their forgiveness was what he craved. He could feel God tugging at his heart, calling him back to Him, but how could anyone forgive Jonah when he hadn't forgiven himself? A little girl died on his watch. Was not the world mourning? Who had time to be nice in the face of such cruelty? Would that he had died instead of her!

"You think I should go back?" she asked, surprised.

"I do," he replied. "I think this is no place for a…" he paused, trying to find the right insult to forever push her away, "...pure and good soul," he managed, disappointed at his chivalry.

"That's very kind of you to say," Mary Lou said, sensing that she had him cornered. "And I have been considering going back. I will go under one condition."

"What?" he asked, baffled.

"That you come with me so that you might forgive yourself."

Jonah shook his head before she had finished the sentence. "I can't do that," he asserted plainly.

Unconvinced, Mary Lou pressed on. "You have to," she said, and she noticed his eyes flash.

"I have to?" he asked, his voice rising. "I *have* to? Why do I have to?"

"Jonah," she said, boldly stepping closer to him. "Don't you understand? This is why I was drawn to taking *rumspringa*. God *wanted* us to meet."

Had he not had biblical training, Jonah would have scoffed at such a notion. Yet, his time amongst the English had not made him an atheist. He was an angry theist wrestling with God, unwilling to pray for he knew all too well that God would comfort him and love him. All Jonah wanted to do was wallow in his self-hatred. But God was calling him. He could feel it in his heart and in his bones. He looked down to keep from crying out to the heavens, to trap his soul in the gloom of his own making. The sheer exhaustion, however, of lying about what God was doing, about His everlasting love, that he was the one sheep the Lord had come out to find as the 99 others waited patiently for him, was coming to bear. God had sent this angelic being to call him back to Himself. What a cruel method to wear him down and to get His way. Touched at the warmth of God's love, Jonah replied in a shaky voice, "I'm not sure about that." His stubbornness would die hard.

"You have to come to my community," she insisted. "Otherwise, how will you ever know about forgiveness and what God is capable of healing?"

"But He can't heal my sister," he insisted.

Oh, how men could be stubborn and dimwitted! Mary Lou knew, of course, that his sister wasn't coming back, but that wasn't her point. Jonah was the one who needed the healing, not his sister. *Give me strength!* she cried to God in her soul. What could she say to make Jonah see that he was wrong? Did men ever learn how to admit when they were wrong?

"Why were you in the park that day?" Mary Lou asked him. Jonah's face wrinkled in confusion, and she could tell instantly that he knew the answer.

"What?" he asked, trying to play dumb, yet knowing Mary Lou wouldn't give up that easily.

"The park," she said. "The day we met, and you told me to go back home, you were in the park. Why?"

"I was just taking a walk," he said with a shrug. "It's a free country."

"Yes, of course it is, but you said that you preferred the hustle and bustle of the city. You said that you preferred the noise to drown out your own thoughts. Why were you in the park, then?"

"It's still noisy in the park," he tried to say, but she shook her head. Mary Lou knew that she had him, so she moved in for the final blow.

"It's not," she said. "I think somewhere, deep inside, you were seeking peace. You won't find it here, and you won't return to your community. That's why you must come with me to mine. Please come home with me, Jonah. My community is peaceful, and you will be safe if you choose to think and feel and pray. If it doesn't work, you can always come back here."

"What about you?" he asked her. "Are you ending your *rumspringa* to go home after just a few weeks?"

She hadn't thought of that. "I don't think so. Not yet, anyway."

Jonah took a deep breath, pursed his lips, and stared at the ground. The silhouette of the slim, sculpted, statuesque man, pensive and vulnerable before Mary Lou, made her stare. His looks were pleasing, his eyes inquiring, and his smile (when he smiled) charming. She had not seen him in this light before. His square jaw, his hairline…her eyes wandered…his broad shoulders. For a moment, he was not a brother in Christ needing help, but an outright man with whom she could spend the rest of her… *No! Mary Lou! That's not your place. Let the Lord do His work. Shame on you!* Yet, she felt no shame. Such is the advantage of being pure in heart; when one is tempted, one can only think of pure and holy things to do with another. There was no desire to sin, just an attraction that she managed to rein in. He was still silent, and she was afraid that he was going to say no. But he must have had a change of heart because he nodded.

"OK," he said. "OK, I will try."

"Thank you," she sighed in relief. "Thank you for trusting me."

Jonah met her eyes, and his next words reached into her very soul. "There is just something trustworthy about you," he said. "Something that I've never seen in anyone else."

Mary Lou blushed. "You are too kind," she felt forced to say.

Jonah shrugged. "You are the one who is being kind to me," he said. Feeling closure, he proposed to continue the tour.

"Yes," she said. "I think there are many other quiet spots in the city that I would like to see. If I do end up staying, it would be good to know them all."

Nothing more was said. They walked in silence, smiling at whatever they saw, looking away from the other in a vain attempt to hide their joy from one another. When they looked at each other, they giggled and smiled all the more. The joyous energy fueled them for their walk. Mary Lou did not realize how exhausted she was until she returned to her apartment. All she wanted was to lie on the bed and close her eyes to replay in her mind the sweet souvenir that was her walk with Jonah. She lay on her back with her feet hanging over the bed, still smiling as she relived her afternoon. She smiled at the thought of hiding her smile from him, then giggled at him as though he were there smiling at her. She could see his physique, his vulnerability, his mind, and reassure herself that he'd make a great husband. That jolted her and reminded her that she had been taught never to be idle. She forced herself to sit at the little writing desk that had been set up in the corner. She was surprised at how much effort it took. However, if she were to put this plan into action, she needed to write to her mother.

Dear Maem,

I have decided to come home for a visit and bring...

Mary Lou stopped as soon as she had started. If she said she was bringing a boy home, it would be scandalous. That was something that the English did, to introduce their parents to their future spouses. Mary Lou had heard stories of English girls being nervous about bringing their boyfriends home, and that wasn't what she was doing. The Lord's work was not to be confused with romance. She and Jonah weren't courting. Except, she couldn't explain the feeling she got when she looked at him. Whenever she met his eyes, and whenever she heard God speak to her with him there, it was as if her very soul was amplified, lifted to the high heavens, only to float gingerly back down to earth in the softest of landings back into his arms. She had once heard that God spoke through the love couples had for one another and that God's love was to be reflected in the love that a married couple had for each other. She had listened to the words in church, yet only now did she understand them. Nevertheless, Jonah hadn't asked to court her, and so she knew that she had to put such thoughts out of her mind.

Dear Maem,

She started over, focusing on the necessary words at hand rather than her feelings for Jonah.

I have decided to come home for a short visit. I miss you and Daed *and my brothers and sisters very much. I hope all is well. There is an Amish boy in town who has offered to accompany me on the journey as an escort. He is very far away from his family, and I have offered for him to visit our village, so his soul can find some peace from the bustling city life. His name is Jonah, and I hope that you will make him feel welcome.*

I have three days off from the boutique beginning Monday, which is when I hope to arrive. I will send another letter if anything changes.

Your loving daughter,
Mary Lou

Mary Lou re-read the letter and thought it good enough. She hoped that she wasn't too late to send it that day. She hurried to put it in an envelope, and then headed to the post office.

"It will be there on Friday," said the clerk, when he took it from Mary Lou. "Is that all right?"

"Friday?" Mary Lou said in surprise. "But I can deliver it myself faster than that."

The clerk smiled at her. "I understand, miss, but the postal service has lots of stops to make. Would you like to deliver it yourself?"

Mary Lou shook her head. "I apologize for my rudeness. It's just the only way I can communicate with my family, and I was hoping they'd have time to write a reply in return."

"There's always the phone," the clerk said.

"Oh, I'm Amish; we don't have phones." Then Mary Lou remembered that the general store had just gotten one. She could call there to let her parents know the news right away. Yet, she had never used a telephone before. She felt in her pocket for the scrap of paper her mother had given to her with the number on it. She had no idea what to do with it. However, what if she brought Jonah back and he wasn't welcome?

Determined, Mary Lou had to call her parents and talk to them. It wasn't an easy situation, and she didn't want him to feel out of place. "Actually, that'd be lovely. I have a number for someone I know. Do you think you can teach me to use it?"

"Not a problem," replied the clerk. He picked up the phone and dialed the number for her. *Rumspringa* was for trying new things after all, and the phone was a new thing. She just hoped that she had the words to tell her parents exactly what was going on.

CHAPTER 5

"Thank you for doing this," Jonah said when they left on Monday. "I don't know how I can ever repay you." They had borrowed a horse and cart from one of the merchants in town who was staying the week to meet with some of the big grocery store suppliers. Mary Lou wished him the best and promised to pay for the rental, but the merchant had simply shaken his head and wished the couple the best of luck. Mary Lou was sure he thought they were courting and heading to get married since Jonah was clearly a mess of nerves. It is uncanny how a man about to reckon with his past is indistinguishable from a man going to ask for a hand in marriage. Mary Lou could only pray that he would find peace.

"I'm not looking for repayment," she assured him. "I just want you to be well."

"Mary Lou," he stuttered, as the cart bumped along. "You realize that it's not as easy as all that. I don't even know if I'll be able to set foot in your village. The memories…" His voice trailed off.

"I can imagine," she said reassuringly. "But I am here so that you can try."

"I wrote to my parents last week after we talked," he said.

She squealed with delight and turned to him. "You did?

Really?"

"I did," he said. "I wrote and rewrote the letter about six times, but I eventually mailed it. I remembered what you said, about it feeling like they were losing two children, so I had to do something."

"That is very brave of you. I am so proud."

"Thanks," he said. Her smile brought him joy. He could not help but feel proud of his actions, too. He felt as though it would be okay. "Now, I hope your community doesn't cast me out."

"They won't," she said. "I called my mother already and talked to her."

"You called her?" Jonah asked in surprise, then chuckled. "*Rumspringa* is much different for you than it was for me."

"Did you go on a *rumspringa*?" she asked, and his face darkened.

"I did," he said. "And I decided that I wanted to be Amish. It was two weeks after that, that…the accident…" He couldn't bring himself to finish the sentence. Jonah merely pursed his lips and looked ahead. Mary Lou couldn't help but do the same. She was dumbfounded. His pain was deeper than she had thought, and despite her willingness to empathize, his pain seemed deeper than anything she had ever endured. Not only was this man cut off from his family, but he was also estranged from his preferred way of life. She began to understand his complicated feelings regarding quiet places in the city. How could he want to visit them if it was merely to remind him of what he couldn't have? How could he not when they were the nearest facsimiles to what his heart desired? It was at that moment that she fell in love with him.

Jonah took a deep breath. "There's a lot that you don't know about me."

Mary Lou remained silent, choosing to support him with her smile rather than her words. The journey out, driven by her father, had flown by because she was so nervous. Now full of nerves, but of a different sort, her community came into view more quickly than she had expected.

"My mother's name is Leah," she informed him, suddenly sensing the urge to prepare for what lay ahead. "And my father's is Joshua. They are kind people, and they have already made up a spare room for you. Mind you, you may not get any sleep because I have four brothers and sisters." She hoped that she did not sound insensitive given the mood.

"Five of you under one roof," he said, in surprise. "That must be quite the household. Do you miss them?"

Mary Lou looked at Jonah to gauge whether he was genuinely relieved at the change of subject. "I do," she replied, once she was certain that he was satisfied at how his confession was closed. She was not used to men; thus, she was unaware that not talking about one's feelings was a man's preferred path. Unbeknownst to her, the silence was exactly what he had needed, and she endeared herself to him. "I miss them a great deal. I am the oldest, and they all came much later, so I helped to raise them."

"You must have had your hands full," he stated.

Mary Lou shrugged. "I liked the chaos," she said. "Perhaps that's why I chose to take my *rumspringa* in the city." She smiled at him, knowingly. He returned her smile and shook his head. She watched him as he looked ahead, turning away only once he turned toward her to catch her gaze. They said nothing more, choosing, instead, to let the glowing embers of their love warm their hearts.

Shortly thereafter, they arrived. Jonah jumped off of the cart and hurried around it to help Mary Lou down. She had seen a few people in the distance who were staring at them, but no one approached. The first person that Jonah met was Mary Lou's mother, coming out of the house with a baby on her hip.

"*Willkumm, willkumm*," she said. "We've been waiting for you." She smiled at her daughter as though she had not seen her in months. Mary Lou was always pleased to come home.

"Hello," Jonah said nervously. "It's so lovely to meet you. Thank you for letting me stay in your home." He sounded as though he were reading from a script.

"You must be Jonah," her mother said, with a kind smile. "Mary Lou has said so many things about you, and we are happy to have you."

Jonah was taken aback by the kindness. He stood mute before her. Mary Lou decided that she had better take charge.

"*Maem*, Jonah worked all night in order to get the time off to be here. Will you please show him to his room?"

"Oh, of course," she said. "What a hard worker. You'll make someone a wonderful husband one day." Amish manners and the warmth of their hospitality cheered Jonah. His awkwardness subsided, and he felt at home again. He said nothing as he basked in the satisfaction of having his yearnings fulfilled.

Mary Lou, oblivious to the positive effects of Amish tradition upon Jonah, blushed. She could now clearly see that, despite everything she had told her parents, they were hoping that their relationship would be deeper than just friendship. Indeed, when the darkness that plagued him gave way to the light inside of him, Jonah was pleasant and kind, able to make her laugh like she had never before. He was doting, offering to help her, lending her a hand, or offering his coat because it was cold outside. Yes, he really would make a good husband someday, but it was painfully obvious to her that that day was far away.

If Jonah's soul remained unhealed, Mary Lou thought, *then there was no hope for "them."* The past few days had borne her own desire that it might turn into something more. His confession that he, too, preferred the Amish way of life had consumed her. She had to come to grips with her passion lest her plans usurp God's plans for Jonah.

Once her mother had shown Jonah upstairs, she and Mary Lou left him and headed to the kitchen to catch up.

"Your father has taken the others to the barn," she said, "to count the chickens."

"To count the chickens?" Mary Lou asked, confused. "Are some missing?"

JONAH'S REDEMPTION: AN AMISH ROMANCE

"No," her mother replied with a smile only another mother would recognize. "We just thought that perhaps you wouldn't want so much chaos the moment you got here."

"Oh," Mary Lou realized. "Thank you, that's very kind of you."

"It is kind of you to offer to bring him here," her mother said. "I had heard about that tragedy. We tried to keep it from you children, for it ripped that community apart. They were all so broken-hearted."

"Of course," Mary Lou said. "I couldn't even imagine. But he blames himself. I can't make him see that it wasn't his fault."

"It's not your place to show him. He must see it for himself." Her mother had always been direct. "Rest assured that no one blames him for it. His parents are heartbroken and pray every day for his safe return."

"How do you know all this?" Mary Lou asked. His community was miles away, and the Amish were never supposed to gossip.

"They started a prayer chain," her mother replied. "For both him and the soul of his sister. All the surrounding communities took up the prayer." Ah, yes! The prayer chain; it is the holy way to spread bad news about good people. One could still sound pious when sharing another's business, so long as it was couched in the righteous act of prayer. "It is not gossip when they tell you themselves and ask for prayer," Leah retorted, as though she had read Mary Lou's mind.

"I didn't know," Mary Lou pleaded.

"You did," her mother corrected. "There is just much to pray for, and you've had a lot on your mind this past year."

Mary Lou remembered her trials and felt relieved that she had a good excuse for being out of the loop. Tilting her head, she declared, "I should be more mindful of others around me. Sometimes, I recite those prayers as my mind drifts. I see now that it is wrong."

"I understand. The important part is that Jonah is here now, and we want to help."

"Thank you, *Maem*. I just didn't know what else to do. God put him in my path, and I know that I am to witness to him, but I could not do it in the city. He was too…distracted, too angry. His mood has changed since he's left the city. It's almost as though he feels at home"

"He'll be fine, now that he's here," her mother assured her. "And once he's all right, what do you intend to do?"

"Oh, I don't know. Maybe I'll finish *rumspringa*."

"I meant the two of you. Do you two intend to court?"

Mary Lou should have known that question was coming. How could she have been caught off guard? One look into her mother's eyes and she thought it best not to deny it. This was her mother, who knew her better than anyone else. "Maybe," Mary Lou said. "I don't know what to feel." She thought it wise to say no more.

Her mother's eyes sparkled. "That's how I felt about your father at first. I didn't know what to feel because I had never felt anything like that before. God was speaking so loudly to me, saying that he would be my husband, and I was confused and overwhelmed. I didn't feel ready, and I didn't know if your father was ready."

"So, what did you do?"

Her mother winked as she prepared lunch. "I listened, and I trusted God. And the rest is history." She handed her daughter a biscuit.

Mary Lou smiled. She had missed being home. Her job in the city was the last thing on her mind. Jonah's fate consumed her. Would he be her husband? Was God putting her in his path not only to return him to the faith but also to make him hers? Why couldn't God speak more clearly? Perhaps her *rumspringa* really was over. Maybe, no matter what happened with Jonah, she would stay. But then, what would she do without him? She was getting older, and it wasn't as if there were many eligible men in the community. All the boys who lived there were people she had known since childhood, and most of them were her cousins. They didn't excite her like Jonah excited her; she didn't gaze upon them like she would Jonah, nor did they monopolize her thoughts like he was presently. If she stayed and he moved on, would she become a spinster? Would she be condemned to raise her brothers and sisters rather than children of her own? To help them find spouses while she stayed behind? To take care of her elderly parents when the time came? Although Mary Lou knew women in the community who did this and could find no fault in it, she felt suffocated at the thought.

Never before had Mary Lou reckoned with celibacy. *It is not good for man to be alone*, scripture says, and she was certain that Genesis 2:18 applied to women as well. She had to do something else with her life. She had wanted to be a mother and a wife for as long as she knew what they were. Her sickness forced her to confront her own mortality. If she were to live, she would live for God and family. *Dear Jesus, give me a family!*

Jonah arose for supper, refreshed after a full night's work and the morning's journey. Her brethren greeted him and asked him to play. She had never seen him smile so wildly when he was presented with a ball. He quickly went outdoors, hardly noticing her, to assume the role of surrogate big brother. The children squealed in delight as he chased them, carried them, and tickled them. She didn't know it, but these were all of the signs of a man who had come home. What a father he would be!

Finally, as Mary Lou stood on the porch, she caught his eye, her backlit silhouette impossible to ignore. "Feeling better?" she asked him.

"Oh yes," he said, smiling broadly. He turned to look at the children's smiling faces. "I think I am feeling much better, already." He grabbed the nearest boy and raised him above his head. The child screamed in delight.

"Jonah, my boy!" her father said, as he twirled the boy around by the hands. "Tomorrow, do you think you could help me in the woodshed? I hate to ask when you are a guest, but none of these boys are old enough, and I really need to get some wood split before the storm comes."

"I---I would be delighted," Jonah replied, putting the boy down, much to the latter's chagrin. His frown let all know that he was not done playing and that grown-up conversations were for the dinner table, not the front yard. "It's been a while since I've split wood though." Jonah wondered if his Amish skills had atrophied in the city. After all, he'd been little more than a delivery boy, which required little manly skill. He had not known how to convert his Amish discipline and workmanship for profit in the English world. Would he embarrass himself? Would he appear to be less than a man?

"Not to worry," her father said, with a reassuring smile. "It all comes back to you. It'll be like you never left."

Jonah looked across to Mary Lou, who smiled at him. "Well, in that case, I'd be happy to help."

CHAPTER 6

Mary Lou realized that she had never felt true happiness until she saw Jonah standing outside her bedroom window, chopping wood with her father. It was at that moment that she admitted to herself that she couldn't live without him. In merely a week, his shoulders were loose, his tension was unnoticeable, and he smiled. She chuckled at the thought. *What would the girls at the shop think of him now?* Her mother echoed the girl's observations, wondering aloud whether he was the same man whom she had brought home.

"You should ask him to return to his community," her mother said. "Either that or stay here. He clearly is happier here."

"*Maem*!" Mary Lou replied. "I can't just ask that of him."

"Why not?" her mother asked, perplexed. "You asked him to come here, didn't you, and he obeyed?"

"That was different. I needed an escort to come home."

"Mary Lou, if you think that is the only reason Jonah came here, then you are sorely mistaken. He is also very taken with you."

"Oh, I'm not so sure. Jonah is just starting to find himself in the world again. He was very lost. I can't say that I've had anything to do with it." Goodness! how she hoped she was wrong.

"I understand that," her mother replied, sensing her daughter's fear of rejection. "But you are the reason he is smiling again."

"*Maem*, why are you so eager for this to happen? Jonah and I have barely had time to get to know each other."

"You know as well as I do that God places a husband before you and that it's not up to you. I'm certain from the way you look at each other that that boy will be your husband. It's just a matter of him seeing the light."

"But he doesn't want God," Mary Lou protested.

"Are you so sure?"

"Even if he healed, and even if he were able to smile again, he's given no indication that he would want to return to the faith. So, if you are certain that he is my husband, then we would have to make a choice."

Leah's face went pale. "Mary Lou, you can't live outside the faith."

"So, what exactly am I to do, *Maem*? If God has placed my husband in front of me, and he is outside the faith, and will perhaps never return, how do I choose?"

"You always choose God first. Seek His kingdom *first*, then the rest will come."

Mary Lou could tell that her mother was upset because Leah never paraphrased scripture. She would always quote it verbatim, chapter and verse, from her trusty King James Bible. Mary Lou sighed. Waiting on the Lord—or seeking His kingdom—when one is in love is easier said than done.

"I do not want that for you," her mother whispered, stepping closer to her as though they were discussing some grave secret, "but if you were to choose to live outside the faith—" she wrung her fingers and looked away— "where would you go? What would you do?"

"I do not want that for me either," she retorted. "I have made a decision after *rumspringa*, *Maem*, that I do want to stay in the faith. The noise of the city and the electricity is too distracting to concentrate. It's too difficult to operate. I don't know how anyone can live with such contraptions. They're so difficult to use. I'd rather be closer to God, here. Here, I can hear Him." She nodded her head as though she wished to continue, but she could only manage to cross her arms over her chest.

"I am relieved to hear you say that, *Dochder*," her mother said, regaining some color and raising her voice as though it were safe to speak again. "Then you must be tasked with converting Jonah back to the faith."

"How? He is angry with God; he blames himself for any pain others have suffered around him. This is no easy task, *Maem*." Seeing how disappointed her mother was at her lack of faith, she added, timidly, "But I can certainly try."

Mary Lou couldn't look her mother in the eye lest she betray her lack of conviction at what she'd just promised. Her mother seemed convinced and wasted no time. "You should take a walk into town today. Jonah has not been into town since he arrived. I think it would be relaxing."

"Possibly, but only if you have some reason for us to go. I don't think I could go without a chore to complete." The task of converting Jonah and wooing him seemed far too daunting. Mary Lou needed a more manageable objective. *At least I could get something done with Jonah*, she reasoned.

"I can give you a list if that would make you feel better," her mother said with a smile. She went into the other room to fetch some ink and paper. Mary Lou wandered outside, figuring that the fresh air would clear her mind and do her some good. There Jonah stood, chopping wood. He smiled when he saw her and wiped the sweat from his brow.

"Hello," he said. "I wondered if I would wake you, as I was right outside your room."

"Oh no," Mary Lou said. "I came down to help mother with breakfast, as always. You've made quick work of that wood." She couldn't help but be impressed. *A fine husband, indeed.* Everything he did convinced her more and more of her love for him, and that she couldn't live without him, and it made her heart ache for she knew that she could not be unequally yoked. The notion of

45

missionary courting unsettled her. She did not like the pressure of returning someone to the faith only to marry him. The stakes would not be so high were he a stranger who rejected God. Now, though, her yearning for him and her yearning for God were tearing her apart. Furthermore, how could she be sure that he would convert unto God and not just for her? How could she know that he was genuine? Indeed, how could she be sure he loved her at all? She was distressed that this might be all for naught (as far as she was concerned) and at the pain of losing him, for she could not live without him. Perhaps a better Amish woman would concern herself only with the glory of the Lord.

"I try," Jonah replied. "I'm not sure that it is as fine as your father would like, but I'm hoping to improve my skills over the next few days."

"I'm sure he will be happy if only for the help because my brothers are not quite old enough for some of the tasks you have been doing. Your assistance with the things that he doesn't normally have help with will relieve him greatly."

"I'm happy to do so," he said and looked out at the sky. "It is so quiet out here."

Mary Lou nodded. "This is where I often come when there are decisions that plague me, and I just want to hear God's voice." She hadn't realized that she was on the cusp of exposing herself to him.

Mary Lou thought it best to change the subject lest he ask her a follow-up question about hearing God's voice. Her wit was not sharp enough at present to avoid an awkward confession. "*Maem* suggested that we go into town to collect a few things."

"That would be lovely." Jonah paused and looked her in the eye. Then he changed his tone as though nothing had happened and added, "I haven't been there yet, and I've been curious about it."

Mary Lou wondered if he had implied that a walk with her would be lovely. *Why did he look at me like that at first? Did he change his tone because he was embarrassed?* She hoped that she hadn't appeared dim-witted. "She has a list," Mary Lou said. "And knowing my mother, it may be quite the list. Is that okay?"

Jonah shrugged. "That's fine. It would give me a chance to truly see this community. I feel as though everyone whom we've met so far has been welcoming, and I am eager to see more of the town." She had hoped that he had wanted to see more of her.

"Had you expected them to be unfriendly?" Mary Lou asked.

Jonah shrugged again, then looked off into the sky. "I just thought... I wasn't sure. You know?"

Mary Lou nodded knowingly. She felt his pain. She wished that she could heal him, that he would stop blaming himself. She wanted to comfort him, but deep in her soul, she knew that he needed God's touch. That theological insight was both liberating and distressing to her.

"*Maem* has probably finished the list. We should head into town before she has a chance to add anything more."

"Yes," he grunted as he chopped the last piece of wood. "I'll fetch my coat, and then I'll be happy to escort you." There was that smile and the same look in his eye. *What was he trying to say?*

Mary Lou's mother handed them an almighty list. Her smile gently reminded Mary Lou of their chat, while Jonah believed she was acting as a child would whenever they saw two young adults together. He half expected her to ask him if Mary Lou was his girlfriend. But Leah was conniving. She was certain that a late morning walk was exactly what would get the flame burning. Mary Lou would see, yet again, just how strong Jonah was, how the community would welcome him and make him feel at home, and her daughter would imagine herself living here, with him, happily ever after. Just a little hope would boost her confidence, Leah figured.

"Please take your time. Enjoy yourselves, explore," she said. "I'm fine for help in the kitchen, and Joshua is all right in the barn."

"We won't be long, regardless," Jonah asserted. "I don't like the idea of either of you without help. It's the least I can do since you're hosting me."

"That's very kind," her mother said, smiling broadly at her daughter. Mary Lou tried not to blush nor roll her eyes. What she managed was to look like a confused lobster. Nevertheless, that was her mother's signal that she would approve of a courtship if Jonah were to ask. She hoped that he hadn't seen her face just then or her chances were *nil*.

Mary Lou admired her parents for being welcoming despite the situation. They encouraged her in her faith–that forgiveness, tolerance, and respect were owed not due to status, but because every human is made in God's image. She knew that some would judge Jonah for the situation he had been in and how he had reacted. Then again, she could not control everyone. What she was seeing lived out before her was Christlikeness; it touched her heart and gave her confidence that God could turn Jonah around. They left the house and strolled down the path into town. Jonah soaked it all in.

"Does it make you miss home?" she wondered.

"A little bit," he admitted. "My community is a little bit different. I try not to think about it, because…" he cleared his throat, "it makes my heart ache."

"I understand," she said. "Surely you can't avoid it forever."

"Why not? There's a whole world outside my community."

"There is," she said, gently. "And I understand why you may have painful memories returning there. But the pain will only grow the longer you stay away."

"I feel fine now," Jonah objected. They were silent for a while. Finally, he turned to her and said, "She loved this weather."

Mary Lou cocked her head, clearly unable to understand him.

"My sister," he continued "She loved this weather the most. She always wanted to be outside, and she thought this was the perfect temperature to play in. The way the air smells, it reminds me of her."

Of course, Mary Lou! Who else could he have meant! "Did she have a favorite color?" Mary Lou asked, unable to think of anything else to say. The Amish women rarely wore color, claiming that shades were more modest. Nevertheless, they secretly had favorite colors. Young girls weren't especially good at keeping them secret.

"Blue," he said. "A dark blue, like a deep ocean, not like the sky."

"That sounds lovely and practical. She would have made someone a lovely wife," Mary Lou heard herself say. Though she was inexperienced at comforting the broken-hearted, even she could see that she was talking too much.

"Yes," he said. "She would have done great things. I just..." Jonah choked up and they both stopped walking. Insecure about what to say, she could only stare at him. He couldn't hold her gaze. He looked away. Self-conscious that her look may have repulsed him, but unsure of what to do next, she froze, unable to take her eyes off him.

You know in your heart that it's not your fault, she desperately wanted to say to him. *There's nothing you could have done. I'm sure she's forgiven you, and that your parents have forgiven you. If you could only forgive yourself, you'd recognize the pearl that you are. No jeweler would reject a diamond for a mere flaw; no father would turn away a mourning son. No God would add to your grief. Come back to Him, and He will run to you with open arms like the prodigal son that you are.*

Utterly unaware of his companion's internal dialogue, Jonah felt he owed Mary Lou an explanation. "She trusted me to save her," he sniffled, desperately trying to hold back his tears. "She trusted me to make sure everything was taken care of. She would bring me rocks to keep safe, along with feathers, flowers, and scraps of paper that she wanted to treasure forever. I still have them." The shame of his latest confession weighed upon him so that he fell to his knees under its burden, his tears now pouring like water from a cracked jar.

"Sometimes, God calls us home," Mary Lou said to him. "And ours is not to understand why." She grew ever more frustrated with her responses, wondering angrily why she could not speak words of comfort in times of need, yet spout, with the greatest of ease, what was proving to be the most useless theological platitudes for the moment at hand. She could only pray that his weeping would drown her nonsense.

"It is easier said than done," Jonah said to her. Mary Lou's heart sank. *She was of no use! How could she re-convert him with such insensitivity?*

Taking her courage in both hands, she changed her approach. "I am sorry, Jonah. I am not being a good friend. Please forgive me."

Jonah took a deep breath and wiped his face. It only seemed to make matters worse. Snot and tears were smeared all over his swollen face, and his sleeve was soaked. He tried the other sleeve to the same effect. Only daring to look at Mary Lou from the corner of his eye, he smiled for his embarrassment. She giggled, relieved. He stood, wiped his face with both hands, and then dried them on his shirt and pants.

"Thank you," he said, to her. "I appreciate it."

Mary Lou cleared her throat to change the subject. "I think we should start at the dressmaker. There was my sister's dress that my mother simply could not alter, so she brought it there. I hope that she has found a way to make it bigger, because..." she stopped herself from saying that it had been 'outgrown'... "it is my sister's favorite dress."

"Fine," he mumbled as he scanned the list. He appeared grateful to have something else to focus on. "And then?"

"And then the general store. It makes sense, based on their location."

"Fine. How do I look?"

Mary Lou nodded, meaning he looked all right. They made their way into town. All in all, it took an hour to go through town and complete the errands. Of course, they stopped to talk to the workers at each shop. By the time they were headed home, Jonah was smiling again.

"Thank you," he said to her. "That was exactly what I needed."

"It's not quite a tour like the tour you gave me in the city," she said.

"Aye," he replied, as they walked. "And have you made an official decision about returning?"

"I have," she said to him. "I have sent a letter to Deliah saying that after a week at home, I can't imagine ever leaving again."

"I am sure they will be disappointed to lose you."

Mary Lou smiled, blushing slightly. "Deliah was very kind to me, but she knew that I wouldn't be there long. I told her I appreciated the opportunity and that I would never forget them. What about you?"

"I haven't been that brave yet," he confessed. "But I will let you know if I make a decision."

"And your parents?" Mary Lou asked. He shook his head. "There's still time to send them a note," she said. She hoped that Jonah would make his decision soon. Until then, she had to support him and offer him strength whenever she could, hopefully, better than she had on the way into town. There should be no rush. She didn't want him to feel unwelcome if he stayed a bit longer.

Mary Lou remembered what her mother said about Jonah being her future husband. Every time he smiled, she could see them growing old together as she stared into his eyes. Every time he glanced at her, she shivered, flattered at his attention. If this were what God intended for her, she would be happy. But it was up to Jonah to submit to God's will.

Once back at the house, her mother was delighted to see them again. "You two did well," she said, beaming. "I won't need to go into town for a month!"

"I am very happy to help," Jonah said. "As I was saying to your daughter, it is the least I can do."

"I have a letter for you," Leah said.

Jonah looked surprised. "For me?" he asked. "The only person to whom I gave a forwarding address was my boss."

"I think it is from there," she said. "Supplier...something?"

"That's them," Jonah said as he held out his hand.

"Is everything okay?" Mary Lou asked, concerned.

"Indeed," Jonah lied, as he opened it. His expression betrayed him, and she could see that everything was not all right. "I'm just going to be outside a moment." He hurried out of the door so quickly he almost lost his balance.

Mary Lou turned to her mother in shock. "What could it say? Do you think he's in trouble?"

"How quickly did you leave?" Leah asked her. "Did you give notice?"

"I thought that we both did, but I don't know. Things were not good when we left."

"Go to him," her mother said.

"Really? I would think that he would want some time alone." Plus, Mary Lou remembered that she had not been very effective the last time she had tried to comfort him.

"Go," her mother insisted.

Mary Lou gulped, and against her better judgment, headed outside.

Jonah was sitting on the tree stump where he had been chopping wood with his letter in his hand.

"Jonah?"

"Hey," he said, quietly.

"What is it? What's wrong?"

"When we left the city…they didn't exactly give me permission to go," he said. "They said that if I left, they would put my absence under review, and then let me know."

"Let you know what?"

Jonah sighed. "Whether I would be granted a leave of absence or whether I would be fired."

"Oh," she said. "So, the letter says…"

"The letter says that I have been granted a leave of absence, but that I must return within two weeks or else I lose my job."

"And it's already been a week. That's very soon," she noted.

"I know. I wasn't prepared to make a decision so quickly."

Mary Lou sat beside him. "Well, it is just a job, isn't it?"

"It's the only job that would take me. I don't have any experience, and I don't have a proper education. If I leave, I leave on bad terms. Getting a new job would be almost impossible."

"Well…getting another English one might be difficult," she prodded.

He put the letter in his back pocket. "Yeah. I guess God is telling me that I must decide about my life soon."

"Well, whatever you decide, I support you."

"You are too good to me," he said.

Mary Lou shrugged as though it were nothing. "You deserve happiness, Jonah. And you have not had much of it these past few years. I'm glad to do anything that I can."

"What about you?"

"What about me?"

"You deserve happiness as well," he said. "And I feel that I owe you a great deal for bringing me here and risking your reputation by being seen with me, a fallen Amish."

"I risked nothing. All I did was to answer the call that was in my heart by ending my *rumspringa* early. I have had my taste of the English world, and this is my choice and my faith."

"It must be nice to be so certain in your choice."

"But I am not certain. And it is because I am uncertain that I know I have to be here."

"How does that work?" he asked. "If you are uncertain…"

"I know that I need to rely on God. Of that, I am certain. What is to be my course of action is, as yet, undetermined. The English world is devoid of Him. I need to meet Him here that I might hear him clearly. Then I will obey."

"I admire you, Mary Lou. Do you know that?"

She blushed. "No one has ever told me they admired me before."

"Well, consider it the first of many compliments I hope to give you," he said. Her heart soared! She could picture their future together. She could see their home, their children, their life fulfilled. And then, rather anti-climactically, he opined, "Come on, we should head inside."

*****

"Wasn't that a delightful service?" Mary Lou asked Jonah, after their second church service together. It had been two weeks since he had come to the community, and neither of them had any plans of leaving soon. Jonah had been fully welcomed by the community. Mary Lou hadn't decided what she was going to do with the remainder of her *rumspringa*. Jonah knew that what he wanted was to stay a little longer, though he kept any specifics to himself.

"It was," Jonah agreed enthusiastically. It was as if his soul were set ablaze. Jonah felt like a new man in the two weeks since he had returned to an Amish community. "I felt as if I understood every word of the message, that it was preached just for me. I could hear God speak to me during the reading. And the singing was beautiful. I do believe your community sings much better than mine."

"I'm sure that is not true," she said.

"Well, I'll have to take you to mine some time, to compare."

She turned to him, at once surprised and hopeful. "Would you?" she asked.

Jonah had been partially joking, but when he saw the look in her eyes, he paused. "Would you like that?" he asked.

"Oh yes! I would love to meet your family, especially now that you've met mine. I would love to see all the places where you grew up and hear the happy memories of your childhood…to meet your friends."

"Not all the places in that community are happy," he reminded her.

Mary Lou nodded. "I know, but I would be with you, to help you find strength when you feel as though you have none."

"I like the way you say that," he said, as he turned to her. "When I feel as though I have none, instead of when I have none."

"Because you always have strength," she said to him, as their eyes met. "Especially when you are at your weakest. Moments like that are when the Bible says we are strong."

"Mary Lou, how did you become so wise?"

She smiled at that. "I wasn't always so wise, but talking to you…" She started over: "Whenever I'm with you, I feel as if God speaks through me. I can hear Him clearly when you are around." She had progressed in how she handled his sorrow since their first walk into town. She leaned heavily on Holy Spirit to give her words of comfort and obeyed when prompted to be still. She was proud of her recent efforts.

"Well, that would explain how you always know the right thing to say," Jonah replied. "I hope that I can hear you inspire me for the rest of my life."

"Of course, I will always…" she paused suddenly. *For the rest of your life?* she mouthed.

"Yes," he said. "For the rest of my life. Do you understand what I'm saying?"

Mary Lou shook her head. Her heart beat faster, her mouth went dry, and her head spun. *What were these words coming out of his mouth? Could it be?* It was so sudden, too good to be true.

"Mary Lou," he said. "Since I met you, you have been kind and inspiring. You have made me laugh, and you have brought me hope when I had none. You have brought me back from the very brink of darkness and shown me the light again."

She blushed furiously. "I just did what was right, Jonah."

"Then I hope you always do such good and always do right. And I was hoping that we could spend the rest of our lives together so I could support you in doing such things."

She felt faint. "Jonah…" she babbled, reaching for him to maintain her balance as he stood in the middle of the road.

"Mary Lou," he replied. "Would you do me the honor of being

my wife?"

She thought she was going to swoon. Words failed her. She looked at him, utterly wooed by his strength, his ruggedness, his voice. He raised his eyebrows as though he were waiting for something, but she couldn't imagine what it was. It would have to wait; this moment would only happen once in her lifetime. Then it dawned on her:

"Yes," she blurted. "Yes, I will marry you."

"Wonderful!" he cried. "Then you've made me the happiest man in the world."

"Mary Lou!" Their happy moment was interrupted by her father, who was running after them. He was shouting and panicked.

"Mary Lou!" he said when he got close. His eyes were red, and he looked as if he could barely breathe. "Naomi...Naomi..."

"What about Naomi?" she asked, confused. Naomi was her youngest sister, and she had been in church with them until about half an hour ago, when she had gotten restless. She and some of the other children had been taken out by some of the older children, to play until the service was over. *"Daed*, what's wrong?"

"She was playing by the river and..." her father could barely speak.

Mary Lou's heart dropped. She put her hand to her mouth. *"Daed*! Say it isn't so!"

Joshua shook his head, and then burst into tears.

Mary Lou turned to Jonah, whose face was dark. She took a step towards him, for comfort, but Jonah took a step away.

"Don't come close to me, Mary Lou," said Jonah. His voice was flat. "Don't come close to me. For I bring doom upon any community I enter."

And with that, her fiancé, her hope, and her happiness turned and ran.

BOOK 2

CHAPTER 1

Mary Lou had always known what to do. She had always been patient, kind, and someone to whom solutions came easily. She had always made contingencies upon contingencies, and she could anticipate a situation before it ever happened. However, she never expected her new fiancé to run. She never expected her baby sister to go missing in the river, just like his. She never expected to be standing in the middle of her community in tears.

It had taken so long to get Jonah to open up to her, let alone trust her. Mary Lou's *rumspringa* in the city had been short, but she understood why she had been led to do it. Her Amish future assured, she had nevertheless felt like she needed to take *rumspringa* to explore the world outside of her community, just in case there was something out there that she'd discover about God. The English world both fascinated and terrified her, and she thought working as a seamstress in a small shop and living above it would be enough to explore it.

Meeting Jonah, an Amish man her age who had left his community after his baby sister's drowning, had been unexpected, as was falling in love with him. Mary Lou quickly came to her senses to realize God's hand in it all, so she had him escort her to her community to try and heal his soul. Not only did it work, but he proposed, yet another blind side, although she had hoped for it. Most devastatingly, she was caught off-guard when her father came upon them, in what should have been the happiest moment of her life, and told her that her little sister had drowned in the river, just like Jonah's.

Mary Lou would never forget Jonah's words as he ran: *"Don't come close to me, Mary Lou. Don't come close to me. For I bring doom on any community I enter."*

Rumspringa had surprised Mary Lou. It had disarmed her and robbed her of her planning abilities. Most notably, it had blocked her capacity to anticipate. Little did she know, love had the same capacity for mystery and suspense.

Jonah hadn't been seen since the moment when he turned and ran. In the days that followed, Mary Lou's sister Naomi was mourned and buried. Life was supposed to return to normal after that, but for Mary Lou, life would never be the same. Jonah was gone, treated by most around her as though he had been a mere moment in her life rather than the person with whom she was to spend the rest of her life. Having nowhere to write to him to beg him to return only increased her longing for him. Unaware of his whereabouts, she questioned whether she had the energy to search for him. Naomi's death weighed heavily on her mind, and her family grievingly dragged themselves through their daily activities. In the evening, they drearily met at the supper table, exhausted by the burden of carrying their heavy hearts since dawn.

Mary Lou doubted whether it would all make sense again. Nevertheless, every morning, she arose, washed her face, and changed her clothes in anticipation of hope. Despite its distance from her despair, each new day was one of hope in God. If He could raise Christ from the dead, surely, He could make a way out of her despair. She would assume her usual routine of helping her mother with breakfast.

"I think I need to go back," Mary Lou said to her mother, out of the blue. They were rolling out dough for sticky buns, and normally, they talked while they did it, although lately this chore had been infected with silence.

"Go back where?" her mother asked.

"To the city."

"What?" her mother retorted in shock. "You finished your *rumspringa*, Mary Lou. You made your choice."

"I left that job, yes," she said. "But I didn't end my *rumspringa*. I was only there for a few weeks. I don't know what to do now, but I don't think I can stay here."

"This is your home," her mother objected

"I know, but I don't think...*Maem*, I don't know what to do."

"You think you don't know what to do?" Leah's voice trailed, overwhelmed by emotion. Mary Lou stopped rolling out the dough and went to hug her mother.

"*Maem*, we've both been through such a hard time. I can't begin to understand the pain you must feel, losing a child. But you must also understand how I feel disoriented now, as well."

Leah wiped away her tears. "Yes. I do understand. My own pain blinds me. You've lost, too. If only God would take this pain away!" They fell back into each other's' arms, weeping.

"I have to trust that God will reveal His plan," Mary Lou finally said. "So, you understand why I have to go?"

"My heart is torn," Leah cried. "I feel like I am losing two daughters."

Mary Lou tried to hold back her tears. "You are not," she said. "I promise, I will come back. I just thought...I had my whole life planned out. I thought that the path was clear, and it was not. So, I have to go back to where it was clear." Her grief confused her, and she forgot how opaque her path in the city had seemed.

"Okay," her mother relented. "What do you need?"

"Well, right now, I just need to finish making breakfast. I will talk to *Daed*, and we can make arrangements as soon as he comes in."

"Do you think that you'll want to go right away?"

Mary Lou sighed. The pressure to find a way forward in the darkness of her mourning only exacerbated her pain.

"I don't know," she confessed. "I don't know if I can get my job back, and I don't know if I can live in the apartment that I left."

"Do you think he's back there?"

"Jonah? I don't know."

"Do you hope he's back there?"

"I…" Mary Lou took a deep breath. "I don't know that either. He left so suddenly, and I know that he has a lot of past trauma. But if he left that suddenly, who knows how he'd hold up against the fact that we are supposed to be together, for better or for worse? I am trying to find forgiveness in my heart, but when I needed him the most…he left." It was Mary Lou's first clear insight since Naomi's passing.

"I hope that God will guide you," her mother wished, "so that you know what the right answer is. If Jonah's meant to be your husband, then God will find the right path to bring him back to you. And if he's not…" she stiffened her back before continuing, "then you will find another man."

"I am certain that Jonah is the one. I have never been more certain of anything in my life."

"And only a moment ago you weren't? I wonder if this time in the city will only make things worse!" Her mother's bluntness irked her. She fought the urge the leave, but then her sorrow ambushed her. Mary Lou wept.

Unable to bring herself to comfort her daughter, yet unwilling to pursue the discussion at hand, Leah carried on with preparing breakfast in silence. Mary Lou gathered herself and resumed rolling out the dough, sniffling as her soul bled. Neither could find joy in their hearts in what was a precious memory between a mother and her firstborn. When Mary Lou's father came in from doing chores with her brothers, she dropped the news on him without waiting for him to eat. Manners failed her. Taken aback by his daughter's unusual lack of tact, Joshua reached for his breakfast and savored the fresh bun. He dropped it like a hot potato when he remembered that he hadn't yet said grace. Catching his sons' surprised looks, he bowed his head and closed his eyes. That morning, grace was longer than usual. Joshua didn't seem to want to return to the situation at hand, choosing instead to blow it away with the hot air of a rambling prayer. Once he finally said, "Amen," the food was cold. He looked up lovingly at his daughter, who had instantly understood his method of calming them all from the shock of her news.

Joshua was emotionally even-keeled compared to Leah's fiery character. He held his daughter's gaze, then grunted in agreement. "You are entitled to finish your *rumspringa*," he said to Mary Lou. "When do you want to go?"

"I'll write some letters and make arrangements," was all Mary Lou could manage.

Her father nodded knowingly. "You just let us know, but I don't think you should pin your hopes on finding Jonah again."

"Why?" she asked, suddenly exposed.

"From what I've heard, he has not returned to the city. I wrote to his father to tell him that his son had been here. He wrote back, thanking me for the news. The last he heard, Jonah had been traveling."

"Oh," Mary Lou muttered as she swallowed her disappointment "Well, returning to the city is not...just for Jonah."

"Indeed," her father said. "I just wanted you to know what you may find."

"*Danki*," Mary Lou said. "And thank you for writing to his father. I should get to writing things of my own."

After breakfast, Mary Lou headed up to her room to do just that. She had a few leads where she could investigate because she had bought an English newspaper with job and apartment postings the week before. This time would be different from the previous time, when the seamstress who had hired her had known of her faith and that she may not stay. This time, she would be on her own. That would be an advantage. Her community seemed glum, particularly towards her and her double loss, leaving her family to themselves. *Blessed are those who mourn, for they shall be comforted* seemed not to be interpreted as a command, but as a promise that comfort would eventually come from the Father. It was no wonder where Mary Lou got her inability to console others. She could forgive herself for her poor showing with Jonah on their way to the general store a few weeks prior. Indeed, leaving this place to return to *rumspringa* would ensure quicker healing.

Many workplaces asked for a resumé that Mary Lou didn't have and didn't know how to prepare. Her only paid work experience was her brief stint at the seamstress shop. Some establishments asked for letters of interest. Perhaps her sewing and organizational skills would be an asset.

Then something caught her eye: *Wardrobe apprentice, entry-level, Sky Theatre.*

The Sky Theatre was well known in town. Mary Lou had never been inside, or in any sort of theatre for that matter. She knew that it attracted many tourists every night, and she had heard them express their satisfaction as they poured out of the matinées (Mary Lou was never about town in the evening). She decided she'd call to express her interest. After all, this was still *rumspringa*.

"Is it okay if I go to the general store to make a phone call?" she asked her parents that afternoon.

"I'll take you there," her father offered.

The general store was just down the road, but Amish women were rarely unescorted in public. The store was the only place in town that had a phone. Mary Lou had used one once before when she called from the city to come home; otherwise, she had no experience using one. She thought that it was going to be easy, but when she got to the store and got permission to use the phone, words escaped her.

"What is expressing interest?" she asked, perplexed. "Is it just...telling them that I'm interested in the job?"

"I suppose," her father grunted as he browsed the store. Mary

Lou took a deep breath and dialed the number. It rang three times, and then someone picked up.

"Sky Theatre," a female voice said dryly.

Mary Lou swallowed. "Hi, I uh…saw your advertisement in the newspaper, so, I am…expressing interest?"

"The wardrobe assistant?" said the voice.

"Yes. I have some seamstress experience and…"

"Have you ever dressed a bunch of little kids really quickly?" the woman interrupted. "It's for a show that has a lot of child actors, so we need someone to help before the show and then for costume changes and such."

"Oh, yes," Mary Lou said. "I have lots of brothers and sisters."

"Great. Will you come in tomorrow for an interview?"

"Oh…tomorrow?" Mary Lou asked. "I don't have a resumé or anything…"

The woman was disinterested. "That's all right, we'll be testing you on the spot. Come prepared to dress a bunch of hyperactive young actors."

"Sure," Mary Lou said. "At what time?"

"6:00 p.m."

Mary Lou agreed before having thought about the logistics. In fact, the speed at which the entire conversation had gone had made her reluctant to ask anything else, fearful that she'd miss the opportunity to get away from the stench of grief and mourning that plagued her. Her parents lived a simple life, as did the rest of the Amish community, and while she had never stayed in a hotel, she knew that they were expensive. Thus, an escort would need to be arranged, and perhaps a second in order to return. She hung up, hopeful that her healing would begin on the morrow.

CHAPTER 2

Mary Lou didn't realize that she wanted the job until it was given to her. She had a fantastic time at the theatre, helping to dress all the child actors, loving every moment of it. Since she was basically made for the job, they had an offer ready for her on the spot, and Mary Lou even signed the contract before she thought about her next step. Being with children soothed her. It was therapeutic. With so many about, she found comfort despite her sister's passing. Perhaps she had been eager to return to the city's anonymity.

Peace and nostalgia enveloped Mary Lou as she rode with her father back into town. She had seen many of the streets where she and Jonah had walked. Every place held a memory: a moment of laughter, a moment of sadness, each a moment of closeness. The buggy rode past the park where they had first conversed. Her father was oblivious. These memories were personal and private, meant only to share with her...love. She would not use the word *fiancé* since their status as betrothed had lasted but a fleeting, death-stained moment. She was lost in thought and eerily quiet until they got to the theatre.

"Do you provide any housing with your job?" Mary Lou asked upon her arrival, contract in hand. She couldn't believe that she had gotten the job so easily.

"Uh, no," Caroline, the lead wardrobe supervisor said. "But I can make some suggestions for a few places to live if you like? What kind of budget are you on?"

"Whatever this pays."

Caroline nodded. "Here, let me write down a few places. I didn't realize you were from out of town. You'll be okay?"

"Yes, my father has put aside some of his chores to take me home."

"Oh, how kind! So, you still live at home? Is this your first time in the city?"

"No," Mary Lou said, uncomfortable with this line of questioning. She didn't want to go into more detail, but Caroline was looking at her expectantly. She felt forced to say more. "I uh...I met my fiancé here."

"Oh, so that's why you want to move," Caroline winked at her. It took a second before Mary Lou realized that Caroline was implying that she and Jonah were going to move in together.

"No, no, it's nothing like that," Mary Lou said. Then, despite herself, she continued. "I don't...really know where he is right now." She instantly regretted opening up that way.

The older woman didn't know how to respond, herself feeling Mary Lou's discomfort at her latest confession. Caroline opened her mouth to discover her verbal constipation, then chose to purse her lips and raise her eyebrows before finally deciding to smile at the girl. Sensing she was forgetting something, her hand shot out before her like a jack-in-the-box. Mary Lou helped herself to the paper and examined the list.

"Well, good luck," Caroline managed. "We'll see you next week."

An embarrassed Mary Lou turned quickly towards the door before heading back out to find her father. He had said that he might circle the block a couple of times, as the horses didn't like to stay still in the big city for long. She stood there, in the darkness, waiting for him, and watched everyone rushing by her. The city was busy, and there were people of all shapes and sizes wearing clothing as diverse as the flavors in a Russell Stover box of chocolates. No one, however, looked twice at Mary Lou. She was strangely grateful for, now, she could understand Jonah's desire to be in the city when he mourned. It was refreshing to see expressions other than pity. She felt normal.

As Mary Lou looked out for her father, her heart stopped. Across the street and turning the corner, she saw a familiar dark head of hair go by. It was Jonah. It had to be Jonah. She had only seen his back, but his back was the last she saw of him. Besides, he had a recognizable gait, an unmissable curve to his cheekbone, and a special place in Mary Lou's memory. She'd recognize him anywhere, at any angle.

"JONAH!" she cried out, but he didn't turn around. He had to know she was there. Surely, he would be glad to see her again. "JONAH!" Still no reaction, and he was getting further away. She set her jaw and took three steps forward, calling out to him again. "JONAH!" She had not realized that her momentum had taken her into the street. Though she had Jonah's physique committed to memory, she was loathe to remember city etiquette. She had forgotten that the city was noisy and that no one paid attention to anyone there. She had forgotten that there were no carriages moving at a slow pace. There were cars, zigzagging through traffic and moving through the intersection at breakneck speed. If she had remembered any of those things, she might have been fine. But she didn't, and so she darted out right in front of a car.

Mary Lou didn't see it. She had no idea what had hit her. She felt the impact and heard the screech of the tires on the asphalt, but all of the driver's efforts were to no avail. He hit her. She hit the pavement, unconscious.

The next thing she knew, Mary Lou was somewhere else, somewhere brighter and familiar, though not warm like home, but stale and bland. Her pain surprised her, but her confusion did not deter her. One memory flooded back, before all the rest.

"JONAH!" she sat up and cried.

In an instant, several people were at Mary Lou's side. They were all wearing white coats or blue scrubs, and they pushed her back down.

"Lie down," one said. "Lie down. Everything is okay."

"Where's Jonah?" she asked. "I want to see Jonah."

"Who's Jonah?" another one asked.

"My fiancé," Mary Lou managed. "I don't know if I should even be calling him that anymore, given that he turned and ran." At that point, her pain and her heartache intersected in her throat, forcing a deep wail from the pit of her soul. City folk had never heard it before, but anyone who grew up on a farm would say it sounded like trapped prey in a predator's grip. Then her cry moved to her eyes, and she wept as a tub overflowing, as though life itself were fleeing her being. In a flash, she could see Naomi dying and Jonah leaving, causing her to feel excruciating pain.

Mary Lou sobbed inconsolably. She just wanted to go home, back to her simple Amish community, back to her faith and the tranquility of it all. She wanted the past few weeks back. Her sorrow deafened her and prevented her from making sense of her surroundings. Panic set in. She convulsed, kicked, and punched at the air and her bed as though it would rid her of her fear.

Those standing to attend to Mary Lou could not fathom her gloom. She had not yet heard her prognosis, which, as bad as it was, would not have warranted her present reaction. Finally, one spoke up.

"Mary Lou, we're doctors," one of the men said loudly. "We're going to help you. You were hit by a car, but you're going to be all right."

"What?" she could barely make sense of that. "But I…there are no cars."

"There are cars, my dear," he reassured her. "And you got hit by a big one. So just relax. The morphine ought to be killing the pain."

The Amish girl took a deep breath, recognizing now that she

was in the city and not in her community.

"We're going to get that all checked out," the doctor continued. "Do you live with anyone? Is there anyone you can call?"

"My dad was with me," she said. "My dad brought me into town and…"

"Okay, we'll find your father, don't worry."

"He didn't come in?" she exclaimed. "He was coming to get to me."

"It's okay. Relax, we'll find him."

"Okay," she said, only half calmly. "Thank you."

"Don't worry about a thing." Then the doctor quickly turned and left. Mary Lou was lonely and confused. She wanted nothing more than to see a familiar face. She tried getting up to see if her father was there, but her limbs were numb, and her muscles rebelled. She lay back down, defeated.

At that moment, she heard a voice she thought she would never hear again.

"Mary Lou?" said a voice beyond the curtain.

"Jonah?" she replied and tried to sit up. Her face lit up as the curtain parted. Her pain melted away, and she smiled pathetically, like a deer on new legs, each emotion vivid and palpable, making her face look like someone who'd never smiled before. Her eyes and cheeks were puffy and red, her skin pale. It was a face only a fiancé could love. With arms open wide, she reached for him, then winced. She had, after all, just been hit by a car. "Jonah, it was you," she whispered, relieved.

Jonah looked ragged, and Mary Lou could only imagine what he had been doing for the past two weeks. He looked like he hadn't had a wink of sleep nor a bite to eat in ages. His eyes were dark rings, his hair unkempt, and his robust physique was now wilted like a diseased man's.

"What are you doing here, in the city?" he asked. "You shouldn't be here. You should be living your life in the community, far away from me."

"I…" she licked her lips. Her mouth was parched, and her breathing laborious. "I came to continue my *rumspringa*," she coughed, then swallowed hard.

"I told you, Mary Lou, that I am a curse on anyone whom I come across."

Mary Lou discovered a new pain in her head and wondered how much more her body had to reveal to her before pain would cease its surprise. With her head pounding, she valiantly offered, "Jonah, you aren't a curse. I missed you…"

"I…missed you too," he confessed. Jonah gazed into Mary Lou's hazel eyes. Under normal circumstances, she would be entranced, but with the residual pain that even the morphine could not kill, her heart and her head contradicted each other in love-filled hurt. Still, he was at her side. What a good husband he would make. She was certain that he would be her husband, though it was difficult to tell whether it was God or the morphine speaking. Probably the morphine, since God would likely have made a man of Jonah who could suffer as Christ suffered. Indeed, his faith was weak, and he knew it. He loved her but felt as though he didn't deserve her. He was not the man he wanted to be, and he was too stubborn to let the Potter mold the clay. "But you shouldn't be here," Jonah continued, then held his tongue, sensing that this argument could have no therapeutic benefit whatsoever.

"Jonah," she finally said. "We aren't married yet, so…"

"Yet? Yet! You still think that we're getting married?" his temper getting the better of him. His mind knew that it was inappropriate, but his mouth had a mind of its own. He had gotten mouthy in his time away from the Amish. Bitterness did that to a soul.

"We…you proposed to me," she reminded him.

"I proposed to you before I remembered I'm a curse on the whole world. You saw me again, and you got hit by a car." He said it like a lawyer making his closing arguments.

"That's not your fault," she said. "It's the fault of the driver.

And maybe me, for stepping into the road."

"I wish you hadn't come here," Jonah pronounced, trying to change the subject. He did not want to talk *marriage*; he wished, instead, to remain in the morass of self-loathing that would keep others away from him. Ironically, he blamed her for what happened as though her mere presence triggered his curse.

The doctor returned. He shot a confused glance at Jonah, then addressed Mary Lou. "Is this Jonah?"

Mary Lou nodded.

"Welcome, Jonah. I'm Dr. Martin." The middle-aged man shook Jonah's hand firmly. He was built like a linebacker– thick-necked, broad-shouldered, with arms like stovepipes. He was slightly taller than Jonah. Hair had evacuated his head and relocated onto his face, which he kept trimmed and neat. His thick, gray whiskers made him look distinguished. His blue scrubs accentuated dark blue eyes, which were paradoxically reassuring and intimidating. He gave Mary Lou the impression that he was seldom, if ever, contradicted. "Have you seen her father, perchance?"

Jonah shook his head. "But I know what he looks like. They are Amish, in case you couldn't tell, so we can't call him or anything."

"Do you think you could find him?" Dr. Martin asked. "I think Mary Lou would appreciate him here."

"Yes, I would," Mary Lou confirmed. "But Jonah, don't be long."

"I'll find your father," Jonah said before heading off.

Dr. Martin had several files in his hand. "I have your x-rays here," he announced. "Do you remember when we did the x-ray?"

"No, I don't remember an x-ray."

"You have been in shock. This must all be new for you since you are Amish. Have you ever seen a doctor before?"

"Not in the English world," she said. "Only in my community."

"And you don't have any past medical history?"

She shook her head, forgetting her sickness the previous year.

"Okay," he continued. "So, I did an x-ray on your arm. It's not broken, and you don't seem to have a concussion. Any head pain?"

"From all of the crying…"

"A drink of water will do you good." Dr. Martin reached for a bottle of water on the table next to Mary Lou's bed. For the first time, she took in her surroundings. Her bed was by a window to her left. There was a small, brown table with two drawers to her right, a lamp above her head, and a navy blue plastic chair at the foot of the bed. A panel of buttons for adjusting the bed's tilt and height was installed on its right guard rail, though she hadn't the faintest idea what they were for. Curtains separated what were certainly other patients in the room, their coughs and moans clearly heard from where she lay. The space was small, cramped even.

Mary Lou looked out. It was dark outside, but there were no stars in the sky. She wondered why, but fatigue set in. Her curiosity vanished. She sipped some water, then lay her head onto her pillow.

Dr. Martin continued. "Sometimes injuries from car accidents can manifest themselves days later. We'll be better able to see if you've suffered any internal damage once the swelling goes down. You might feel stiff or sore for a few weeks. We'll give you medicine to manage the pain. You'll stay here overnight so we can keep an eye on you. Another doctor will chat with you in the morning."

Someone pulled open the curtain. "Mary Lou!" It was Joshua. He reached for his daughter and pressed her to him. Mary Lou yelped like a dog whose tail was trod upon. He released her, afraid that he might have caused more harm. "Is this where you've been? How are you?"

"I'll be fine, *Daed*. Nothing's broken. I just need to rest here tonight."

Jonah was lingering in the background. Mary Lou caught his eye and thanked him.

"*Gern gschehne*," he said. "I should leave you two alone

73

now."

"No! Stay!" Mary Lou cried more frantically than she expected. She looked at the other two men, composed herself, then pleaded once more, "Stay, Jonah. Please, stay."

Jonah was torn. He feared Joshua and any reaction he might have, but he couldn't bear the thought of breaking Mary Lou's heart anew. He held her gaze, took a deep breath, then acquiesced. "Okay. Just for a little while."

Joshua was perplexed. It pleased him to see Mary Lou relieved, but he was in no mood to tolerate Jonah's self-pity. He said a little prayer.

Mary Lou figured that a little while was better than nothing. She could quiz him about his whereabouts and make an appointment to see him in the morning. Surely, he'd agree.

Dr. Martin answered Joshua's questions, excused himself, then quickly resumed his rounds. Joshua, seated on the bed, turned to his eldest and squeezed her hand. He inquired briefly about her condition, then bowed his head. They prayed for Mary Lou, for good health, and for Holy Spirit's blessed calmness when Leah received the news. Jonah had remained just outside of the curtain. He thought it wise to remain in Mary Lou's line of sight whilst avoiding Joshua's. Also, he was giving the pair a moment to themselves.

"I could stay in the city," Mary Lou suggested. "I'm supposed to stay and find an apartment."

"You can't stay alone!" her father objected. "Not when this has happened to you."

"But I won't be alone. Jonah will be nearby if I need any help, won't you?" She looked expectantly at her betrothed.

Jonah looked like he was put on the spot. He froze, mouth open, surprised at Mary Lou, who hadn't bothered to ask if he lived in the city or if he planned to stay around to help her. Then he thought about it to realize that she knew exactly what she was doing. How shrewd!

"Because we're getting married," she added. "And he's going

to help me get well."

Jonah swallowed hard and turned to Mary's Lou's father. "Yes, that was my plan," he lied.

Joshua teetered between pleasing his daughter and pleasing his wife. He could not contact another Amish person to stay with her in his stead, nor could he rely on his younger boys to tend to the farm. He had chores to do at dawn and a long way home in the dark. No one else could take his place there, whilst at the hospital, the failed Amish boy was a tolerable substitute. It was less than ideal, but it solved Joshua's dilemma. Returning home was his only option. He felt as though he were leaving the one to tend to the 99. *However*, he reasoned, *they are engaged*. His wife would not approve, nor would she be pleased if the farm were neglected. So, he acquiesced to the woman at hand. Satisfied, he nodded in agreement. "If you're sure. Jonah, do you have a place to stay here?"

"Yes, I have a place," Jonah confirmed.

"And you can help my daughter find a place of her own?" he asked, sternly.

"Yes, sir. And I will take good care of Mary Lou."

"Please, call the general store if there is anything amiss," he instructed both of them. "I must get back to the farm before dawn."

"I will," Jonah promised. "Thank you, sir, for trusting me."

Joshua gave his daughter one last hug, then turned to shake Jonah's hand. "Thank you for doing this," he said, half relieved. Mary Lou understood farm life, so she did not resent her father for leaving. Plus, the time alone with Jonah would allow her to work on him uninterrupted. She bid her father goodbye and then turned to Jonah.

"*Danki*," she said.

He took a deep breath and looked away.

"I don't know if I can do this," Jonah said.

Mary Lou didn't respond. They didn't know what the future held, but they were going to try to make one together, and that was what mattered. Jonah was going to have to be coaxed along, was all.

All would be well. At least, it was for now. God had returned Jonah to her, and she was grateful. She was worry-free. Tomorrow could worry about itself; each day had enough troubles of its own.

CHAPTER 3

Jonah kept his word, though he was torn. He had left the hospital shortly after Mary Lou's father did to discuss matters with his housemates and to prepare a place for his...friend. He could not bring himself to call Mary Lou his *fiancée*, not because there was another girl, but because of his conviction that her life would be better without him. Morose and feeling responsible for her fragile state, he returned to her side in the afternoon in order to take her home with him.

"Where are you staying?" Mary Lou asked, looking somewhat stronger than she had the last time he had seen her. The sleep had done her good, and, as ever, she was in good spirits. Jonah did not realize that her perky demeanor was elevated to joyousness on his account. Indeed, his self-pity made him miss a great many things about her, like her gasp whenever she countenanced his presence in a room, the quick inhalation of a woman whose breath had been taken away.

"I'm actually staying just outside the city," he answered. "There are several theatre performers renting a big house out there. They needed someone on-site to do the maintenance and yard work. It's an old house, so they need someone more experienced in that area."

"And older houses are our specialty." Mary Lou winked. Then

her mood sobered before she asked, "Are they…they aren't all men, are they?"

"No. It's co-ed. I talked to them last night, and they are happy to have you stay in one of the guest rooms."

Mary Lou grabbed Jonah's arm with both of her hands and almost squealed. "Well, that's exciting. They know I'm Amish, don't they? And do they know that I'm working in the theatre, too?"

"*You're* working in the theatre? Since when?"

"Since yesterday. I'm the new assistant wardrobe stylist."

"Well I'll be…" his voice trailed off.

"Why? You think I can't do the job?"

"No, it's not that," he replied, truthfully. "It just seems…like an odd twist of fate."

"Everything about us is an odd twist of fate. God works in ways that we cannot understand."

There was a moment of silence as Jonah reckoned with her latest confession. Peculiarly, his spirits lifted, like a cobra out of a basket to the tune of the charmer's flute. He felt hope. Then, almost automatically, the mongoose of sorrow sank its teeth into the cobra's neck.

"Well, so far, God's ways haven't been positive," he said, gloomily.

Mary Lou turned to him in shock. "What?" She could not believe that he wasn't overjoyed that they'd been reunited. This, him before her, was all she had wanted for weeks. And he was going to have that attitude?

"You heard me. God's ways have not been positive."

Then it dawned on Mary Lou: she had a mission from God to return Jonah to the faith. She chided herself for forgetting and for expecting something more. It was clear that her work had not been complete. Besides, he was unreasonable in the city. There was something about nature that soothed him. It was clear to her that they were back where they had started when they first met. She settled into her wheelchair and resumed her role as a servant of God.

"You can say that," she said calmly. Then she added, "But we can agree that His ways aren't always clear to us, can't we?"

Conflicted and unwilling to give any ground, Jonah declared, "I don't really want to talk about it right now, if that's okay."

"Well, we have to talk about it if we're going to get married." Mary Lou had only meant to say that under her breath, the last vestige of a girl in love, but he had heard her, nonetheless.

Jonah stopped the wheelchair in the hallway and crouched down before her. "Mary Lou, I can't marry you." Then in staccato, he added, "We're not getting married."

"Why not?" she asked, her tone more like that of a petulant child than a servant of the Most High. "You told my father that you were going to marry me." Now she did sound like a little girl who was not getting her way. *Perhaps it's the medicine?* she thought. God's mission was fading out of her mind. Mary Lou felt vulnerable in the chair and desperate to keep Jonah around as she gazed into his dark green eyes. She could not suffer the thought of losing him again.

"I know I did. I told your father that because I wanted him to let you stay here. I was afraid he'd insist on taking you home because of some stupid Amish rule. It would kill you! I knew you needed to stay in the hospital; I knew you wanted me around, and I knew that you wouldn't rest until you got what you wanted. You needed to save your energy, so I gave in. I admire you for knowing what you want and knowing what to do to make it happen."

"I don't always know what to do," she sighed. All planning, strategizing, conniving, and manipulating escaped her at present. *I am doomed to be with him for but a short while; then he'll be gone again, and I'll be alone*, she thought.

"Let's go to the house. You need rest." Jonah rose to take his place behind Mary Lou. They did not utter a word as he pushed her to the parking lot, then to a car. She balked.

"Jonah! This is a car," she said. He stopped. There before her was a matted gray automobile. She couldn't tell how old it was or whether its two-tone coloration was a good thing or a bad thing. There was no way for her to tell its condition since she had no experience in any horseless carriage. All that she knew was that it was a car, and she couldn't believe Jonah expected her to ride in it.

"Yes?" he replied, trying not to sound too sarcastic for fear of being overheard and reprimanded, given her present state. Then he changed tack and continued, reassuringly. "I know you may be a little scared after what happened last night…"

"No, it's fine," she interrupted, shaking her head, for he had misunderstood her. Unwilling to appear rude, but still wanting to convey her Amish beliefs, at least subtly, she asked, "You can drive?"

"I was a delivery boy," he reminded her, gently. Mary Lou had a way of curbing his most unpleasant tones, willing him to be kinder, at least to her.

Mary Lou shook her head, then exhaled forcefully, incredulous at how far Jonah had strayed from the faith. "I guess I didn't think of it. Or I didn't realize how long you had been in the English world."

"I need it in the English world. Without it, there's little I can do to move about or prove who I am. Besides, I had to adapt quickly in order to survive here."

Mary Lou clearly wasn't getting her point across. "I don't believe that," she objected. "I believe that I can keep my faith intact and still live out here permanently."

"It's not that easy. You're surrounded by electricity and distractions all the time."

"But that's what makes it faith," she replied, obstinately. "You have to try very hard. That's what God wants."

"I don't want to get into a discussion about God right now. You need to rest, so let's get you in the car and go home. You are still on *rumspringa*, aren't you?"

Mary Lou had forgotten. *The fact that I am on an exploratory journey through the English world will make being in a car just fine,* she reasoned. She was buckled up before the engine started, and they were off.

"Ah!" she yelped as Jonah accelerated into traffic. Her pulse quickened, and she had to concede that she was a little scared after what had happened the previous night. However, she trusted Jonah, and looking out the side window took her mind off of the road.

"My father wrote to yours," she told him. "Yours said that you were out of town."

"Technically, I am out of town. I mean, this house is pretty far out in the boondocks."

"Yeah but…your parents don't know you're in the city. Is that what you want them to believe?"

"I don't know," he answered, honestly. "I wrestle with wanting to see them some days and not being able to face them on other days."

"When you were with me, in my community, you said you wrote to them. You said that you were going to make amends."

"I don't want to set foot in my community now," he retorted sternly. "Not with such a curse."

"Why do you keep saying that?" she cried out, but she was weak, and it made her head hurt.

"Is your sister not dead, Mary Lou?" he snapped.

Mary Lou sat quietly. She wanted to say vile things to him. She didn't deserve this. She was suffering, too. Hurt people hurt people. Her Amish upbringing gave her pause. The Bible's teachings were held fast in her soul. That is how her head could rule her heart, even when she felt lost. She said a prayer.

Jonah stared at the road. When he finally glanced at her, her face glistened, soaked with tears. He fought the urge to pity her.

"Yes, but it's no fault of yours," she said to the man she loved, though her voice did not quiver as one would expect from a woman in torment. Rather, it was firm, stoic, and full of conviction. "I wish you could see that."

She sounds like she actually believes it! Jonah thought. "I said

I didn't want to talk about this," he spat, coldly. They rode in silence out of town and onto a dirt lane. A giant house welcomed them at the cul-de-sac. Mary Lou gasped.

"That's where you live?" she asked. "That house is beautiful."

Before them stood a three-story Victorian home, with crimson red siding and white trim, on a plot cleared from the forest. The front porch ran the length of the house and had two swinging benches at either end. White pillars marked the entrance, and stone slabs, flanked by flower beds, made a meandering path from the porch to the gravel driveway where they had parked. Three tall lamps stood apart evenly to light the stone path. Several small trees stood in the front yard, each on beautifully mulched mounds sitting in rings cut perfectly into the grass. Two rose bushes sat perfectly centered between the driveway and the house, and between the door and the swinging benches. *When the grass and leaves are green in the summer, this sight will be perfectly divine*, thought Mary Lou. She stopped herself from adding children to her mental image.

"I split the rent with eight other people," Jonah informed her.

"This is much better than any apartment I could find in town," Mary Lou declared through bated breath. The change of subject did her good and lifted her spirits.

"Exactly," Jonah agreed. "And if you can do the job with the theatre, there'll be someone to take you there and back every day."

"Do you ever go there?" she asked.

Jonah shook his head. "Not normally," he replied. "I don't need to. All my work is around here." He then got out of the car and made his way around the front of the vehicle to open her door. Mary Lou did not remain seated for Jonah's sake (after all, if a man is to be a gentleman, a lady needs to patiently cooperate with him as he performs such duties as opening doors, taking coats, and holding chairs as one sits), nor because she was in pain, for she still was, but because, in staring at her surroundings, she did not feel like she had been hit by a car on the eve. Instead, she was utterly in awe of the house that lay before her. Its beauty pleased her.

Jonah opened her door and stretched out his hand. Mary Lou remained seated, soaking it all in. She had no idea that the English had such good-looking homes. She then looked up to Jonah, whose hand was still suspended in mid-air, and stated, "It almost looks like a giant homestead."

"Almost," he acknowledged, smiling at her for the first time since they'd reacquainted. "No one understands me when I say that."

"I do," Mary Lou reassured him.

Getting out of the car would have been a simple task if Mary Lou were English and well. But she was neither English nor well, so her first time getting out of a car was, to say the least, an unpleasant one. First of all, she did not realize her seatbelt remained buckled. Her first attempt at getting up jerked her back into her seat and took her breath away. Once unbuckled, she placed her hand in Jonah's, who tugged slightly, thinking he was being helpful. Mary Lou winced and gasped, then quickly let go. She turned her torso to exit, hoping her feet would follow like they do when climbing down from a carriage, but the lip at the threshold of the door trapped her feet in the vehicle, leaving her hanging head-first out of the car. It was a painful ordeal to use her core to return to a seated position, and, once there, she looked down at her feet to understand what had just happened. *It looks like I'm sitting on a chair in a basin*, she thought, since the floor of the automobile was lower than the threshold over which she had to get her feet. Jonah instructed her to come out feet-first. Mary Lou took a deep breath and swung her right foot onto the gravel, then lifted her left one over and out, but she found that she had slid off of the back of the chair and onto the armrest. Her ribs throbbed as she struggled to sit herself up, reaching out for anything on which she might find leverage to sit up. The previous incident had left Jonah too shy to offer her a hand, so he chose to point to the various places where she might gain the leverage she sought. His advice proved helpful, and she was able to sit in the car with her feet on the gravel. Feeling hopeful, the Amish girl thrust herself upwards, only for her head to meet the top of the opening in an inglorious *thud.*

Jonah, heartbroken at the pitiful display before him, and sensing that they were being watched by his housemates, decided that he had had enough of this. He bent over and, in one motion, took Mary Lou in his arms like a husband carrying his bride over the threshold, stood up, and shut the door with his foot. He headed towards the house, and that was how his seven roommates beheld Mary Lou for the first time. In retrospect, Jonah felt that it was not the most convincing way to persuade anybody that they were not engaged.

Sitting on the front porch, on a swing, was a slender and delicate young creature of pale, rosy skin, auburn hair, a pointed nose, and piercing green eyes. She wore blue skinny jeans and an emerald green top, both of which tightly caressed her Barbie-doll figure. She was, Mary Lou concluded, the most beautiful woman she had ever seen.

"Hello!" the woman called. "Jonah, you brought us another Amish friend? That's exclusivity."

"Ignore her," Jonah commanded Mary Lou. He put her down on the porch and gave her a minute to find her legs. She held his arm. Normally, the Amish wouldn't touch, but she needed support. "Her name is Porsche, and she is the lead dancer at the theatre. She's also crazy."

"She's beautiful," Mary Lou noted.

Jonah shrugged as though he hadn't noticed. "If that appeals to you," he rejoined.

"It doesn't appeal to you?" she asked him.

Jonah shot her a look that was almost a glare were it not softened with pity. "No. She doesn't."

Hope surged into Mary Lou's soul.

"You must be Mary Lou. I'm Porsche," the dancer said as she introduced herself with a smile and an outstretched hand.

"Nice to meet you," Mary Lou retorted. Then, as though to excuse herself, she added: "Sorry, my arm is a bit sore."

"No worries. Jonah told me what happened. So scary."

"Indeed. I must have had an angel looking over me." Mary Lou looked up at Jonah, her head resting on his shoulder. Embarrassed, Jonah shook his head and guffawed.

Porsche changed the subject. "Well, the guest room is all set up."

"Thanks," Jonah said to her, still feeling awkward.

"Can I talk to you when you come back, after Mary Lou is settled?" Porsche asked.

"Sure." Jonah led Mary Lou upstairs to her room.

"What does she want to talk to you about?" Mary Lou wondered.

"I don't know. Maybe the garden?" Jonah speculated.

Mary Lou was self-conscious as she eased her way up the stairs. She probably looked hideous after a day in the hospital. Though she didn't care about her looks, she did worry about first impressions.

The interior of the home did not match its exterior, which looked like it was meticulously looked after and well-maintained. The inside of the house, however, looked like eight theatre people lived in it. Clothing and shoes, plates with food still on them, and bottles all lay haphazardly about the floor, the furniture, and even the stairs. There was music playing somewhere deep in the house, and a thin, black frame that hung on the wall across from a couch spewed light and babble to no one in particular. Mary Lou noticed, however, that all of the books were neatly in place on the bookshelves.

The Amish girl thought it strange that she met no one else. There had been no welcoming party, or, at the very least, someone to offer her a warm drink and a snack as it was in the Amish tradition. It may have reminded her of a homestead, but Mary Lou was not in an Amish community.

Thankfully, the room was on the second floor and not all the way at the top. It was more elaborate than she was used to, with crown molding on the ceiling, thick windowsills that could hold any number of plants or flowers, regal drapes, and painted walls. Its four-post bed stood daunting against the far wall, though it would have looked better in a more spacious chamber. At present, it seemed like a baby elephant in a telephone booth. Still, Mary Lou was grateful for a soft bed to lay down her weary head. It had been a long morning. Jonah put her bag on the floor between her bed and the bathroom. He lingered at the door, waiting to see if she needed anything else.

Mary Lou broke the silence. "*Danki*. For everything"

"*Gern gschehne*." Jonah shifted his feet. "Just worry about getting better and then we'll…talk about the future."

"About our future?" Mary Lou exclaimed.

"About the future." Jonah turned and closed the door behind him. Mary Lou took a deep breath, sighed, then lay down. *Better to look on the bright side*, she figured. Jonah was with her, and they had another chance together. She shuddered. *At least, I think we do.* Between his emotional state and the goddess-like Porsche, she wasn't so sure.

Mary Lou didn't want to be put off by the fact that Jonah was trying his best to act as if they weren't engaged. She knew that they both needed time to heal and time to mourn, but she was going to fight for their love. Then she remembered that God had commissioned her for a task; she resolved to complete it. *I hope I'm on the right path*, she pondered, then fell fast asleep.

CHAPTER 4

I am going to have a good day, Mary Lou promised herself before opening her eyes. She had recently chosen to make this conscious decision every morning lest the weight of her grief crush her. A ferocious hunger had interrupted her sleep, though she could see by the sunlight that it was morning and time to eat breakfast. She arose, said her prayers, thanking God for being alive and for finding Jonah, who, perhaps, would have a change of heart, and also for grace in her dealings with the English housemates from whom she did not know what to expect. Upon freshening up and changing her clothes, she headed downstairs.

The kitchen was a flurry of activity, unlike the order Mary Lou was used to in her mother's kitchen. There seemed to be no one in charge, with the preference being "everyone for himself." The disorder was shocking. Her mind tried to find who was in charge so that she could get her orders and properly fill her role as servant, but the logic that the disorder was caused by a lack of leadership eluded her. Thus, she stood in the doorway, eyes wide and mouth agape, frozen by the confusion, yet burning to devour a proper Amish breakfast. She took a step forward, then froze again, hoping no one had noticed her. Perhaps she could simply return upstairs and wait until the kitchen was empty, but how could she go unnoticed? A plain, gray dress, a bonnet, the posture of a servant, and the look of innocence was as out of place in a kitchen full of actors as Santa was at Easter.

"Mary Lou!" cried one of them. "Welcome. I'm Johanna." Mary Lou spotted a barefooted, curly-haired brunette skipping towards her. She wore the same style jeans that Porsche had worn on the eve, a white, V-neck t-shirt, and a silver chain that bounced against her bosom as she walked. Her smile was warm and sincere, revealing perfectly straight, porcelain teeth. As her face lit up, her eyes disappeared into her face.

"Hello," Mary Lou obliged. "Sorry, I don't mean to intrude."

"Nonsense, you aren't intruding." Johanna put her arm around the famished creature. "It's lovely to meet you. Jonah has told us so much about you."

"He has?" Mary Lou looked surprised. "What did he say?"

"He's always talking about you," Johanna stated, and Porsche chimed in.

"Well, he's always talking about the girl he loves," the latter corrected.

Mary Lou blushed as her spirits soared! She forgot that she was hungry. If Jonah was talking about her, it couldn't be that he didn't love her. "Well, that's good," she heard herself say.

"Yeah, why did you two even break up?" Johanna asked.

As high as they had soared, her spirits were now a libation dripped all over the floor. Mary Lou felt hungry again. "What?" she managed.

"He said that you broke up," Johanna stated, bluntly. "So, are you just friends now?"

"We're uh…oh," Mary Lou bumbled.

"Johanna," came Jonah's voice from the other room, "could you not?" The offended man entered the kitchen, a portrait of irritability.

"I just thought I'd give the girl a chance to tell her side of the story," Johanna defended herself before adding, "because you certainly won't tell it."

The kitchen was quiet. No one was chewing or drinking, and those who had been rushing were suddenly dawdling. Though not everyone was looking at the quartet arguing, it was clear to Mary Lou that all ears were tuned in to their conversation. Her stomach growled.

"Poor thing," Porsche exclaimed. "Here, let me make you something to eat. Do you like peanut butter on toast?"

Mary Lou nodded.

Jonah continued the confrontation. "I don't really think that matters," he said. "What matters is that it's eight in the morning, Mary Lou hasn't had anything to eat, and you two just pounced on her."

"Hey, I'm making her breakfast," Porsche objected. "Would you like to join us, Prince Charming?"

"Let's just eat breakfast. You can ask questions later." Jonah seated himself and gestured for Mary Lou to do the same. "I'm sorry about them."

Mary Lou decided to speak to him in Pennsylvania Dutch, the language that most of the Amish community used. She trusted that Jonah, like most of the young folk in the nearby Amish communities, was fluent. Today, she was grateful for a second tongue.

"Why did you tell them we ended our relationship?" she asked.

"Because we did, when I walked away," he said in a low tone, as though he did not want the others to understand.

"You didn't walk away! You ran away."

"I don't want to talk about this now," and Jonah ended the conversation swiftly with a swig of coffee. Mary Lou wanted to scream at Jonah for fighting with her, for being so loose-lipped. What business was it of his roommates to know of their engagement? A heavy heart only compounded her sorrow.

"You two okay?" Johanna asked.

Mary Lou looked down at her hands. "Of course," she lied,

and forced herself to smile.

Porsche placed a couple pieces of toast slathered with peanut butter before the famished girl, but Mary Lou could not eat. How could she swallow with a lump her throat? She left Jonah at the table and joined another girl at the sink to dry the dishes. Jonah offered to drive them all to the theatre, though no one expected the Amish girl to work. When everyone had left, Mary Lou helped herself to a mug of hot water and lemon on the front porch. She sat, covered in a blanket, woolen socks on her feet, and gazed at the perfectly manicured front lawn. It was just after dawn, though the days were getting longer. The birds chirped while the hot drink soothed her throat and warmed her heart. Mary Lou began to daydream of children dancing in the front yard. Her children. Jonah's children. She still loved the man, though she was furious. *Is there such a thing as furious love?* she wondered. The conflict within her appeased, and she resolved that she would not find the answers she sought within her own wisdom. Waiting on God seemed to be the only sound strategy.

The crunch of tires on gravel announced Jonah's return. He did not notice Mary Lou and would have continued into the house had she not kicked her foot to swing the bench upon which she sat. Once he saw her, he froze.

"I really don't want to fight anymore," he declared, finally breaking the silence.

"I don't want to fight either," she replied.

Jonah held her gaze for a moment, and when he was sure she meant it, walked forward. "I told them we broke up because it was easier than telling them the truth. It was easier than explaining everything." His words betrayed his pain, and his vulnerability unsettled him.

Mary Lou reflected for a moment. Then, with empathy and sincerity, she replied, "I understand. I wouldn't want to pour my heart out in such a setting either. The English are…different."

Jonah sat next to her. "They are. It's a nice distraction."

"Is that what you want? A distraction?"

"The ultimate sin," he rejoined with a smirk, as he leaned against the step, "being distracted from God." He was not feeling so vulnerable anymore.

"I think it is the ultimate sin if you intend it to continue," Mary Lou said softly.

"So, everyone who's different from you is a sinner?" he retorted.

Mary Lou shook her head, for that was not what she had meant, though Jonah did not offend her like he would have an English woman. "No. You aren't that person, Jonah. I know you have Jesus in your heart."

"God betrayed me," he said, though not as bitterly as he had intended. Her presence softened him, he noticed. Still, Jonah was comfortable playing the victim, so he continued, uncertain of the reaction he was trying to get from her. "And He betrayed you too."

"No, he didn't!" she protested.

"He didn't?" Jonah replied. "So, he kept your sister safe then?"

"Jonah, that's not betrayal," she replied. "It's just..." Her voice trailed off. She did not have the energy for this.

"What is it then?" he goaded. "What is it when *kinner* get taken back to Heaven before they reach double digits?"

Mary Lou gritted her teeth. "I don't know," she surrendered, unable to fathom how someone could have witnessed her accident but two nights ago and not have the wherewithal to give her peace of mind. Still, she couldn't let him have the last word. "God kept me safe yesterday," she added, softly. "And we found each other again."

Jonah snorted and shook his head. "God also put you in the way of that car. I thought..." The incident flashed before his eyes and took his breath away. He felt a lump in his throat, but he did not want to give in to his sadness. Hate made him feel protected. But it was all too much. "I thought I would die on the spot when I saw it was you," he admitted despite himself. "I couldn't breathe. I panicked." He said it as though he were reliving the moment. Then he paused to catch his breath.

Mary Lou looked down in front of her. "It's okay to be scared, and it's okay to not know what to do sometimes. You just have to trust God."

"Well, I can't trust a God who does those things. And I am sorry I just…left you. Clearly, I am being punished, and I carry my curse with me."

"I don't feel it's that way at all," she said, partly exasperated but with the patience of Job. "I feel that God put us together and that we must trust in Him. We can better weather the storms together."

Jonah closed his eyes and inhaled deeply. Mary Lou was implacable. He thought it best to change the subject. "What do you plan to do today?" he asked her.

"I'm supposed to go back to the hospital for a follow-up in a week, but the doctor said to return sooner if I felt…odd."

Alarmed, Jonah turned to her and asked, "And do you?"

Mary Lou shrugged, timidly. "I think so. The thing is, no one tells you how you're supposed to feel after such an incident."

"If you don't feel right, we need to get you to the hospital right away." Jonah leaped to his feet like a frightened cat.

Mary Lou had not wanted to be a bother, though the longer she sat on the porch, the stranger she felt. Like a deer on new legs, she stood only to sit back down. "Just give me a minute."

"If you cannot walk, I will carry you," he said, pale-faced and scared.

"Jonah, it's okay." She sounded like she was trying to reassure herself more than Jonah.

"That's easy for you to say. You don't have to be on the other end of a tragedy."

"I was," she reminded him, "not too long ago."

They fell silent, collecting themselves. Once settled, certain that they would not bicker, Mary Lou let Jonah help her to her feet. He held her waist, unwilling to let her go, entirely focused on her every move, blaming himself for her condition every step of the way to the car.

"You look pale," he said, as he started the engine. "Tell me if things get worse, okay?"

"I will," she promised. "But don't you have work to do?"

"Work can wait," he answered. "You're more important than work." They were then slammed back into their seats as Jonah drove like a Lamborghini test driver on the narrow roads of Bologna, weaving before oncoming traffic to pass any and all in his way. His grip tightened about the wheel, and he clenched his teeth. Mary Lou felt queasy. Her face became wet as something trickled over her lip.

"Jonah…" she started.

"What?" he turned to her and saw the blood.

Dear God, Mary Lou thought woozily. *Protect us.* Then she passed out.

CHAPTER 5

Mary Lou knew where she was when she awoke this time. The hospital's sounds and atmosphere were now familiar to her. A tube attached to her hand, another under her nose, and some wires protruding from patches on her chest confused her. Her arm hurt, and she was feeble. Her clothes were not her own.

Déjà vu, she thought because Jonah was not beside her. She heard steps. A nurse entered the room. Mary Lou's heart sank.

"Hello! You're awake."

"Yes," Mary Lou sighed. "I was hoping for Jonah."

"Ah, that's your fiancé, eh?" the nurse asked.

Mary Lou nodded. "Is he here?"

"No, honey," the nurse informed her, kindly. "The officer let him bring you in, then took him away."

"The officer?"

"From what I understand, he was driving erratically, and the officer was going to take him away to charge him for reckless driving, but when he saw you had passed out, he agreed to let him drop you off at the hospital first. They should be at the police station now."

"What?" Mary Lou cried. "No! No, he can't. I need him. He was just trying to take care of me."

The nurse smiled condescendingly as she crouched beside the

bed. "Can I tell you a secret, honey?"

"Yes," Mary Lou agreed, although she had a feeling that it wasn't a secret she was going to like.

"I see girls your age come in here all the time with boys like that, and they are best off without them."

"Boys like what?" Mary Lou wondered.

"Reckless drivers. Boys who are young and addicted to the speed of life rather than settling down. He's just not ready." The nurse stood up again.

"No," Mary Lou objected. "It's not like that at all. He loves me. He…" She didn't have the energy to argue.

"You don't have to decide right now," she said. "Right now, you need to get some rest."

"I don't want to rest! I want to see Jonah. Please, do you know how I can contact him?"

"Not if he's been booked," the nurse replied, regretfully. "You'll just have to wait until he gets out."

"Booked?" Mary Lou was unfamiliar with the word. It was yet another example of how the English were different. She was frightened and cold.

"Jail," the nurse said. "Not if he's in jail."

'Oh," Mary Lou moaned, sinking her head into the pillow. Her stomach churned.

"The doctor is going to be in soon to talk to you. Just stay calm. Is there anything else I can get you?"

"Can I go home?"

The nurse forced a smile. "I don't think so, dear. There's a lot that we need to talk about."

"Is something wrong?"

"Just sit tight until the doctor comes, okay?" The nurse quickly turned on her heels and left. Mary Lou sat up and looked around the room. She was alone. The view from the window was different. The room was cozier and warmer, with wood paneling, a private toilet, padded chairs, and a coffee table. It was a large private room with many machines in it. Fear struck her heart. Prayer was all she could manage.

Dear God, please help me. Please protect me. She was going to say something about Jonah, but her mortality preoccupied her.

After what felt like an eternity, the doctor came in. Mary Lou could tell from the consternation on his face that he would bear bad news. She braced herself. Standing at the foot of her bed, he looked down at her. There was something cute about watching a short man trying to be authoritative. The neon lights reflected off of his shiny, bald head. *Black skin is not supposed to reflect light*, the Amish girl thought. He peered over his spectacles at her, then through them and down at the clipboard that rested against his potbelly like a butter knife on lard. His hamster-like voice completed the farcical sight.

"Mary Lou, do you have any family around?" he asked in an unnaturally high-pitched voice for a man. "Someone we could call?"

The girl collected herself, remembering the somber events that had brought her into the doctor's care. "My family is far away," Mary Lou managed, "in the Amish community."

"Do you have a way to contact them?" As he said this, he turned the clipboard on its side and pressed it against his navel, which, instead of flattening it, caused the fat to move down over his belt, creating a muffin top. His buttons looked like they were about to pop off.

"I could call the general store, and the owner could find them," she suggested. "Is there something I need to tell them? You could just tell me, and then I could call them."

"Well, when you were brought in the day before yesterday, we ran a couple of blood tests, just routine ones. Your white blood cell count came back as abnormal, and your red blood cell count is quite low."

None of that meant anything to the poor girl, so Mary Lou nodded, not knowing what else to do.

"With the additional blood tests that we ran today and the scans we did, we've diagnosed you with leukemia." The words spurted from his mouth like a bus driving through a puddle to spray the very passengers about to board. They were cold and insensitive. He was a hard fellow who thought it best to deliver bad news directly. In fact, he delivered all news nonchalantly. A woman might discover her pregnancy in the same manner that the Amish girl was informed of her cancer.

Mary Lou stared at him. The word had never been mentioned to her before, though, given the mood, she did not wish to discover what it meant. She craved her people, and she missed Jonah. "So…may I go home?"

The chubby doctor raised an eyebrow. *The girl is taking this better than I thought.* "You might be able to go home for a little bit, but you need regular treatment here," he said. "Chemotherapy, for at least six months."

"And that will cure me?" Mary Lou had hoped that her latest question had not betrayed her ignorance. She was hearing too many words that she'd never heard before, and she had neither the strength nor the inclination to learn anything new. All she wanted was for this to end so that she could go home.

"Maybe," the doctor posited. "The treatments are very harsh, and there is no guarantee that they will work. Your disease is in the advanced stages, and we….do our best. You must have been feeling unwell for quite a while."

"My sister just died. I've been feeling unwell ever since."

"Sometimes, a traumatic event can bring to light what we've been really feeling," he declared academically.

"So, the trauma caused it?" she asked. Jonah had said that he was being punished for what he did. Maybe she had done something to deserve this. *Was God punishing her?* A shake of the head quieted her inner dialogue.

"No," he said. "It probably just made you a little more tired than usual, and then you noticed it. I'm glad that you were brought in when you were. Any later, and we wouldn't be able to help you."

Mary Lou now appreciated the gravity of the situation. She

swallowed. "What are the chances I'll be cured, according to your medicine?"

"I don't have an answer for you," he said matter-of-factly. "You are young, so your chances are better than if you were older."

Mary Lou stared at the sterile bed sheets. "All right," she said, at last. "Thank you for being honest with me."

"Do you want to discuss the treatment?" he asked. "I understand it can be a lot to take in right now, so if you prefer to wait…"

"Is it something that I can do from home?"

"There is nothing you can do from home. I know some in your community believe in remedies that the hospital may not. And while I do not object to herbal medicine, rest, and prayer, I am telling you that there has never been a case of cancer like this cured outside of a hospital. You need to be here, every day." He left without another word.

Mary Lou closed her eyes, wondering what she ought to feel after such an exchange. Regret is what she settled upon since she hadn't asked the crucial question: Was she going to die? Death had no sting since Heaven, where Christ—and Naomi—awaited her, was her reward. Would she die without ever seeing Jonah again? Even if they weren't to marry, even if it was to break her heart, no cancer could pain her as much as his absence.

CHAPTER 6

Mary Lou had telephoned her parents, via the general store, to tell them of her diagnosis. She waited as the owner fetched one of them, rehearsing what she was going to say about her health. Her mother was the one who took the call. From the moment Leah spoke into the receiver, her daughter was on the back foot because all she wanted to talk about was Jonah. For the first time since she had met him, Mary Lou did not want to talk about Jonah, at least not with her mother, whom she hadn't realized, was fuming over her husband's decision to let her eldest live in sin with a backslidden Amish boy. Jonah was living with women who weren't relatives. Jonah was driving a car, and recklessly at that. Jonah had almost gotten Mary Lou killed, twice if you counted the first time she was sent to the hospital. And now, Jonah was in jail.

"Wasn't Jonah supposed to be taking care of you?" her mother asked, rhetorically. This was before Mary Lou had had a chance to tell her mother of her cancer diagnosis. How she regretted having let on that she was alone in the hospital for the second time in three days! Mary Lou feebly defended her former fiancé, saying that she was certain he would offer to help her once he was out of jail. Her mother put her foot down.

"No. Absolutely not. You are banned from ever seeing *that*

boy again!" Leah could not bring herself to say his name lest her fury cause her to say what she really thought of him. "If God is punishing you for anything, Mary Lou, He is punishing you for being with Jonah," she continued, only a smidgen more calmly than before. "That is not a man who is meant to be your husband. That is a man who is leading you into temptation."

"But he's just lost," Mary Lou protested. "He needs me, *Maem*, and I need him."

"No," her mother repeated, coldly. "Stay away from him. I'm sending your father to get you." Then she hung up.

Mary Lou never had the chance to tell her mother what the doctor had said. Now, there were two daunting choices to make: one about her treatment, the other about her love. Worse still, her father did not come to get her that day or the next. She was a balloon leaking energy rather than helium. Every sentence that she had spoken since Jonah's return had made her eyes pour and her face humid, transforming her countenance into the Irish weather. Gloom beset her, slowly consuming the hope of Christ in her heart like a gourmand savoring a French dish. She had to make a heartbreaking choice, alone, as disease ate away at her life.

The walls seemed to expand, and the door seemed to shrink, both conspiring to isolate her. Mary Lou's weakness made itself acutely conspicuous, more so than the last time she was bedridden. She had more over which to fret this time. One more over whom to worry. She prayed, but it brought her little comfort, and the silence that followed "Amen" highlighted, underlined, and underscored her loneliness. Finally, she sang. *Jesus loves me, this I know, for the Bible tells me so. Little ones to Him belong. They are weak, but He is strong.*

"Hey," said the voice that Mary Lou had been dying to hear. It may as well have been the voice of an angel. The gloomy gourmand stopped chewing. She had imagined a list of a thousand things to say to Jonah when she finally saw him. Now that he was right in front of her, she had no idea what to say.

"Hey," she parroted, happy to have said nothing more, for the very sight of him moved her.

"How are you?" Jonah asked.

A geyser erupted from the Amish girl's face.

Jonah rushed forward to hold her. "Mary Lou, what's the matter?"

"Where have you been?" she howled. "Why didn't you come to me? Why didn't you call?"

"I wanted to," he answered, "but I couldn't."

"Why not?" she asked.

"They don't let you make calls in jail, except for one, and I needed to call...someone else."

"Who? Who did you need to call?"

"I needed to call a lawyer," he answered with what was left of his patience, "to get me out of the ridiculous mess that officer put me in."

"That officer?" Mary Lou's tone was indignant. "Jonah, you put yourself in that mess."

He raised an eyebrow. "Is that what you think? You think it was my fault? Excuse me for hurrying to get you to a hospital when you were near death!"

"You were right about that," she whispered.

"I'm sorry?" he asked.

"They say that I have cancer and that it's bad."

"How...how do they know?"

"I don't know. They did tests. It's in my blood. They said that if I had come just a few days later, they wouldn't have been able to cure it at all."

Color evacuated Jonah's face like the galloping tides at Mont Saint Michel, though Mary Lou was beginning to understand that he was more concerned about the effect his perceived curse would have on her than for her own well-being. "So... they can cure it?"

"I don't know," she answered. "They said it's really bad, and there is no cure."

"Mary Lou," Jonah said, his voice drowned under billows of self-contempt, "this is my fault. This is my curse."

"NO!" Mary Lou's voice erupted. "Jesus!" she cried, though not like the non-Amish would in frustration, but more like someone calling out for help. "Your curse, Jonah, is that you can't seem to stay around and sort things out."

"What exactly do you mean by that?" Jonah's back stiffened. "You think I don't deal with my problems! Excuse me if I don't want to curse anyone else."

Jonah's self-centered proclamation precisely illustrated Mary Lou's point. For once, though, she did not argue with him so that he would see things her way. Instead, she chose to cut to the heart of the matter. The prospect of dying left the girl in no mood to waste time. "Jonah, I could die. Do you really want to be away from me if I do? Do you really want to run, knowing you'll never see me again?"

Jonah turned away. "I don't know. If it means that you'll live, then yes. All I know is that I missed you every second that I was gone."

"So, don't run away again," she begged. "Don't run away. Stay."

Jonah breathed deeply as though it would get rid of the ball in his throat. "What if you went home?" He turned around, suddenly hopeful. "Is there a way to treat you from home?"

"The doctor said there isn't," she said. "I'm certain that my parents would bring the horse and carriage in every day."

"That's at least several hours of travel. That's miserable. You can't!"

Mary Lou shrugged. "The other option is to stay here."

"Well, that's what you should do," Jonah said, satisfied as though that were the end of it. He was proud of himself for having stayed around to prove Mary Lou wrong and was glad to have been of service.

"Where?"

Jonah bit his lip. *Oh, that!* He hoped that his face hadn't let on what he was thinking. "Where are you going with this?"

"I just want to be well, Jonah," she stated as though the obvious weren't clear to him. "And I want a chance at life. A chance that I don't feel I've gotten yet."

"You should have one," Jonah agreed. "You deserve it, more than anyone I know."

"If I choose to stay here…" she paused to catch his eye, "I am sure that my parents will disown me."

"Why?" Jonah couldn't imagine the couple he'd met ghosting their offspring.

Mary Lou finally had the man she loved eating from the palm of her hand, so she decided it best not to repeat what her mother had said over the phone, lest it crush him. Instead, she decided to give another reason before moving on to her true motive. "They think the English world is full of temptation and curses, and that even if I am on *rumspringa*, this is different."

"Is that really how you feel?" he asked. "That is a big choice to make all by yourself."

"But I wouldn't be by myself, would I? You would be here."

Jonah ran his hand through his hair. "Mary Lou, if you think that I don't want that more than anything…"

"So, it's simple," she said. "Just stay with me."

"But I can't! I'm cursed!" He looked ready to sob.

Mary Lou pulled her blankets aside and swung her legs over the side of the bed.

"What are you doing?" he asked her.

"Come and pray with me," she said.

Jonah shook his head.

"It's because you feel that you can't that we must," she said, gently, then held out her hand.

Jonah reached out his own to begin what was now a familiar dance. The music was their longing, a haunting anthem to all that was and all that might be, the lyrics the sonorous beating of their hearts, each synchronized in tune but not in harmony, hers sung in the key of hope, his in despair. Like the morning after the accident, he felt her limp grip in his robust hand, pitying her for her weakness, yet her eyes betrayed a fervor—a fire—almost contagious were he not infected with hope's antidote: lies. He stepped forward and helped her up. Being near him again was precious to Mary Lou. Her heart jumped an octave. He helped her into the wheelchair. She closed her eyes to thank God for the little moments, cherishing all these things and pondering them in her heart.

Jonah understood that her hope and delight were stored in him, a jar of clay. *Does she not realize that, in doing so, she was placing her joy like a fool stores new wine in old wineskins?* He fought the urge to flee, gripping the handles protruding behind her with unusual force.

"There's a chapel just down the hallway," she said. "I know it's not quite our way of prayer, but it will do."

The two of them remained mute as Jonah wheeled Mary Lou down the hallway, their tune a mere murmur. They found an empty chapel, for which they were both grateful. They entered from the rear and worked their way towards a large, wooden pedestal, atop which sat a vase of fresh flowers whose colors were muted by the soft, amber light. The chapel was unadorned save for one, round, stained glass window of a dove, so none could tell which religion it served.

Jonah sat beside Mary Lou, poorly hiding his state of unease, yet persisting so as not to upset the fragile creature next to him. He felt Mary Lou's tender, silken skin on the top of his hand as she interlaced her fingers with his. A rare Amish moment of affection, indeed! He looked up to hold her still fervent glare. He was soothed, but his curiosity was piqued. *How can one so frail seem so strong?* Mary Lou closed her eyes, then led the prayer.

"Dear God, we come before you, two lost servants. I am sick and in need of healing, both physically and spiritually. Jonah feels cursed, and he needs to be shown your light again."

"Mary Lou, it's not that easy," Jonah interrupted, but she hushed him.

"Please God," she continued, "please give us a sign. Please show us what to do. Be a light unto our path." She paused as though waiting for an answer. All was silent.

Theologian Blaise Pascal once said that man's problem is his inability to sit quietly in a room alone. Jonah shifted in his seat, then coughed. He was suddenly itchy. He scratched softly at his forearm, and then his neck, before the back of his calf called out for attention. He felt discomfort in the arch of his foot. Not daring to remove his shoes at the risk of asphyxiating the girl, he ran his hand through his hair, then rocked softly back and forth like one might do to calm an infant.

Mary Lou sat perfectly still. Perhaps her weakness made it so, though she did not slouch as one might expect. She sat erect and attentive, as though waiting for a reply that would come like a whisper from afar. Her eyelids brightened. She opened her eyes and saw the sun streaming through the stained glass window. The sunbeam came across the floor, and then, to her delight, fell on both of them. The dove shone brightly. Alas! Her answer came.

Jonah leaned into the light. He closed his eyes and finally sat still, though it was plain to see that he was calculating, thinking, resolving. Mary Lou could practically see the thoughts churning in his head. It was a new and unexpected pleasure for her to watch a pensive man. *Is marriage filled with moments like these? she wondered. If so, I am ready to cherish them, dear Lord. Amen.*

Time paused, though it did not seem to for Mary Lou. Their quarter of an hour in that chapel passed like a mere flutter of butterfly wings. Eventually, Jonah spoke up.

"If you stay with me," he began, "your parents will likely follow through with their promise. I have broken all the rules. You can't call it a *rumspringa* anymore. I am lost, Mary Lou, and I don't know that I will find my way back to the light."

"I know that you will," she said, calmly. It was the most

frightening thing in the world to tell him that she was sure when she wasn't. *Is it a sin to say you believe when you doubt?* she wondered. In her mind, it didn't matter since she knew that he needed her to be strong in that moment. "And I know, more than that, that this is the right choice." A cloud covered the sun and returned the room to amber.

"I will take care of you," Jonah promised. "Have no doubt about that. I promise you that I will. I just can't promise that at the end of it, I will return to the community."

"I'm not asking you to. If it is God's intention, then we will do so."

"And if it's not?"

Mary Lou took a deep breath. "Maybe it's not God's intention that I live," she confessed. "Maybe it's not God's intention for my parents to abandon me. We don't know God's intent. We just have to trust that He has a plan and then walk in it."

"Are you sure about this?" he asked, looking her in the eyes.

"Which part?" she asked, chuckling nervously.

"All of it. This medical treatment. Staying with me."

"I do know one thing. I know that God placed you in my path. You bring me joy." Mary Lou swallowed, halting her monologue when she sensed it wise to do so, for she was discovering that men prefer to take the lead. She waited as he held her gaze.

"All right," he said. "Yes. Let's do it." He was cocky. Something had changed. He was assured that God answered prayer, but annoyed, too, like he took offense at God answering *her* prayer. He spoke with a heretofore unseen confidence, like he had found a new comfort zone in caring for the sick whilst rebelling against Amish tradition.

"I have to tell my parents," Mary Lou reminded him. "I know that if they hear what I feel in my heart and the assurance that God has given me, they will understand."

"If you say it as confidently as you just spoke to me, I don't know how anyone could remain unconvinced," Jonah said to her with a smile. He helped her back to her room. Mary Lou felt at peace for the first time in weeks. She was certain that this was the right decision, and she was certain that her parents would understand.

Mary Lou picked up the phone in her room and called the general store. It took the shop owner a while to find her parents, and she held Jonah's hand as they waited.

"I love you," he said. "I know that I'm not supposed to say that…but I love you."

"I love you too," she said, gazing into his eyes. She was confident in her course of action, so much so that she felt as though God would speak to her folks through her.

Finally, Mary Lou's mother picked up the phone. Her father could be heard as though he were standing behind her. "*Maem*," she began, "*Daed*, Jonah has returned, and we have prayed. We have decided that it's best that I stay in the city with him to continue our courtship—"

"Mary Lou," her mother interrupted, "if that is the choice you are making, do not consider coming home. You are taking the path of the devil with that boy."

Mary Lou's hand shook as she spoke. If only her mother would listen, then she could tell her about her cancer and the logic behind her decision. "But *Maem*, God—"

"This isn't God speaking. It's you." And with that, she hung up.

BOOK 3

CHAPTER 1

"And after you take care of the garden, can you make sure to repaint the front porch? It's probably the last thing that needs to be done."

"Yeah, sure," Jonah said, as he sat at the kitchen table. "Everything will be done by the 26th."

"That's perfect," the landlord said. He was a bald, middle-aged man with an air of congeniality. His oversized nose, broken repeatedly in the ring, made him look jolly and approachable. His broad shoulders and thick biceps gave the short man an air of strength and respectability, but his potbelly placed the man's more intimidating days firmly in the past. A warm smile endeared him to many. "And then you and the little Miss will have a few days alone in the house after that, before the next batch of actors moves in."

"We'll be...alone?" Jonah asked.

The landlord nodded. "That's not a problem, is it?" he chuckled.

"No," Jonah said, even though he wanted to say more. Instead, he just looked down at the list in his hand again. "Is there anything else you want done?"

"I think that's it. Thanks, Jonah."

"No problem." Jonah stood to shake the man's hand. "I'll get

111

it all done."

"Thank you, son," said the landlord, returning his firm grip. "You've been a godsend." Then he turned and left.

Jonah glanced in the mirror and ran a hand through his hair. For a normal couple, it would not be a problem to be left alone for several days in the house that they were living in. He and Mary Lou had lived with eight housemates since the day she moved into the house. However, they were far from a normal couple. Jonah was formerly Amish, having left his community after his sister passed away in a tragic accident. When he met Mary Lou while she was on *rumspringa*, he thought that he had met his soulmate, and he was ready to recommit to the Amish way of life. He expected that his life would turn around, until he went to her community, and her sister tragically drowned.

Jonah was certain that he was a curse on the world. He was afraid to get attached to Mary Lou lest she die, too. Thus, he had convinced himself that they should not be together for her own good. He had left her to hide in the city so that she might have a chance at a good life. He intended to stay away, but when she found him, unrelenting in her devotion to him, he softened. She even tried to continue her *rumspringa* to stay in his line of sight. Once she was diagnosed with cancer, however, he was certain of his fate. Still, her cancer was rough, and he hadn't the heart to leave her side though he was certain to be the death of her. Unperturbed, Mary Lou manipulated the situation to have Jonah by her side. Knowing full well that neither Jonah nor her father could refuse her as she recovered from having been hit by a car, she had arranged for Jonah to care for her in his home—out of wedlock—with her father's approval!

Mary Lou was to stay with Jonah so that she might more easily visit the hospital for her treatments. He was to care for her, be her chauffeur, and help her recover. He had not anticipated Mary Lou being disowned by her parents. Some of their housemates were able to assist when Jonah was occupied but going it alone with no respite would require a Herculean effort on his part.

No longer full of her usual zest for life, Mary Lou moved through her days as if underwater. Chemotherapy, grieving the loss of family and community, as well as a noncommittal fiancé all contributed to her depression. Pain, both physical and emotional, was her new companion. She hardly smiled.

Jonah tried everything he could to make Mary Lou happy and comfortable. He wanted desperately to see her smile, but he was not a funny character, nor was he charming. He would have to coax a grin through service, he figured, though he guarded himself against anything romantic so as not to draw close to her lest his curse caused her to die, too. Afraid to lose her, he failed to realize that he was losing time with her. He performed his gestures of service to Mary Lou with no encouragement nor presentation, as a cat might give his mistress a dead mouse. Though helpful, these acts of service were not endearing. Unable to get the desired reaction, he withdrew, blaming his curse for her sadness. He let the others in the house take a more active role in her care, blind to the fact that his mere presence would be enough to raise her spirits. It should have been obvious during their devotionals, something he offered on the days when she was faint and unable to hold her Bible. For, although she accepted help for many other tasks from the housemates, she could not tolerate anyone reading Scripture to her but Jonah. Mary Lou cherished this little pleasure, so much so that she would sometimes feign fatigue just to hear her true love's voice recite the word of God. Jonah naïvely thought that it was because he was the only one who could correctly pronounce the difficult Old Testament names.

Jonah had never found himself in such a complicated situation. Had he been a zipper, he would have wanted to remain opened and closed at the same time. Mary Lou's elegance and sweetness compelled him to want to draw her near and to push her away so that he wouldn't suffer loss. Her sincerity and fidelity made him want to be a better man and to douse her with sarcasm so as to prevent it. Her love and gentleness found their way to the deepest recesses of his heart, and he both loved and hated her for it. Never had he been so conflicted, but he had to help her; she had to smile.

Being alone together might bring undue stress on the Amish girl. Mary Lou's faith was her strength, yet living alone with Jonah would violate her sensibilities and accentuate her anxieties. She was fighting for her life and fighting for their love. A fight to keep her faith could not be in the mix. Jonah thought long and hard about whether to stay or go, whether to keep on as they were, or to call Mary Lou's parents and ask them to reconsider having disowned her. He would care for her only if it made her comfortable. Approaching her with such a concern would only upset her, defeating the purpose of bed rest. No, he had to handle this on his own. He figured it was better to keep this to himself for now.

Jonah found it interesting that such things mattered to him so much, even after so long away from his community. The English didn't think twice about living together unmarried. He had been immersed in the English world for a few years, yet the virus of their ways was slow to infect him. He still found himself thinking like an Amish man and doing Amish things, like lighting candles instead of turning on the lights, or waking before dawn. He thought that they were just old habits to be broken, for his soul no longer felt Amish. Now, he viewed them as creature comforts that allowed him to find his bearings in these trying times. If he were honest with himself, he would admit that he loved the Amish ways and Mary Lou for staying true to them.

Jonah now longed for his childhood community. If somebody fell ill, the others took care of him. The populace prided itself on being self-sufficient. The English world was black and white, with a sense of community hard to come by. If only he had someone to help him!

"Dear God," he prayed to himself, "help us." Jonah didn't pray very often because he never felt as though God heard him. He never admitted to Mary Lou that he was jealous when she spoke to God, for, she always seemed to get an answer. Why wouldn't God speak to him some of the time?

Pushing thoughts of God and Mary Lou aside, Jonah decided to return to the tasks at hand. The to-do list that the landlord had given him was long and would most definitely keep Jonah busy right up until the moment the actors all moved out. It was a mansion that hosted touring theatre performers, after all. There was much work to be done caring for the English, picking up after them, and repairing and repainting any door, counter, or toilet they used. They were not as neat as the Amish, nor were they as careful with their belongings, much less with those of others. Mary Lou had been hired to work with the actors as a wardrobe assistant in the same theatre. Sadly, she never got a chance to work, though she was a natural with the children and their costumes. Luckily, Jonah's wages took care of both of them, and their housing was free. Thus, the backslidden Amishman felt it his duty to offer the landlord his best work, assuring him that the house would be in top condition for the next tenants.

Jonah was supposed to mow the lawn and get the paint for the house during the hardware store sale, and he needed to pick Mary Lou up from the hospital, all within two hours. He decided that he could mow the lawn when he got back. He didn't much like the English mower because it was loud. He had to use it, however, since there was no way he'd get anything done with the push mower.

Jonah made a quick sweep through the house to complete the shopping list before he headed for the truck, something about which he had mixed feelings. He had been driving without a license the day that Mary Lou had needed to get to the emergency room, and he had gone to jail for it. If he hadn't rushed to the hospital, she might have died. Going to jail had been the price to pay to save her life, but it was also one of the reasons her parents had disowned her. He'd since gotten a learner's permit and bought the truck after his car was impounded. For Mary Lou, climbing out of the truck was akin to climbing out of a buggy, which suited her much more than climbing out of a car.

After making the drive into town, Jonah noticed that even though the hardware store was busy, no one had the courtesy to say, "Hello" to him. Such was the English world, which Jonah had craved for its anonymity once his sister passed, but with the burden he carried, it had cost him more than it had blessed him. Home, for him, was where everyone greeted each other in congenial and friendly tones since they'd all known each other since birth. Strangely, on this particular day, Jonah had to resist the urge to speak to others waiting in line as he would have amongst the Pennsylvania Dutch. Mary Lou was having an effect on him...

Once he had gotten the items he needed, he headed to the hospital where Mary Lou, certain that Jonah had been placed in her life to be her husband, awaited. She believed that they were courting with the intention of marriage. However, her first impression (coming straight from the Almighty) was that she needed to win him back to the faith, not marry him. Such was the man's effect on her that she could even forget an edict of God in his presence. Still, the couple had endured more in three months than most couples went through in a lifetime. Perhaps she could do both.

In order to save money, after treatment, Mary Lou would wait outside of the hospital for Jonah to pick her up, rather than in her room. That way, Jonah would not have to pay the parking fees. He hated that, because she always looked so pale and sick after her treatments, treatments the doctors said were helping, though he found it hard to believe because she looked sicker than before her treatment. True to habit, he spotted her on a bench as he pulled up to the front of the hospital, a tall, dominating edifice seemed intent on intimidation rather than benevolence. She looked like any Amish girl would, dressed in a bonnet and long skirt, in stark contrast to the English girls who gawked at her attire as they entered the hospital in halter tops and hoochie shorts.

Jonah thought Mary Lou to be the most beautiful woman that he had ever seen, and he made sure to tell her that as she climbed into the passenger seat. They weren't supposed to value looks, but she blushed nonetheless like she always did after a compliment. He found it adorable.

"*Danki*," Mary Lou said. "I feel like a mess."

"Well, you don't look it," Jonah said. "Do you just want to go straight home?"

"Yes, please. I'm exhausted. But I have good news."

"Oh?" he asked her in surprise as they pulled away from the curb.

"Yes. The doctors said that things are going so well that I can take a few days off, to give my body a chance to heal."

"Really?"

Mary Lou nodded.

"When?"

"Somewhere around the 26th," she answered.

Jonah felt like he'd been jolted by a defibrillator. "The 26th?" he asked as he drove.

"Yeah." She turned her head towards him. "Is that a problem?"

"No. It's just that the landlord came by to talk to me today. He said that our current housemates will be moving out on the 26th."

That unsettled the good Amish girl. "Oh! That's sooner than we thought."

"Apparently, their other booking extended, so they have to go as soon as this show is closed."

"So, we'll be alone. In the house. Just as I have a break from treatment."

"Yeah," he confirmed, then glanced at her. "Is that okay?"

She bit her lip. She seemed to be wrestling with her soul for a moment, and then she spoke. "No. I'm sorry."

"Yeah," Jonah sighed. "I had a feeling that you were going to say that."

"What are we going to do?"

Jonah tried to smile, but he looked constipated. "I'll figure it out," he replied, unconvincingly.

She looked at him, half wanting to believe what he said, but entirely sure he hadn't a clue.

"I'll take care of it," he promised her. "You just worry about relaxing."

"Okay. I trust you."

CHAPTER 2

An epiphany is when an individual comes to realize that there is a God, usually when He manifests Himself. Jonah had heard of them, but he had never had one. This had made him insecure, especially since, he felt, too many of his relatives and friends had had one or multiple. It was as though God were ignoring him.

Per his routine, Jonah was up at dawn the following day in order to get things done before Mary Lou got up and needed his attention. Before he had opened his eyes, God spoke to him.

Go home, God told him.

Jonah was suddenly filled with a sense of peace, one that passes all understanding, and the conviction that he must obey. Still, had he heard correctly? After all this time away from home without a word to anyone there, was he supposed to just go home? A thousand reasons why he couldn't go home came to mind, but none were convincing. Usually, anxiety and self-pity elbowed their way into his inner dialogue to assert themselves and to reassure him that he was, indeed, cursed. Today, however, they stood aloof, like a gang of teenage boys at a school dance. Indeed, it would have been artificial to recite the usual worries in light of what had happened. Instead, he was left to ponder what force could tame his angst with a mere pair of words!

Jonah trembled. He hurried out of bed trying to find something else to do besides reckon with what may very well have been the Almighty. Unaware, he wandered to Mary Lou's room. He paused with fist raised as though he were about to knock. He stared ahead, with only the slightest sense that she was on the other side of the door, and went through his plan in his head. He could see it in front of him: Mary Lou reassured that they would not be living in sin—a smile at last!—then a drive to his community where his parents would greet him, his mother with a hug, and his father with so firm a handshake that he could squeeze water from a stone. Then he felt peace.

Jonah returned to his room to get dressed, freshen up, then head down to the kitchen. As usual, it was a hive of activity.

"Do you want me to bring Mary Lou some tea?" Porsche asked. She was kind, even if she was unusual in tone and tact. Jonah was glad that she had been there for Mary Lou on days when he had not managed to be.

"Actually, I'll do it," he replied. "I have something that I want to talk to her about."

"Something like a shotgun wedding?" Porsche quipped with a Cheshire cat grin.

Jonah shook his head. "You English girls are far too quick on the draw."

"I'm just saying, if you married her, you could stay in this big old house alone after we leave."

"She told you?"

Porsche shook her head. "No, I just put the pieces together. I'm not completely ignorant about your Amish ways, you know."

"My Amish ways? I haven't acted Amish."

"Jonah, you think you don't act Amish?" Porsche asked, slightly indignant but mostly incredulous. "You may wear English clothes, but you're still an Amish boy at heart."

Jonah was hurt, but he tried not to show it.

"Did I say something to upset you?" she asked.

He shook his head, disappointed with his vulnerability. "No," he lied. "You didn't."

Porsche handed him a cup of tea. Jonah took it, nodded, and returned upstairs.

It was quiet. Jonah wondered if Mary Lou was still asleep. He rapped lightly on her door, prepared to turn away, when he heard her voice, still angelic despite the horrors of her treatments.

"Come in," beckoned Mary Lou.

Jonah pushed the door open and found her sitting on the edge of the bed, dressed and looking weary.

"I've brought you a cup of tea," Jonah said, presenting it to her.

"*Danki*. That's just what I was after." Her smile was that of a healthy young lady, warm and endearing. "I was wondering whether I had the strength to go downstairs."

Jonah put the tea in her hands, then took a step back. She had prayed with him in the chapel at the hospital, and since her faith was ever foremost in her thoughts and actions, he knew that he could tell her about his epiphany. In fact, he wanted her to be the first to know. For months, he had been telling her that he wasn't sure he trusted God, that he disbelieved. It had clearly broken her heart, yet she had always been cordial, respectful, even. He knew that he could trust her; he just didn't know how to announce it.

"I heard God speak to me this morning," Jonah said unceremoniously.

"You did? What did He say?"

"He said…*Go home.*"

Go home, Mary Lou mouthed. "What do you think it means?"

Jonah rubbed the back of his neck, looking sheepish. "I don't think there's a hidden message in it," he confessed. "I think it means exactly what it means: we should go home."

The thought of facing her parents in her condition was out of the question. "Jonah, you know that I can't." Mary Lou looked down at her hands.

"My home," he clarified. "We should go to my home."

"Can you do that?" she asked, suddenly interested.

"I don't know. I want to believe that I can...I heard it, Mary Lou, as clear as the birds singing outside."

"I don't doubt that you heard it. I just want to know whether you are going to obey."

Jonah turned and sat at the edge of her bed. "You know how hard it would be for me to go home. And I don't know what kind of reception we would receive. But it would solve our problem."

"It would," Mary Lou nodded. "And it would just be for a short while." She took a sip of her tea, content to sit in silence, letting it work on her love's conscience.

Jonah could not sit in silence. Impatiently, he asked, "What do you think I should do?"

"I think it's up to you," Mary Lou replied, then sipped her tea again.

"Don't do that," Jonah cried.

"Don't do what?"

"Don't make me decide," Jonah moaned. "I don't want to bear that burden. I don't know if I can bear that burden. I've enough on my mind, right now."

"But you heard God speak. That has to mean something."

"Maybe it wasn't God," Jonah speculated. "Maybe I'm going crazy."

"Jonah!" she gave him a look. "Give yourself more credit than that. You heard God, and now you are wrestling with whether or not to obey Him."

"Why should I obey Him?" he asked. "It's not like He's been—"

"I will not hear a word against God this morning," Mary Lou interrupted, raising her voice as well as her hand. She did not seem frail at that moment, but strong in her conviction, as though she were animated by a power greater than herself. Jonah's train of thought stopped in its tracks. "I know you feel that He hasn't been kind to you, that He's been ignoring you, that He's let you down, and that you haven't heard Him speak to you in the past, but you heard Him this morning, Jonah, so what are you going to do?"

The Amish apostate was taken aback. It had not occurred to him that he was accountable to God. He had only thought of how returning to his parents' place would benefit Mary Lou and solve the inconvenience of her conscience. Now he was scared, not of returning home, but of confronting God. Any decision taken was not merely to be weighed in his favor, but as an invitation to trust in the Omnipotent Creator of the universe, something he was unwilling to do, given their past. Confronted with having to choose to remain closed to God for his own sake or open to the same for Mary Lou's, he clenched his fist. "I don't know," Jonah said through gritted teeth. He then relaxed his jaw before continuing. "I mean, when I first heard it, I couldn't believe what a perfect solution it was. I thought it was the answer to our problem. But now, having to deal with God, too…" His voice trailed off since the only way he could finish that sentence was to say something against Him.

Mary Lou tried to sound reassuring. "I know it won't be easy, but maybe it's worth it." She began to hum softly. After all, David would play music to calm a king's tormented soul. Jonah recognized the hymn, and, despite himself, began to sing it in his head:

He leadeth me: O blessed thought!
O words with heavenly comfort fraught!

Jonah rolled his eyes. "That's not fair."

Mary Lou continued.

Whate'er I do, where'er I be,
still 'tis God's hand that leadeth me.

"I haven't heard that in so long." The hymn soothed Jonah. The tension left his neck and jaw, and he looked up to the ceiling as though searching the heavens.

"Jonah, God is speaking to you, and to you alone. This is between you and Him. If you choose otherwise, God will provide a place for me to stay."

"You are not doing that," Jonah declared. "You need to rest.

Running around looking for a hotel isn't going to make you better. And you can't stay alone here either." He inhaled deeply and exhaled loudly and slowly. "You're right. I heard it, for whatever reason, and I need to obey. So, we'll go and stay with my parents for a while. Maybe the country air will be good for you."

"I'm sure it will be," she smiled. "Even though we are not in the middle of the city, things will be quieter out there. I believe I will heal faster."

"If it makes you heal faster, I'll move back there," Jonah blurted out.

Mary Lou smiled all the more, her eyes widening with delight. "Don't tease me with such things," she retorted.

Jonah leaned in toward her, and, with an air of sincerity, declared, "I mean it, Mary Lou. If you truly feel better out there…."

Mary Lou put her hand on his arm as though to halt him so that he wouldn't get ahead of himself, and smiled. "Why don't we take things one step at a time?" she asked him. "Do your parents have a phone?"

"At the general store, same as yours, but I don't know the number."

"Is there a way to find it?"

"I can ask one of the actors," Jonah suggested. "They seem to have a way to find anything. I could also write to my parents, although I'm not sure I'd get a reply in time."

"I will pray for you while you make the call," Mary Lou said, feebly. "I don't think I'm going to go downstairs today." The morning had taken a toll on the Amish girl. She lay back down in her bed, setting her teacup next to her.

"You look pale," Jonah said. "Are you sure that the doctors said it was a good idea to take a break from treatment?"

"They said sometimes, a little break is what makes all the difference. And I know that a little break right now will make all the difference to me."

"Right, then." Jonah stood up and headed downstairs. The

actors were still there, although they would have to leave soon given what time it was. He took Porsche aside and asked her quietly for what he wanted.

"What, do I just Google "Amish general store"?" Porsche asked, as she pulled out her phone. "I'm pretty sure there will be a million of them."

"I don't know what that means," Jonah confessed.

"Do you have anything more specific?" Porsche asked.

"It's to the north of here," Jonah said, hoping that was specific enough.

It was clear to the dancer that she would have to rely on her own abilities. Jonah watched as she thumbed away at her screen, curious as to what was going on. "Found it," she announced. Porsche turned her screen to face him. It had a familiar address and an image of the storefront he had grown up playing around. His heart rate rose.

"That's it!" Jonah exclaimed.

Porsche turned the phone back to her, pressed on the screen, then turned it back to him. "Here," Porsche said and handed over her phone. "Just give it back when you are done."

Jonah put the phone to his ear. It rang several times. *Was anyone going to answer it?* he wondered. A gruff voice answered the phone.

"Hello?" he said, in Pennsylvanian Dutch.

Jonah inhaled. "Philip? It's Jonah. Can you find one of my parents, please?"

There was such a long silence on the other end that Jonah was sure the shopkeeper had hung up.

"Jonah?" he finally asked. "Really?"

"Really. And I really need to speak to my parents."

"It'll take a while," Philip said.

"That's fine," Jonah said. "I'll wait."

"Well, all right then," Philip said, and then he put the phone down. Jonah could hear steps, then a door open. He leaned against the wall and closed his eyes as he waited. *The worst they could say*

JONAH'S REDEMPTION: AN AMISH ROMANCE

is no, he thought. Except that they could say much worse than no, and he prayed softly that it wouldn't come to that. It was his first prayer in a long time. He had to confess that it was a good thing. He must be on the right path.

Jonah's prayer was interrupted when someone picked up the phone.

"Jonah?"

"Hello, *Maem.* I'd like to come home."

CHAPTER 3

"**I** don't know what to wear!" Mary Lou exclaimed. She was standing in her bedroom on the morning of the 26th, feeling free yet nervous. It shouldn't have mattered what she was wearing, but the intoxicating feeling of change for the good made her worry, nonetheless. She wanted to wear her best dress to meet Jonah's parents, but she couldn't decide which one it was.

"You can wear anything you like," Jonah said. "As long as it's, you know, within—"

"Jonah!" Disbelief mixed with amused indignation was the look Mary Lou gave her on-again-off-again fiancé as he lingered in the doorway. "I don't own anything that isn't Amish."

The sounds of everyone moving, carrying their suitcases, small furniture, and lives of the past months into their vehicles, harried the Amish girl. The pressure of leaving soon, coupled with her frail state, distracted her, when normally, it would focus her attention. The cancer had made her cognition out of sorts. Jonah's petty suggestions did not appease her.

"Well, that's good," Jonah stated. "Would it help if I picked one?"

Mary Lou smiled, playfully. The notion pleased her, though she did not know why. Romance was new to the girl, so it was hardly surprising that it escaped her. "Yes," she answered. "Yes, I do want you to pick one."

"All right." Jonah stepped forward and picked the first in a row of near-identical dresses. "That one."

"You weren't even looking!" she accused him.

Jonah grinned. "I'll see you downstairs." On his way down, he saw Porsche lingering in the hallway. She was standing, arms crossed, straddling her suitcase. It was clear that she'd been waiting for him. "So," she said, "I guess this is goodbye."

"It is," Jonah said. "Although, who knows, maybe you'll be booked by the theatre again."

"Maybe." Porsche shrugged. "It's a big world out there."

Jonah gazed past her, out the door. "Yeah, it is."

Porsche smiled. "Any chance of wanting to see it?"

"Maybe. I once wanted to see it more than I do now. Things have changed."

Porsche looked down at her feet. "I get it. You'll probably be married the next time I see you."

Jonah grimaced. "I don't know about that."

"You will be," Porsche predicted. "That girl has you hook, line, and sinker."

"That's a funny English expression," he said, smiling and cocking his head, searching her face for meaning. It gave him no explanation.

"It's true, isn't it?"

Jonah shrugged, then played along, hoping that she'd be none the wiser. "I guess. I never doubted that I loved her. It's just that things are—" he paused, searching for the right word, "—complicated, and I wish they weren't. It's a sin to be envious, but I'm envious of you and the freedom your life affords you."

Porsche chuckled. "You think the English life is so easy?"

"You aren't bound by the same rules."

"I agree with that. But we do have other rules that we have to follow." Porsche looked up at him. "I think your life is the one to be admired."

"No one would ever admire my life!"

"Really?" The dancer raised an eyebrow. "Well, if you feel that way, you can change it to something that your grandchildren can admire."

Jonah smiled and shook his head. "You always know what to say."

"I do. See ya around, Jonah. I'm the last to leave, so, unless you want to get struck down by a bolt of lightning, you two should head out soon."

"We will," he said. "Bye."

Porsche headed out the door with all of the grace and elegance one could expect from a dancer. Jonah stared, comparing her freedom of movement to Mary Lou's stiff and restricted posture. *I envy their life*, he thought. *Porsche moves free from constraint, whilst Mary Lou walks as though burdened by a myriad of Amish edicts and commands.* He sighed, then looked around the house. It was quiet now, a lovely place to live in peace with Mary Lou. However, he knew that Porsche was right. They needed to leave.

"Mary Lou?" Jonah called up the stairs. "Are you ready?"

"Yes," she answered, then presented herself at the top of the stairs. She was wearing the dress he had picked out and a smile from ear to ear. He smiled back at her, then held out his hand as he made his way up to her. Using his hand as a brace to descend made her feel special. It was the little things in life that people cherished, and Mary Lou was adding this to her mental scrapbook.

"I'm not going to see a doctor," she began. "I'm not going to have some horrible treatment that will make me ill. I'm leaving to go to an Amish community where I can be myself again. This is worth celebrating."

"I agree," was all Jonah could manage. Envy for the English lifestyle distracted him from what was, for Mary Lou, a momentous occasion. Left behind were her loneliness and sense of antipathy. Ahead of her were familiarity and a sense of belonging. They could not have been together on more different paths.

"Now, remember the plan," Jonah said as they headed out the door, "I'm going to drive us as far as the outskirts of my community, and then my father will pick us up in the buggy and bring us the rest of the way unless you're unwell. In that case, I'll drive all the way to my parents' house."

"People will stare," she objected.

Jonah shrugged. He had more important things to consider than to make an impression. "They are going to stare, anyway."

The young couple drove off, making their way down winding roads in silence. Neither one of them knew that there was a radio in the truck, nor did they know how to use it. Mary Lou leaned her head against the cool glass and closed her eyes as they drove. She did feel a bit ill but said nothing. Though she wanted to thank Jonah for his efforts with caring for her, and for his tremendous sacrifices, she was afraid that, should she open her mouth, the feeling in the pit of her stomach would race out before the feeling in her heart. Relief came at the sight of a horse and buggy on the side of the road.

"Are you sure it's okay?" Jonah asked her after he parked the pick-up.

"Yes, of course," she said. "I never feel ill in an Amish buggy, only in English carriages."

Jonah chuckled. "I've never heard cars referred to as *English carriages* before."

Mary Lou smiled, content that she had made him laugh.

The buggy driver looked on. He was, without a shadow of a doubt, Jonah's father. They shared the same eyes, jawline, cheekbones, and stature. To Mary Lou, the man's appearance was uncanny, as though she were getting a glimpse of what her fiancé would look like in 25 years. The older man glimpsed his son's face for the first time in years. Grief and elation scrunched his face like a squeezed fruit that squirted tears from every crevice. Jonah got out of the truck. Father and son embraced, pressing each other tightly in a vain attempt to dam their saline flood. Mary Lou's eyes teared up before she recalled what a momentous occasion this was for Jonah.

The two had not seen each other since Jonah's sister drowned. The girl had been enveloped in her own cares, insulated from the consequence before her, one that she could have easily anticipated had she been herself.

Mary Lou let the men have their moment. Their weeping, moaning, and occasional snorting drowned out the sounds of nature and traffic. Their tears cleansed the dust and cobwebs from their deeply shared, yet neglected, love for one another. She could only sit quietly as grief did its work.

It began to rain.

The men did not notice. Father and son stood embraced, still weeping. Mary Lou looked down at her hands, wondering how much more time would be appropriate to give them in their sorrow before suggesting that they head home. She cleared her throat.

The men loosened their embrace as though they had heard her. Father cupped his son's face in his hands as though he were about to kiss him. He inspected it, then smiled, satisfied that before him was his son. He turned to look at the girl, who waved at him and smiled. The older man approached her and opened the truck's door.

"I'm Mary Lou," she said. "And it's so nice to finally meet you, sir."

Jonah's father smiled. "It's so nice to meet you, too, Miss," he said. "I am honored that you will be staying with us."

Mary Lou blushed. "It's just a few days," she replied. "But it will be a lovely break."

Jonah licked his lips, conscious of the rain and Mary Lou's feeble state. "Perhaps we could go, *Daed*? It's not good for Mary Lou to be outside for too long."

"Indeed," he agreed. "Please, come this way, *milady*."

Mary Lou blushed again. *Milady* sounded at once quaint and archaic, even for the Amish who live perpetually in the past for fear of modern vices. He offered her his hand and gently let her down. She hurried to the buggy and settled in. A blanket was wrapped around her, for which she was glad. But the wind was chilly, and she shivered.

"Are you okay?" Jonah asked.

She nodded. "Yes. I'm just tired."

"Well, when we get to my parents' place, you can lie down," Jonah said. "I'm sure the whole town will want to meet you."

"Oh my!" she said, alarmed. "I really don't think I'm up for visitors."

"I was joking," Jonah assured her. "I mean, the part about everyone wanting to meet you is probably true, but they won't be pounding down the walls."

"That may not be such a joke, *Soh*," his father piped up. "News has spread through the town like wildfire."

"Of course!" Jonah rolled his eyes. "No one has anything better to do." And he again yearned for the freedom of the English.

"Jonah!" Mary Lou hissed.

"It's not good for her to have too many visitors, *Daed,*" Jonah said, "because of her immune system."

"We understand, *Soh*," he replied. "Your mother and I will take care of it, don't worry."

"*Danki,*" Jonah said, as the buggy rolled along.

Mary Lou wondered about what to say to Jonah's mother, how she'd answer his siblings' questions about her health, and imagined other mundane things along the way. She hadn't yet had time to picture the sort of house that Jonah had grown up in. She looked up as they slowed down, then stared, mouth agape. The house wasn't as large as the large Victorian mansion they had just left, but it was bright red, with blue shutters. The colors surprised and pleased her, for it was rare for an Amish home to be so bright.

"They were Jennie's favorite colors," Jonah said. He then leaned forward to whisper into Mary Lou's ear. "Tradition be damned." The apple did not fall far from the tree.

The buggy stopped. Jonah's father helped with the luggage, and Jonah took Mary Lou's arm lightly to help her out of the buggy. She stopped on the step to gaze at her surroundings, happy to be amongst her Amish brethren once more. The sight of trees, birds, and blue skies, along with the smell of horses, flowers, and freshly clipped grass overwhelmed her senses. She closed her eyes to let the Amish sun shine upon her face, smiling all the while. A giggle escaped her as she exhaled.

On the front porch stood a short woman looking at Mary Lou with piercing, green eyes, portals deep into an aged soul. They had seen turmoil and suffering, forgiveness and redemption. One could tell that their owner was studious, not of books, but of life. She had seen many things—some that were not Amish—and ever sought to learn. A sage's wisdom and a child's curiosity happily cohabitated in those eyes. Mary Lou fixed her gaze upon the emeralds. They looked upon her as though she were the jewel, grateful to behold one so precious.

Mary Lou stood a full head above the woman. Now standing next to her on the front porch, it felt strange to be looking down at her, for Mary Lou was sure that she had contemplated a giant of the faith. Without word or action, she could deduce that Jonah's temperament and stubbornness came from the matriarch.

"Thank you for bringing my son home to me." Her gratitude was a carrier pigeon fluttering away with the weight of her grief.

"What do you have in here?" Jonah's father quipped. He held up a suitcase. "Bricks?" No one answered him, so the man laughed at his own joke.

"You'll be staying in the front room," said Jonah's mother. Jonah stopped in his tracks. Intuitively, Mary Lou knew whose room it had once been. "Why don't you go and get settled?"

"*Danki*! I will," Mary Lou said, then turned to see Jonah, who hadn't moved, staring at the stairs to the porch before him. She decided it best to give him time, so she proceeded to the bedroom.

The front room was painted a pale blue, with red trim. There was no sign it had ever been anything but a guest room. Jonah came in behind her.

"This was *her* room, wasn't it?" she asked.

Jonah nodded. "She was so happy to move into her own room. Nobody wanted it because it gets so hot in the summer and cold in the winter. The air doesn't circulate, but she didn't mind. It was hers, alone, and that's all that mattered." He put her bag down next to the bed, then turned to her. "You should rest."

"I should," Mary Lou agreed, "but I feel like you need to talk."

Jonah shook his head. "I don't. I knew what I was getting into when I came here."

"Have you been in here since she—?"

"No," he cut her off, desperate not to hear the end of that sentence, "but I'll be fine." He did an about-face and left the room.

Mary Lou sighed, then and sank into the soft bed.

CHAPTER 4

"**D**id you know that her parents called here?" Jonah's father asked.

"Recently?" Jonah asked.

"No. A little while ago. Mary Lou's father wanted me to know where you were. We wanted to tell you that our souls soared on eagles' wings when we got that call—"

"—But then you were gone again," his mother interjected. "You told us you were out of town. You told us that you had left."

"I know that I told you things that weren't true, *Maem*, and I'm sorry for that," Jonah said. "I just needed to be alone."

"Jonah," his father said, "I don't want to have a big conversation right now, but I want you to remember that you are not the only one who is suffering."

Jonah knew that the words rang true, but his return home was not as soothing as his visit to Mary Lou's community had been. He was angry, self-loathing, mournful, and unforgiving. Seeing Jennie's room void of her things had unsettled his fragile soul, exposing deep, emotional wounds that had not healed. Verbal pus spewed from the open wound that was his sister's death. He wasted no time with formalities, did away with pleasantries, and continued straight away to pick a fight with his father as though the prodigal son had never left. "Will the suffering ever end, though?" Jonah asked, contemptuously. "This is a burden that I will carry the rest of my life, *Daed.* It is an impossible yoke. She was my sister. I was her guardian." Enraged, he stood up from the kitchen table. "What am I even doing here? Why do you allow me to be here? How can you even stand the sight of me?"

His mother stepped forward and looked him in the eye. Her green orbs were mesmerizing, almost magical. Anything she said upon making eye contact would ring true. "Jonah, you are still my son." Soothing words for his infected gash.

Jonah closed his eyes and took a deep breath. Perhaps it was his mother's eyes, perhaps it was her conviction, or, perhaps, it was Holy Spirit Himself that caused his father's words on suffering and Mary Lou's saying about his parents losing two children to slowly convict him. "I know," he said. "I am." His rage subsided. He was home now, the place where he belonged.

"So, no more of this talk," ordered his mother. "Tell me what your lovely Mary Lou likes to eat."

"She hasn't been able to eat much, lately," Jonah said. "I suppose she wouldn't refuse homemade bread."

"Lovely, I'll make some," said the matriarch. Then she bustled off towards the kitchen.

Jonah sat back down, then sighed as he looked at his father. "Go ahead," the younger man said.

"With what?" his father asked.

"I can tell you aren't done," Jonah replied. "I know you better than that."

"All I will say is there are things in my past for which I, too, feel guilty. But the day I met your mother, I knew that none of those things mattered."

"Go on," Jonah encouraged. Whether his father's next words were of any importance remained to be seen, but he thought it wise to let the old man continue.

"*Soh,*" his father continued, "the day you meet the woman that God has put in your path as your wife, everything changes. You are responsible for her; you must take care of her. That is your first priority. Everything else is secondary."

Jonah nodded.

"Well, then things have to change, don't they?" his father asked. "Your heart is still broken, as is ours. But the world turns, and we must keep up with it."

Jonah chuckled. He couldn't help it. He knew that he shouldn't, but it escaped like a determined creature from his captor's clutches, nonetheless. "Isn't that what the world says the Amish forget to do?" he asked. "That we don't keep up with the world?"

His father threw his head back and exhaled a loud, "HA! I suppose so," then shook his head. They both enjoyed the moment before the older man added, "Now that you are home, you must get back to normal."

"What exactly is normal, *Daed*?"

"Well, you could help me with the chores."

Cunning, thought Jonah, but he hid behind his charge. "I shouldn't leave her alone."

"Well, she's not alone, is she? Your mother is here."

"But she won't know what to do."

His father rolled his eyes. "So, run and tell her, *Soh*. We are not so behind that we can't understand some simple instructions." He then folded his arms and leaned back in his chair.

Sheepishly, Jonah arose to go find his mother in the kitchen. He asked her to keep an eye on Mary Lou, gave her a few instructions on how to help her should she feel unwell, then rejoined his father.

The men made their way to the barn, the Grand Central Station of chores for the Amish. It was *the* place to go if one were bored. Indeed, Jonah had often been promised that if he had nothing to do, his parents could always find something for him to do in there. It had changed little since he had last seen it, save for a few more goat stalls, which was easily explained by his mother's preference for their milk to make cheese and soap. The massive complex had been raised in a day by 30 men in Jonah's youth, though he remembered little of the event *per se.* His day had been spent in the safety of the kitchen where his mother had wanted the toddler to be kept in the house for fear of any injury. Since it was her responsibility to feed the masses, his day had been spent savoring melted butter on biscuits and bread, as well as cheese on toast. He could almost taste it, now.

"I have been waiting for this day for quite some time," his father announced, "hoping that you would stand beside me out here once more."

Jonah looked around, trying to compare his mental image of the place with what he saw presently to find any other changes. *Alas!* he thought, *the only thing that changes in an Amish community is the weather.* "I did miss it," Jonah finally admitted.

"Of course, you did. I would not be able to survive in the city. I am not young anymore, Jonah, but I do understand why you left. It's just that, the city is not a place I would run to."

"It's not so bad," Jonah said. "Yes, it's noisy and hectic and cramped, but nobody knows who you are."

"You are making my point for me," his father said.

Jonah shrugged. "There are parks. Actually, a park is where I met Mary Lou."

The old man smiled. "Is it now?"

"Well, we met at work, but I wasn't too kind to her when I met her. So, I went for a walk in the park to reflect on how I treated her, and then I came upon her on a bench."

"And so, it was fate," his father said.

"Maybe," Jonah replied. "She was seeking peace and quiet in the noisy city. I suppose I was, too." He gazed into the distance, as though longing for a more urbane setting. "It was nice to be surrounded by people who didn't know what I had done."

"Now that you are back, you see as clear as day that your mother and I welcome you with open arms," his father said. "Do you intend to return, then, when all of this is over?"

"When her treatment is over?" Jonah asked. "I don't know.

Maybe."

"Why would you not return?"

"Family is very important to Mary Lou as well," Jonah said, "but hers has had a lapse in judgment."

"Do you think that it's permanent?"

"I don't know them well enough to answer that," Jonah admitted. "I suppose that people can surprise us."

"Some people do surprise us," his father replied, as he headed towards the horses.

Jonah followed. He went straight to one of the gray mares and smiled. "I missed you, girl," he said to the horse, who neighed and rubbed her nose against him. He put his hand on her, and she stood still.

"You haven't been to her grave, yet," his father said to him.

Jonah looked up quickly. "I can't go to her grave," he said. The fact that he had just arrived would have sufficed to silence this topic, but Jonah's unresolved issues polluted his mental state. He was always ready to flee at the mention of his sister's death. His father, on the other hand, was keen to get him back in the saddle. A wiser man would have solicited Mary Lou's help, like the matriarch had planned to do, for who could refuse a dying woman her wish? But the old man did not see the folly of his approach.

"Why not?" he asked.

"Because she's gone. It's not like it'll bring her back."

"You know, Jonah—"

"I don't want to talk about it," Jonah barked.

"Well, you might want to," his father said. "I don't want to be harsh, *Soh*, but your fiancée does not look well."

"Of course, she doesn't look well," Jonah snapped. "She has cancer."

"I meant that she may not make it to the wedding," his father said with candor.

"How could you?"

"You must be realistic, *Soh*. I am not trying to hurt you."

"What? How is that not hurtful?"

"It's just the truth," his father said. "Are you prepared for that? For one so young, you have an enormous amount of pain, Jonah."

Jonah thought about throwing a milk pail at his father's head, but, instead, breathed deeply, thrusting his chest out to breathe in the cool, late winter air. Proud of himself for having remained calm, he turned to leave. "I love her," he said, then added, with his back turned to his father, and a wave of the hand, "The rest doesn't matter."

"Then I will pray for you," his father called after him, "because you know that prayer works when we are faithful and obedient."

"No, it doesn't," Jonah said only to be contrary. "It hasn't worked for me so far."

"Hasn't it?" his father said with open palms. "Because it seems that you have been provided happiness again when you thought that you would have none." He yelled the last sentence, for Jonah had picked up the pace on his way to anywhere-but-with-him.

The son knew that he had been happier, though not as happy as he could be, since he'd met Mary Lou. He didn't deserve her, and she deserved a far greater fate than the one she had endured since he'd known her. Her smile brightened the darkest corners of his soul, her eyes twinkled whenever she saw him, thus flattering his fragile ego. Jonah was standing still now, unable to multi-task with his imagination and his legs.

"I am happy that you have found happiness, at least," his father added. "And I am happy that she has brought you home."

"To be precise, I'm the one who brought her home," Jonah said, walking back towards his father.

The old man raised an eyebrow and grinned. "Is that what you think? Once you marry her, you will see that it's her who is taking you everywhere."

Jonah smiled as only one can after having been enraged one moment, only to find oneself giggling the next. His father's laugh made him giggle all the more. He looked away to regain his composure.

"Why are you waiting?" asked his father.

"Waiting for what?" Jonah was still breathing heavily.

"Why are you waiting to marry her?"

"Oh," Jonah replied, then he composed himself. "Because it's not November?"

The Amish married after harvest, in November and, sometimes, early December, when farm life was at its quietest and winters were not yet at their coldest. Being that it was still winter, but almost spring, most of the community would be gearing up for sowing season, sharpening tools, and mending harnesses. It simply wasn't the right time to announce a wedding. Besides, an Amish wedding was hosted in the bride's home, hardly a place where they'd be welcome.

"Life is short," his father pointed out. "I don't mean to sound macabre but..."

Jonah took a deep breath. "I'd thought of it, actually," he confessed. For the first time, he was being honest with himself about Mary Lou aloud. "But I was worried about what people would think."

"*Soh*, who cares what people think?"

Jonah snorted. "Yeah, that is true. But Mary Lou is still faithful to the Amish traditions. She couldn't just have a civil ceremony; she would want a traditional Amish ceremony. Plus, we'd have to be baptized first."

"So?" his father asked. "We're a traditional Amish community, overjoyed for you and ready to celebrate."

Jonah put the pieces together. "Wait, you would do that for us?"

"We would, if your future bride agrees."

"Not to mention the bishop," Jonah added. "And, I don't know if Mary Lou would agree. She would want her family there."

The older man sighed. "Of course, but, realistically, would

they come?"

"Not right now."

"You should talk to her," advised his father. "Your mother and I will be happy to support you, if that's the case."

"Are you sure the bishop will approve?"

"Let's just say, he owes me a favor."

"Very well," Jonah said. "*Danki*."

Jonah nodded, then convinced himself he had worked up the courage to go and talk to Mary Lou. He headed back towards the house and entered through the kitchen. He had fallen for the girl, and he hoped that she would marry him despite his dark past. He was not filled with the certainty that a man has when all the signs that a girl wants to marry him have been shown and that the answer is obvious. Rather, he felt like he might still lose her, that she would be the third in an unholy trinity of lost girls. Or perhaps because she would never agree to marry him without her family present.

Upon entering the kitchen, his mother presented him with a cup of tea. "I think she's awake," she informed him. "Would you like to take this to her?"

"Yes," Jonah said.

"Your father spoke to you?" she asked.

"You knew?" Jonah asked.

"It was my plan!"

A woman taking you everywhere, indeed! thought Jonah.

"I came up with the idea last night," she continued. "We weren't sure what you'd say, but as soon as we saw you two together, we knew that we had to suggest it."

Jonah turned his shoulders square to his mother. "Are you not afraid that the community will throw stones at us?" Jonah asked.

"Let he who is without sin cast the first stone," his mother replied with a threatening glare he was sure was intended for his accusers. Jonah had forgotten how much Bible verses comforted him, though he had just realized that they could also be used as a threat.

"Wish me luck," he said.

"God is with you," she said.

Jonah started up the stairs. Mary Lou's door was open, and she was sitting at the edge of the bed. Jonah had rehearsed this moment privately a dozen times before. Upon seeing her, his mind went blank, and he forgot why he was there. He stood still because his legs could not function when his mind was trying to work.

Mary Lou smiled. "Is that for me?"

Feeling the tea's warmth in his hands, he thrust the cup out towards her, spilling a little tea.

Politely, Mary Lou took it and pretended like all was well with the love of her life. "*Danki.*"

"Hi," he said, as though he needed to announce his presence. "Are you feeling all right?"

"Yes," she said, still pretending like Jonah was fine. "The bed was comfortable. I don't usually take naps, but this was perfect."

He smiled and leaned against the doorway. "My parents would like me to talk to you about something."

"Oh? Are we in trouble?" she asked. "Do they want me to leave?"

"No quite the opposite, actually."

"Opposite?"

"Yes," he said, with a smile. "They want us to get married, as soon as possible."

CHAPTER 5

"Get married?" asked Mary Lou. She put her cup of tea down and turned to him.

"I know," Jonah said. "There are a thousand things wrong with the situation, but there are a million things that are right."

"We're past the wedding season, for one," she said, holding out her finger and pressing down on it with her opposite hand to begin enumerating her objections.

"Everyone can take time off for one day," Jonah said with a shrug, "one morning, even. There are some here who aren't farmers."

"Secondly, I thought that you didn't want to get married." Mary Lou pressed down onto a different finger.

Jonah sighed. He paused to look down on the bed next to her and to choose his words carefully. "Mary Lou, it's not that I didn't want to get married. And it's not that I don't love you."

Mary Lou licked her lips and looked him straight in the eye.

"It is so complicated." Jonah hesitated before continuing. "My father said something to me that resonated with me. He said, 'Life is short.'"

"You think I'm going to die," Mary Lou said.

"No, I don't. I think that you are the strongest person I know."

"But you still think there's a chance."

"Mary Lou," Jonah said, quietly, as though begging her to shut up so that he might let his feelings out. He decided to get straight to the point for fear she'd misunderstand him again. "If my sister has taught me anything, it's that any one of us, in any given moment, could be called back to God. I think that waiting any longer would mean losing precious time with you."

Mary Lou breathed deeply, then shook her head. "We can't get married. My family won't come."

"We could ask them. You never know whether they'll say 'yes.'"

In a rare show of condescension, Mary Lou opined, "They are stubborn and insistent. They won't come."

"We'll be your new family," Jonah offered, unrelenting in his conviction. Mary Lou tried to recall a time when she had seen him with more conviction. *Ah, yes,* she thought, *whenever he was clinging to his misery.* "I'll be your new family," Jonah continued. "This community is willing to support us."

Mary Lou pursed her lips and raised her eyebrows, as though she were trying to tell him, *I told you so.* "Not what you had expected?" she asked, just on the right side of sincerity from sarcasm.

"No," he replied. "Not at all what I expected. I suppose I had created a world in my mind that didn't exist. I had used my own pain as a weapon rather than looking for a place to heal."

Mary Lou's eyes watered. She reached for a third finger and said, "I always said that if I got married, Naomi could be one of my *newehockers.*"

The pair were silent and bowed their heads at the memory of their lost siblings. One might have expected them to cross themselves were they Catholic.

"We have no celery," Mary Lou continued to object, softly, though the thought of wedding decorations inadvertently made her imagine their wedding as an imminent reality. Her mind searched for solutions.

"We can go buy some in the city. I still have the truck parked on the outskirts of our village."

"I don't have time to make a dress, or the dresses of my *newehockers*," she continued, daunted not by the task, for she was a capable seamstress, but by doing it on such short notice with a fraction of her usual energy.

"My mother would be delighted to help you," Jonah offered. He made a mental note to check with her, later.

"I'm not going to have the energy to clean up afterward, nor the will to travel to meet the relatives on the weekends."

Jonah noticed that Mary Lou had thought through the wedding to the honeymoon, though not a typical English one. An Amish honeymoon was one of visiting half a dozen relatives in as many homes per weekend to collect one's wedding gifts, a monumental task to ask of Mary Lou. Visiting households with as many as a dozen people in each would tax the girl's weak immune system. The exhaustion of the trips between farms, the perceived rudeness of her naps, a different bed to sleep in three nights in a row would be, by far, the most demanding part of their early married life. Jonah, however, could only focus on the fact that she had gone through the entire wedding preparations in her mind to formulate her objections. She was close to agreeing to it. He waited.

Finally, Mary Lou wiped the tears from her face and looked up at him. "Yes," she said, at last. "We should do it."

Jonah's face lit up. "Really?"

Mary Lou nodded. "Life is short, and none of us know when we will be called back to God."

Jonah suddenly turned pale. "We are going to get married."

"We are going to get married!" Mary Lou cried.

The color returned to Jonah's face. "We're going to get married!" He leaned out the door and shouted down the stairs. "*MAEM!*" *MAEM*, COME HERE!" He had yelled with such urgency that his mother came rushing up the stairs.

"What is it?" she asked. "What happened?"

"She said yes," Jonah squealed.

"You didn't have to yell like that," she said, then turning to Mary Lou, she added, "Congratulations, my dear."

"*Danki*," said Mary Lou. "I would like to write to my family if you wouldn't mind. I'd like to hear from them before we have the ceremony."

"Of course," Jonah's mother said as she turned toward her son. "But first, does this mean that you will accept the faith?"

Jonah should have seen it coming. He couldn't bring himself to answer her quickly, for his excitement had waned once his mother had shown him the other side of the coin. Knowing Mary Lou, his baptism into the faith was a prerequisite for her hand, though joining the Amish merely for love seemed as though he were doing it for the wrong reasons. Conscious that four eyes were on him, eagerly waiting for an answer, he nodded.

"AH!" the matriarch shouted approvingly. She hugged him before hugging her almost daughter-in-law. "Congratulations! I am so excited! Welcome to the family."

"*Danki*," Mary Lou said, in a sweet and sour tone. She would have desperately wanted her parents at her wedding, but a life with them and not Jonah was unbearable. She had found the man whom God had placed in her path as a husband, and she had returned him to the faith. *Hallelujah!* she thought. It was cause for celebration, but....Her thoughts trailed off.

"Now, is there anything you need?" Jonah's mother asked Mary Lou.

"Only some pen and paper," Mary Lou said, quietly, "and the postage, please."

The elder woman nodded and assured her she would be right back before rushing down the stairs. Mary Lou turned to Jonah and smiled.

"Well, this is not how I thought we'd spend our week."

"No," Jonah said, "but it's better than anything I could have ever imagined."

"Could you get me another cup of tea?" Mary Lou requested, with a chuckle. "It's gone cold."

"Yes," he said, reaching for the cup. "Anything for you."

"Jonah?" Mary Lou asked, quietly. "Would you do this, even if I weren't sick?"

"I think so?" Jonah faltered, then tried to recoup his loss. "I just don't know if I would be brave enough to do it right away."

"That's God giving you courage," Mary Lou said, matter-of-factly. She leaned back against the pillows on the bed. "You know that, right?"

"How do you keep such faith?" Jonah asked, grateful that she had not taken his blunder the wrong way. Still, he felt exposed.

"Because I know it to be true," Mary Lou replied, "and I know that God challenges us sometimes to make us grow."

"We've been challenged enough for now," Jonah said. "Tell God, 'No more challenges for the foreseeable future.'"

"I'll be sure to," his fiancée said like a mother promising her child she'll deliver his list to Santa. "But if there are more, I won't question it. I will just trust in God's plans and purposes."

Mary Lou had hoped Jonah would say something before heading back downstairs, where his mother was informing the rest of the family of the double good news. But the man had an errand. He smiled courteously on his way to the kitchen to boil the kettle and leaned against the wall while he waited. He took it all in, only faintly aware, in the depths of his soul, that he had made the right choice. Mary Lou's inquiry had unnerved him. Would he be moving so fast were it not for his pity? Would he have had the weight lifted from his shoulders if he hadn't? Of one thing he was certain: he could see clearly for the first time in a while.

CHAPTER 6

T he letter from Mary Lou's parents finally came at the end of the week. Jonah recognized her mother, Leah's, handwriting, relieved that it had come. With only two days before they had to return to the city, he hurried to hand it to his fiancée. The latter sat quietly reading the Bible in the parlor, bathed in the sunbeams of a dying, evening sun.

"I used to read that copy of the Bible all the time," Jonah remarked. "I love that it doesn't have a worn spine, so it falls open to random places whenever it's picked up. Some of the Bibles always open to the same place, you know?"

"Yeah," Mary Lou related. "I had one that continually fell open on the verse about not shaving the sides of your head. It may have been important, but..."

"Irrelevant," Jonah chuckled. "I understand. That's why I liked that one. I almost took it with me when I left." He shifted his weight to the other foot.

"Did you bring a Bible with you?" she asked.

He shook his head. "No. I should have."

"We can't change the past," Mary Lou said.

"I know." Remembering why he had sought out Mary Lou, Jonah held up the letter. "Your mother responded."

Mary Lou reached for it immediately. Jonah considered giving her some privacy, but, on the other hand, she'd need support. She tore open the envelope and scanned the letter quickly. Dejected, she shook her head. "They won't come." The dim light, the open Bible, and the letter on her lap made her the most pitiful sight Jonah had ever seen.

"Mary Lou, I'm sorry."

"They said that they'd be happy to support me," she paused in a vain attempt to hold back her sorrow, "if I weren't marrying you." Satisfied at having held it together, she put the letter away. "I don't want to read the rest of this."

Jonah felt like he had been winded by a punch to the gut. He struggled to find his breath and control his rage. The pause between her last words and his next one seemed interminable. Her tears made matters worse. Sorrow having muted him, he spoke up through clenched teeth. "I am angry at them for making you choose between them and me."

"I'm not," she said, though her tears betrayed her conflict. "If they want to be that way, there is no choice."

Jonah sighed and closed his eyes, glad that he had retained his composure, but not yet soothed by her conviction. Putting away fury, he tried a different tack. "Maybe this isn't right," he said.

"No," Mary Lou objected, quickly. "It is right. I want to do this. And I want to do this before we go back to the city." The girl was all-to-keenly aware of Jonah's tendency to run from conflict and avoid resolution. She was on the cusp of returning him to the faith, and of marrying him. Putting her foot down just might catch him by the tail before he bolted.

"Before we go back to the city?" Jonah repeated.

"Life is short," Mary Lou reminded him. "Is it possible?"

Jonah stared blankly, incredulous at the speed at which the bed-ridden could move. A battery of objections, calculations, and possibilities ran through his head. There wasn't enough time. He had to be baptized. The deacon had to publish marriage announcements. He raised his eyebrows and exhaled through his mouth. "We'll have to try," was all Jonah thought appropriate to answer.

"*Danki*," Mary Lou said, wiping her eyes. "I know there's a purpose for all of this."

"Seriously?"

"Yes," Mary Lou said with more conviction than the moment required. "Perhaps this is the only way God could get you back on the path. And if that's what it takes, then it's worth it."

"I don't know that God would ask you to pay such a price for me," Jonah wondered.

Mary Lou shrugged a lone, bony shoulder. "It's not so great a price. Christ died, after all." She paused, gauging whether she had said enough to convince him to stay. She then added, "God oversees my parent's hearts, and I believe that He will change them. In the meantime, I finally get to dedicate the rest of my life to you."

"I do not deserve you," Jonah exclaimed in a low voice with a half-cocked smile.

Mary Lou returned his smile, satisfied that she had a firm grip on him. There would be no running this time. "I believe that we will have a long and prosperous marriage, as long as we remain true to Christ and His teachings."

"Do you even want to go back to the city after we are married?" Jonah asked.

"Yes. As much as my heart is happier in an Amish community, the commute for treatment each day would be impossible for me to handle."

Jonah nodded his agreement. "I will tell my parents the news. We've much work to do." He turned to leave and hurried down the stairs. *Just how big of a favor does the bishop owe my father?* Jonah wondered. Love made his heart skip and his head dizzy, as though Cupid had popped a bottle of champagne in his head.

"*Maem*?" Jonah said to her, still lightheaded.

"I'm in the kitchen."

"Her parents aren't coming."

"I suspected as much," the unflappable matriarch said. "It will then fall on us to make it *wunderbaar* for you both. What is your plan after that?"

"To head back to the city after until her treatment is finished," Jonah said.

"And then?" his mother pried.

"And then I suppose we will take up life here."

Jonah's mother jumped for joy, then hugged him. "I can't wait to have you back with us again."

"Do you think we should build a little house on the spare land?"

"Yes," his mother said, her eyes gleaming like a woman whose ship had just come in. "And your *kinner* can play with their cousins, and Oh! I asked God to bless me and He has." Her glee was such that Jonah could not tell the woman had buried a child.

"Your faith is *wunderbaar*, *Maem*, unshakable, even after such tragedy."

"God leads us through difficult times so that we might grow, and I am willing to rise to those challenges," she stated proudly.

"You sound like Mary Lou."

"That's why I like her so much," she said, her face grimacing to hold back a smile lest she be thought to laugh at her own joke: "She is just like me!"

"She is *wunderbaar*, isn't she?" Jonah agreed. "Oh my goodness, I'm actually getting married."

"You should tell the community," his mother said. "Samuel has been asking for you."

"Samuel!" Jonah exclaimed with a mix of hope, melancholy, and despair. "I haven't seen Samuel since I've returned. I'm a horrible friend!"

"He understands," his mother said. "Go now, before rumors reach him. He should hear it from you."

"I should," Jonah said. It was all he could do to make things right. "Will you be able to stay here in case Mary Lou needs anything?"

"I shall," his mother reassured him.

Jonah scurried out the door, then bounded up the road to see his best friend from childhood. Samuel had not heard a word from Jonah, save for the pious rumors of the prayer mill, and had kept his distance once he had returned. Though desperate to see him, Samuel figured that his friend had to reconcile with his family before visiting anyone else. Still, he wondered if Jonah had forgotten about him. There was a knock at his door. "Hello!" Samuel said. "What took you so long?"

"Took me so long?" Jonah parroted. "Did my mother send a letter ahead of me?"

"I mean, you've been here for a week, and I've been waiting by the door ever since."

"I've been a terrible friend, haven't I?" Jonah asked.

Samuel grinned. "I'm just happy you are here, my friend. Come in, come in!"

Samuel's house looked almost exactly the same, but Jonah spared him any sarcastic remarks. Indeed, he was lighthearted, giddy, and refreshed to be reconnecting with a past he had cherished.

"I wish you could meet my family," Samuel said. "My wife and daughters have gone to the market."

"Your wife and daughters? You've gotten married? You have *kinner*?"

"Indeed," Samuel confirmed. "I married Sarah."

"Oh, my goodness," Jonah said. "I always knew that you were sweet on her. Congratulations."

"God gave me courage," Samuel asserted. "And, how are you?"

"God has given me courage as well," Jonah said. "I am getting married."

"Really?" Samuel asked. "Where?"

"Here," Jonah replied. "In two days."

Samuel's eyes nearly fell out of his head at that. He then sighed, shook his head, and smiled, like someone who had just conceded to being tricked. "Okay, you got me. Always the jokester."

"No, Samuel, I mean it. I'm getting married in two days."

"Why? What's the rush?"

"It's complicated," Jonah replied. "My fiancée is…ill."

Samuel's face fell. "I'm very sorry. I heard rumors, but I didn't know whether they were true."

"It depends what you have heard," Jonah said. "I have faith that she will heal, but after so much tragedy, Mary Lou and I have learned that life is short, so we're going ahead with it."

"Yes, God does call us home unexpectedly," Samuel nodded. "My wife and I lost a child early on. It was hard. We were in a dark place."

Guilt laid a stone egg in Jonah's heart. He had not been there when his closest friend had needed him most. "My condolences. I should have been here for you. I apologize."

"There is no reason to be sorry. You have been through much pain of your own, my friend. I wish that I could have suffered through it with you."

Jonah was unsurprised at the man's generosity, yet it overwhelmed him. "You and Mary Lou and my family have been so kind to me. I don't deserve any of you."

Samuel clapped him on the shoulder. "God often gives abundantly, but sometimes what we perceive as abundance is measured exactly to what we need."

Jonah inhaled and smiled. Little had changed in the Amish community since he'd left, but nothing needed to. Their lifestyle made it so that loving God and one another was natural—primary, even. *How could I have thought that the English world was where I'd find fellowship?* Jonah thought.

"Would you like a cup of tea?" Samuel asked.

"Yes, please. And I would like to hear what else you have been up to."

"Oh, so much," Samuel said, as they headed into the kitchen. "Now, let's see if I can figure out how this works."

"The kettle?" Jonah raised his eyebrow.

"The stove," Samuel replied.

Jonah laughed. "Let me tell you about life in the big city with electricity."

"Sounds complicated," Samuel said, with a smile.

The men spent an hour trading stories of what had happened while they were apart. Jonah couldn't believe that Samuel had been through so many life changes in such a short time. His friend was all grown up, married with children, and had suffered a character-building tragedy. Samuel was happy, content with what life had dealt him, optimistic about what lay ahead, sure that God had given exponentially more than He had ever taken. Jonah left with a full heart. This visit had been exactly what he had needed. Jonah could now admit to himself that God had found a way to bless him, had given him everything that he had been missing in his life, and allowed him to marry the love of his life. Everything was perfect.

Jonah took a moment to sit on the porch, looking out on the land beyond the house, to bask in the moment. He sat on the same swing that Mary Lou had enjoyed only the day before. It was peaceful, it was quiet, and he was whole. "Thank you, God," he whispered. Time stood still.

Suddenly, the peaceful silence was broken by a screech from inside. Jonah tripped over his own feet to rush inside. "*Maem*?" he asked. "Mary Lou?"

There was a crash and another scream from upstairs. Jonah took the stairs two at a time, his heart beating quickly. His foot slipped, and he crashed down the stairs. His chin hit the wooden step. He tasted blood. Panicked voices spoke unintelligibly to each other. He pulled himself up. "Mary Lou?" he called again.

Once up the stairs, his worst nightmare awaited him. Mary Lou was lying on the floor, in his panicked mother's arms, who shook the unconscious girl in a vain attempt to stir the tortured wonder.

"*MAEM*! What's happening?" Jonah slid to the floor beside

her.

"She just fell. She just fell and now she won't wake up."

"Mary Lou," Jonah said sternly, as though a threatening tone might bring her back to her senses. "Mary Lou!" He then realized that she wasn't breathing. "Mary Lou, don't leave me now. Please don't leave me now."

"What do we do?" his mother asked.

"We need to call a hospital."

"You know there's no phone!"

"FIND ONE!" Jonah shrieked. He gathered Mary Lou into his arms, freeing his mother to run out of the room. Mary Lou was limp in his arms. "Mary Lou! Please wake up! Mary Lou!"

She didn't stir.

Jonah looked up to the ceiling, searching for a power beyond it. "Please, God," he begged. "Take me instead. Do not take her away from me now."

BOOK 4

CHAPTER 1

J onah never realized it was possible to be surrounded by people yet still feel lonely. The hospital, full of nurses walking purposefully, doctors asking just enough to know what to prescribe, interns observing silently, and visitors awaiting news of loved ones, was a building full of people unwilling to make eye contact. Jonah was forced to spend his days by the side of his comatose fiancée, Mary Lou, deprived of the pleasantries of conversation, and, at the very least, signs of life. The silence was even tougher on Jonah because he was Amish, and he couldn't entertain or distract himself like others did by staring at a screen in his palm. Thus, he was relegated to staring at an unmoving Mary Lou.

Jonah thought that with so much time on his hands, he would be able to reconnect with God through prayer and meditation, but the quiet in the room didn't translate to quiet in his mind. The rise and fall of Mary Lou's chest, the flicker of the lights, the traffic of the hallway, or the vehicles scurrying about below stole his attention and kept him from introspection. Biologists figure that it was an evolutionary advantage to notice movement, developed either to attain lunch or to avoid being it. However, with Jonah, it was a spiritual issue, a wrestle common to every man, and the problem with the world today: he was unable to sit still alone in a room.

Should he have been able to, he would have felt God in that place sustaining Mary Lou and ready to comfort him. Instead, his gaze fleeted from one movement to the next. If nothing moved, something itched, so he moved. The wait was unbearable, and the loneliness, palpable.

Anxiety took Jonah's breath away, and he felt as though his heart was about to stop. His mind blurred, unable to make sense of what had happened, unable to anticipate what would happen, and incapable of formulating what he wished would happen. To make matters worse, he couldn't stop shaking as though he were trying to wake himself up from a nightmare. Denial was strangely comforting. He wasn't supposed to be there, sitting on a hard, plastic chair, staring at every moving thing like a cat teased by a laser. He was supposed to be happily married!

Jonah's life had turned for the better once he'd met Mary Lou. He had gone from a self-shunned Amishman unable to forgive himself for his sister's drowning, to a man on the cusp of being baptized into his faith and blissfully wedded. He didn't deserve his fiancée, not with his past. Nevertheless, she was smitten. Mary Lou stayed with him despite her family's disowning her on his account. Her radiant character and honest, optimistic demeanor had won over his parents, who were prepared to host their wedding.

Mary Lou, however, did not deserve the situation that she was in. Cancer had sapped her strength for weeks, teasing her with its remission, only to return seven times stronger. A short trip to Jonah's Amish community was supposed to be good for her soul. Jonah had been reunited with his parents, his best friend, and his community. He had popped the question. Everything seemed perfect, as though God Himself were smiling down on them.

But Mary Lou had collapsed and remained unconscious. Jonah was spending his eighteenth hour in a plastic hospital chair awaiting news—good or bad—of her recovery. Mary Lou was a tangled mess of wires and tubes, unresponsive to any stimuli.

"*Soh*," Jonah's father said, "why don't we go home?"

"What if she wakes up?" Jonah asked. "What if she wakes up and I'm not here?"

"We have left the general store's number with the doctors," his father replied. "Someone will come and get us if they call."

What would Mary Lou think if she awoke and Jonah wasn't by her side yet again? He would be unable to explain to her that he had stuck around this time, that he'd matured. He desperately wanted to stay, but sleep beckoned, and he knew he'd be useless to Mary Lou in his state.

As Jonah was determining the best course of action, a doctor entered the room. He wore black Crocs, blue pants, and a white coat. If it weren't for his stethoscope, he'd look like he'd hurried out of bed rather than a professional at work. His glasses sat where his salt-and-pepper hair was receding, though he otherwise looked fit for a middle-aged man. Soft hazel eyes and rounded facial features gave him a friendly appearance.

Jonah recognized the doctor and stood up, anticipating news. It was refreshing for him to finally make eye contact with someone in the building.

"Are you Jonah?" the doctor asked.

"Yes," he said. "And this is my father, Timothy. Do you have any news?"

"I am afraid I do not have any news," the doctor said. "I was just coming to tell you both to head on home. In cases like this, it's best to let the patient rest."

"It'll take me a long time to return if she wakes up. We're Amish, so we don't have a car. I came by ambulance with her, but it took my father over an hour to get here."

"I understand," the doctor said, handing Jonah a slip of paper. Jonah looked at it, confused. "This is a taxi pass. You can call a taxi, and this will cover the cost."

"We live far away."

"It's fine," said the doctor. "When we call to say she is awake, this will allow you to get here more quickly without having to drive a car."

"So, she will wake up?" Jonah asked, hopeful and desperate for some good news.

The doctor winced. "It's hard to tell."

Jonah turned to his father. "Very well. We'll go."

"Thank you," Timothy said, reaching with his large paw to shake the doctor's hand. He escorted his son out of the hospital doors and into the awaiting buggy.

"I am so sorry, *Soh*," Timothy said. "This is not something that you should have to go through at such a young age."

"Perhaps it's some sort of punishment," Jonah muttered.

"No," Timothy said, holding up a hand as if to tell him to stop. "God does not work that way."

"I hope that He would not punish Mary Lou for something I did," Jonah replied.

"He wouldn't," Timothy assured him. When he made a *kick-kick* sound with his mouth and shook the reins, the horse began to walk.

"*Daed*, how is it that your faith is never shaken?"

Timothy guffawed and slapped his thigh. "What?"

Jonah was confused. He had not meant it as a joke, nor had he felt it appropriate to lighten the mood. Now he was uncertain whether his father wanted to chat on the way home.

"I am honored, *Soh*, that you think my faith is never shaken." Timothy shook his head and chuckled.

"But has it been?" Jonah wondered. "For as long as I can remember, you have always provided me with advice rooted in solid faith."

"Because that is what is expected of me. And have you always listened?" Timothy rejoined.

Jonah ignored the question. "So, your faith has not always been strong?"

"No," Timothy declared, much to his son's surprise. "Your mother and I have had quite a journey to get to where we are in the faith."

"What? You never told me!" Jonah exclaimed, feeling betrayed. Still, he pressed on with his interrogation. Could it be that he was not alone in his suffering? Jonah had never before considered the possibility that others have had crises of faith, that others besides him may have mourned. He was now beginning to realize that others might even understand his pain. This was Mary Lou's effect on him.

Timothy was mute. Jonah wondered if he had heard him. *"Daed?"*

His father licked his lips. "Why don't we wait until we get home, *Soh*? Your mother and I can tell you, together."

"If I do not perish of curiosity first," Jonah muttered.

The journey home was long, and the silence had an unusual effect on Jonah. The steady pace of the buggy, plus the sound of the horse's hooves, relaxed him. But the silence between the men, and the anxiety of Mary Lou's condition, interrupted his peace. The guilt of being away from her in her time of need deafened him with its negative thoughts, denying him the calm usually created by the rhythmic beat of horseshoes on pavement. Only exhaustion could quiet his brain's babbling, allowing his ears to hum to the equine beat on the road home. He napped until the carriage stopped.

Taking a moment to orient himself, then recognizing that he was home, Jonah bolted to the general store.

"Any calls for me?" he blurted out, disturbing the otherwise peaceful ambiance of the shop. The shopkeeper raised his eyebrow, and heads turned towards Jonah to see what the commotion was all about.

"No," the shopkeeper replied.

"I'm expecting one," Jonah explained. "We gave the number to the hospital."

"I will tell you as soon as I get the call," the shopkeeper assured him. Jonah had no choice but to accept his answer. He was powerless to rouse the telephone from its slumber, so he tucked his tail between his legs to return home. Something caught his eye as he turned around: a life-sized, hand-sewn doll sitting in the corner.

"Where did this come from?" he asked the clerk, pointing to it.

"Donna sewed it," he said, naming one of the older women in town known for making high-quality trinkets and other things that weren't particularly useful to a people wary of idle hands. The irony was that she kept her hands from ever being idle by making things only idle hands could enjoy. Indeed, her work was better suited for the English world since they prized toys over tools. The Amish were kept busy with a lack of luxuries, so her creations usually sat in the corner of the store.

Jonah admired it for a moment. "I'll purchase it."

"You will?" the shopkeeper asked in sheer amazement, for he had never met the son of a farmer who had time for enormous dolls.

"My fiancée would love it. I want something for her when she wakes up."

Every woman in the store placed her hand over her heart and stared at Jonah, doe-eyed.

"We are all praying for her," the shopkeeper declared.

Jonah thanked him as he paid, then headed home carrying the giant lovey. When he returned to his parents, they were surprised.

"Where are you going to keep that?" Timothy asked.

"It's for Mary Lou," Jonah informed him.

Timothy smiled and rephrased his question: "Where is *she* going to keep that?"

"In our house, I suppose, once we build it."

Father gazed at son admiringly, for the son still had hope. Timothy was awash with the weight of the work the young woman had done to his son's heart. God must have been behind all of it.

Jonah continued to stand in the doorway, unsure of what to say next. What could a man holding a huge Muppet say to his father? He probably looked ridiculous, but he didn't care. It was for Mary Lou. Everything was for Mary Lou. Eventually, he sat down on a kitchen chair and placed the doll on the chair next to him. His mother had made some tea that sat in cups and saucers on the table, along with her homemade buttermilk biscuits on a plate in the center. His father took one look at the scene and shook his head. His mother smiled, expectantly. Jonah looked at his mother, looked at the table, then looked at the doll. Aware that no serious conversation could take place because of the optics of the scene, Jonah excused himself and headed toward the front room with the doll. There, he propped it up so that it sat watching the door where it could be noticed by anyone walking into the room. He'd done something similar in the same room before, for Jennie, his little sister.

Jonah inspected his work, then hung his head for the weight of the memories he had with Jennie in that room. He was twice burdened by Mary Lou's plight and her place in the front room. He rubbed his forehead with his palm, determined not to shed a tear. He turned to walk out the door, searching for purpose. Hadn't his parents something to tell him?

Before Jonah could return to the kitchen to ask his parents about their past, his eyes registered movement at the front door, but five steps away from him. There Samuel stood, getting ready to knock, but Jonah quickly opened the door to let him in.

The two men had been boyhood friends. When Jonah left, suddenly and without warning, he assumed their friendship to be destroyed. He was forever grateful that Samuel had welcomed him back with open arms and that they had simply picked up where they had left off.

"Jonah, I heard what happened. Are you okay?" asked Samuel, concerned for his friend.

"I'm not all right," Jonah answered. "But I'm here now."

"And Mary Lou?"

Jonah sighed. "She will remain in the hospital. She's still…sleeping."

"My friend," Samuel said as he put his hand on Jonah's shoulder, "I am so sorry. Is there anything I can do?"

"Just pray for her," Jonah replied. "Pray that she makes a full recovery."

Jonah's tone made Samuel grimace. "You think she might not?" he asked.

Jonah bit his lip and looked away. "I'm not sure. And neither are the doctors. But they don't know Mary Lou. They don't know how strong she is."

Samuel nodded. His time mourning for his baby had taught him that people in grief seldom remember what others say, but they do remember who was present in their suffering. Jonah would need to be heard, not told what to do. Thus, Samuel stood and said nothing, listening attentively.

Jonah wanted to say more, but instead, he decided to ask Samuel for a favor. "I was wondering, would you help me build our house?"

"The house you and Mary Lou are going to live in?"

"Yes."

Samuel grinned, his eyes sparkling. "Does that mean that you have decided to stay in the community?"

Jonah nodded. "And I've decided to make myself useful while she is recovering. When she is ready to come home from the hospital, she will find our life together ready to be lived."

"Of course, I'll help you!" Samuel exclaimed. Suddenly, the mood was not so somber. Rather, there was cause for celebration: the prodigal son had returned! "That is a *wunderbaar* idea, and I would be honored to help you."

Timothy approached them, having overheard their conversation. "*Soh*, I'm not trying to dampen your mood, but do you know how long it takes to build a house?"

"I've seen some go up in the community," Jonah said, trying to sound informed.

Timothy smiled. "I will help you, too," he said.

Jonah smiled. "*Wunderbaar*," he said. It had been a long time since he'd felt hope.

"I will enlist my sister," Samuel said. "Catherine has been

looking for something to occupy herself with while her fiancé is visiting his mother."

"Catherine is engaged? Really?" Jonah was surprised. Jonah had only ever thought of Catherine as a child. He hadn't been prepared for how fast she'd grown up.

"Yes," he replied. "She met a *wunderbaar* Amish man from another community, and they had a short courtship. This is his final trip home to his family before the wedding. I'm sure she would like to help by cooking for us each day."

"That is very generous," Jonah said. For the first time in a long time, he felt like he belonged in the community again. Everything was going to be fine.

CHAPTER 2

It was late before Jonah managed to ask his parents what his father had meant in the carriage and why his mother had to be present for the story. All of the children had to be in bed before the three were afforded a moment of privacy. They sat by the fire when Theresa, his mother, began.

"I don't believe that we have ever told you our story. We hid it from the community, but also from you for fear that it would cause you to lose faith in God."

"If I knew what? What happened to shake your faith so much?"

Timothy reached for Theresa's hand before proceeding. "You are aware that your mother and I were born into the Amish faith. Our *rumspringa* was one of youth groups and singing. We were certain of our choice to remain Amish. We were married when I was 17 and your mother, 16. Just after you were born, we were new spouses with a young child, and we were exhausted. We couldn't drag ourselves to church, we couldn't drag ourselves to family functions, we couldn't manage anything because we were so tired—"

"Which every new parent goes through," Theresa interjected. "And we know that now, having so many *kinner*. But everything was a mess! So, we just started doing things that we shouldn't have. We started going into town to buy readymade meals. We went to the diner half an hour away. We couldn't afford to keep it up."

168

Timothy leaned forward. "So, I took a job in town to make ends meet. Before I knew it, we had more money than we knew how to spend. We dabbled in the English life, enjoyed some of their conveniences. A cell phone, electric lights—"

"And before we knew it, we realized that we were not living the Amish life," his mother said.

"But you needed to?" Jonah asked.

"No," Theresa said, "we certainly did not. We couldn't bear to keep it a secret, but we didn't confess, so we left. If we were to live the English life, we figured that we might as well do it with them. We first thought that maybe God didn't support the Amish lifestyle because we had been struggling to live it. But, living amongst the English made us question God's existence."

Jonah leaned back in his chair. He had never heard his parents speak of this.

"And it was because of how we felt about you," Timothy said. "We were struggling so much in the Amish way, and you were suffering because we wouldn't ask for help."

"Where did you go?"

"We went to the big city, and we got an apartment," Timothy said. "We lived there for two years, with no Amish contact, godless and miserable."

Jonah covered his mouth in shock.

"At the time, we were certain that we had made the right choice," Theresa said. "We dressed in modern clothes; we liked our electricity. We liked our life, even if we felt alone."

"What happened?" Jonah asked. "What brought you back?"

"It took a lot," Timothy said. "English money went further in Amish country than in the English world. All of their conveniences cost money, and I couldn't make it fast enough. I was hardly home; your mother spent her days alone with you. She knew no one. We found it difficult to connect. It seemed as though everyone had their friends and didn't need new ones. We didn't want to come back to the community just to ask for help because we were lonely."

"But then there was New Year's Day," Theresa said. "You were only three years old, and the three of us were out for a walk."

"There was an old man, also out for a walk," Timothy said. "We greeted each other and spoke for a little while, and then we started walking again."

Riveted, Jonah leaned forward. "What happened?" he asked, sensing that the old man was important to the story.

"He suddenly fell to the ground," Timothy said. "He had a heart attack right in front of us."

"Oh my," Jonah said. His heart was pounding. "That must have been so frightening."

Theresa nodded. "I had taken a first aid course, so, I knew how to do CPR. Your father called an ambulance, and you sat on the sidewalk, watching us."

"I don't remember any of this," Jonah said, probing his earliest memories for a hint of familiarity. Nothing.

"Even though your mother was doing CPR exactly right, the poor man lay there, unresponsive."

"Did he survive?" Jonah couldn't help but ask.

His mother smiled, pointed at him, and said with tears in her eyes. "At the time, we were certain that he wasn't going to. The ambulance wasn't coming, and we were ready to give up."

"And then three-year-old you just started praying," Timothy said.

Jonah gasped. Then he cocked his head. Something didn't add up. "But you said I had been in the city for a couple years without a church. How would I know how to pray?"

"We don't know," Timothy said, shaking his head. "Your mother and I had long stopped praying around you by that time. Yet somehow—"

"You knew," Theresa squeaked, then redoubled her effort not to sob. Still, her emerald eyes beamed with pride.

"So, I prayed?" Jonah asked. "A real prayer?"

"More real than any three-year-old who was raised in an

Amish community could say," Timothy recounted.

Theresa inhaled to get a hold of her emotions. "I was shocked, but I kept performing CPR."

"As you prayed, the man woke up," Timothy said. "The ambulance arrived just in time, and they loaded him up. The paramedics thanked us—"

"And you shouted that we should thank God!" Theresa shared with a smile, shaking her head. She was laughing, almost hysterically. The weight of that day, coupled with her son's present situation, taxed her system. She shed tears for past mistakes and for the joys since. She laughed in hope for the present and at the folly of hoping in light of so great a plight.

Timothy squeezed his wife's hand. "It was then that we realized that we were the ones in the wrong," he continued. "We had trusted the cell phone, fallen in love with English conveniences, and we had even trusted in modern medicine, but nothing was working until you started praying. We hadn't trusted in God." Timothy then opened his mouth, touched his tongue to his top front teeth, and looked up in a vain attempt to pour the tears back into his eyes.

"We knew that we had to go back," Theresa said. "We didn't pack up that night, but the more we thought about it, the more we knew we had been misled. We had lost our faith, but God had given us another chance through you."

"That's why you welcomed me back after I had left," Jonah said.

"I would like to think that we would have done that regardless," Timothy said. "You are our son, and we love you no matter what."

"But it was easier knowing we had been through something similar," Theresa said, sniffling the last of her tears away.

The atmosphere was palpable, as though a transforming power were present by the fireplace with them. Jonah played the scene in his mind over and over again. He reflected on what it meant, what it taught him about God's character, and whether he would ever find

Jehovah's ear again. *Would He hear Jonah pray for Mary Lou?*

Timothy broke the silence. "We blamed ourselves when you left. We were never satisfied with how we had brought you up in the faith. If only we had done more to bolster your belief in God and to grow it, maybe you would have reacted differently to Jennie's death."

"It certainly was not your fault," Jonah offered. "It was mine." He paused, then said, "Thank you for telling me about your past."

"I am surprised you did not know already," Theresa said, "the way the community talks."

"Gossip is a sin," Jonah reminded her.

"I know it is, *Soh*, but that does not mean people don't do it."

Jonah tilted his head to the side as though something had occurred to him. "Did you ever think that you were being punished for something you had done?"

Timothy looked to his wife. She was looking down at her feet. "We did," Timothy confirmed.

"But for what?" Jonah asked.

"All we could think about was everything we had done that was possibly considered a sin," Timothy said. "We recalled every moment when we hadn't followed the *Ordnung* to the letter and assumed it was because of those mistakes that we were miserable."

"Is that really a good reason to be punished, though?" Jonah wondered aloud.

"It is if you promised to abide by it," Theresa said.

Jonah grunted as he nodded. Keeping one's word was a family value. He should have seen that answer coming. "I am sorry that you went through that."

Both shrugged as if it were nothing. "Trials and tribulations make us stronger," Theresa said.

"Well, then, I must be as strong as a mountain!" Jonah exclaimed.

His parents were glad to see their son in high spirits. "You have been through quite a bit," Theresa said to him. "You should get some rest."

"Yes," Jonah said. "Thank you, for telling me. I won't tell anyone."

"You can tell anyone you please," Timothy said. "We are not embarrassed by the trial we went through. Everyone has tests of faith, and perhaps hearing our struggle can help someone else."

"Well, it's helped me," Jonah confessed. "Thank you for sharing it with me. *Gut nacht.*"

"*Gut nacht,*" his parents said.

Jonah headed to the front room. It was eerie to look in the room and see all of Mary Lou's things without her there. *Please God,* he prayed. *Please bring her back soon.* He lingered in the doorway a moment longer in case the Lord might answer before heading to his room. His conversation with Samuel had triggered his imagination, and he was able to picture the house that he would build. Certain that he would be unable to sleep, he took some paper and a pencil from his desk, and, by candlelight, began to draw his and Mary Lou's home.

It was a common adage that some people were called home before they were ready to go. Some people were only meant to be on this earth for a short time, usually to serve a specific purpose. Jonah hoped that Mary Lou was not one of those people. To hedge his bets, he designed their home to rival her mansion in heaven in the hopes that she would choose to stay with him on earth.

Jonah wanted a family and a large house with many rooms in order to fit all of the children and pets he imagined having. *Children would make her want to stay on earth with me,* he figured. *After all, no one is married in heaven, so it can be assumed that no one has kids in heaven. Thus, the mansion promised to all believers would likely be lonely, cavernous places. Women want to be mothers; this will ensure that she wakes up.* He then added a sunroom where Mary Lou could relax in the early morning as she drank tea. It would be inviting and warm. He pictured a hammock, some swings hung from the ceiling, and a reading nook with fitted cushions. In there, more than anywhere else, they would grow old together. Their grandchildren would visit especially to play in that room, and their children would fight for their place in the will because of that room.

Mary Lou had given Jonah space to think, reflect, and fight with himself. She had not learned how to manipulate a man to do her bidding, though, at times, she wished she knew how for it would seem her task of shaping Jonah into a proper Amishman would have been made easier. But men respond much better to patience and encouragement than to nagging for hurried action. The little things are what inspire a man—the acorns of expectation grow into the oaks of commitment. Mary Lou expected great things, so Jonah was drawing out his plans to deliver a home and a legacy together. The girl had made him into a new man. Her love had given him life; she now needed him to do the same for her.

Jonah continued to draw, rejuvenated with hope, and motivated by a purpose for which he had, unbeknownst to him, searched. There is something inspired about a man with a purpose; greater still, is the listless swain who finds meaning and duty—a calling, even—in the gentle vulnerability of the fairer sex. He got carried away sketching layouts of various rooms, assigning each a purpose for a happy life together, then planning all the furniture he would build for each. Done with the house, he began to draw the landscaping, the fencing for a garden, and where he was going to plant all the crops. Flower beds for the walkway, a running bond pattern for the same, mulch beds for the trees, and even a pergola was thrown in. As the candle reached its end, Jonah had drawn a dozen pages of sketches, most with detailed layouts, and all of them with notes explaining his thoughts to his love. It was ridiculously extravagant, and possibly too big to fit on any plot of land he might find in the community. He decided not to show anyone his plans. Prayer for his fiancée's recovery, hope for the future, and reflection were all needed before he could be vulnerable again. As much as Mary Lou inspired him, he'd have to trust God again. That evening was the first step in moving forward since Jennie's passing. He tucked his sketches into his desk drawer and finally got ready for bed. He had been inspired by his parents' story. Tomorrow would be a new day, and tomorrow, Mary Lou could wake up.

CHAPTER 3

Day 7: *Mary Lou is still asleep. Today, we will start the dream house for Mary Lou.*

Jonah kept a journal of Mary Lou's progress. There had been little to write about in the last week. He'd visited her thrice with no change—good or bad—so he decided that he would take action. When he wasn't with her, he obsessed about the plans for the house, and he prayed short prayers since he was still insecure about his standing with the Lord. Nevertheless, he had purpose, and he was turning his life around.

Jonah had spent the week secretly reworking his plans, drawing up a manageable central structure that could easily be added to as his and Mary Lou's family grew. Windows could serve as entrances to other rooms when additions were built, sunlight could still bathe each room with light via skylights, and hallways leading to the various rooms would easily connect to the existing ones.

Samuel had promised to meet him at the plot Jonah had been given by his father to look at the plans, and by the sun's place in the sky, Jonah could see that he was running late. He grabbed his sketches and drawings, then managed to head down the stairs and out the door before anyone called out to him, a rare feat those days. Jonah loved his family, but he found that he got lost in their day-to-day, making it impossible for him to envision his own. He needed to take steps to secure his independence and to renew his mind. Helping with menial tasks about the farm made him feel like he was turning his wheels in butter. Samuel was a necessary reprieve. Jonah could see him waiting patiently.

"It's hard to envision a house here," Jonah said to Samuel when he arrived.

"I suppose that it will be here soon enough," Samuel said. "May I see your plans?"

"They are just sketches, brainstorms, really," Jonah said, as he handed them over. "So, beware."

"Jonah, have you lost your mind?" Samuel blurted out after looking at the first three pages. "We can't build this."

"Look closely. I've tried to make the central structure the core that we'll need, with the kitchen, some bedrooms, the den, and the sunroom. Everything else can be added to it later, so as not to overwhelm us. We don't need to do everything."

Samuel exhaled. It was difficult to decipher whether he was overwhelmed or relieved. Finally, he spoke: "Look, if this is what you want, then this is what we will do."

"*Danki*," Jonah said. "I know it will take a while, but right now, all I have is time."

"Well, you can't start anything on an empty stomach." The voice startled Jonah since he had believed himself to be alone with Samuel. He turned to see Catherine standing behind him with a basket of food. The woman before him was not the same Catherine he remembered. That girl was a scrawny kid, all elbows, knees, and teeth. This one, now, had grown into her joints and limbs, had a grace about her height, high cheekbones that made her pearly whites fit beautifully into her face, and deep blue orbs that, were he to dive into them, he was sure to find a tropical array of fish and coral inside.

"Catherine!" Jonah exclaimed, in shock. "My goodness, I didn't recognize you at all."

"You look the same, just as I remembered you," Catherine teased.

"Really?" Jonah asked. "Because I feel like I've aged about a hundred years."

"You do have a single gray hair," Catherine said, pointing to his hairline.

Jonah's hands flew to his head, his fingers groping about as though they could feel discolored follicles. "Really?" he asked.

Catherine smirked and shook her head. "No, I'm just teasing you." She opened her basket. "I made good on my promise, and I've brought you some sandwiches for your first day."

"Fantastic," Jonah said. He unwrapped the sandwich and took a bite. "Mmm, this is good," he said with his mouth full.

Samuel decided to fill his sister in before enjoying his portion. "We were just looking at the plans. Do you want to see what Jonah has dreamed up?"

"Of course," Catherine said. She looked at the first page, then nodded. When her brother turned the paper over to the second sketch, her eyes widened. He then showed her the third and fourth pages. Catherine had seen enough. "You have big dreams, Jonah."

"Yes," he confessed. "I want the best for Mary Lou."

"I have an idea," Samuel said. "Why don't you take some measurements while I head to the general store to see how soon they can order the supplies? We'll need a lot more than anyone has on hand for this project."

"That will be perfect," Jonah said. "Will you ask if there are any phone messages for me while you're there?"

Endeared, Samuel nodded and smiled. "I will. Hopefully, I will return with good news." And he headed off.

"Let's hope," Jonah said to himself.

"May I help you with the measurements?" Catherine asked. "I love numbers."

"Really?" Jonah asked, surprised.

"Indeed," she replied. "I never really get a chance to use them, except in baking."

"Sure." Jonah didn't see any harm in accepting Catherine's

offer, and he would certainly need some help if he wanted to get it done in any reasonable amount of time. He didn't see anything improper with it, given the fact that they were in a wide-open field. Jonah took out his measuring rope, eager to get to work.

Having known Jonah her whole life, but not having seen him in the past couple years, Catherine started up a conversation in hopes of catching up with her brother's best friend. "I heard about your fiancée," she said. "I'm so sorry to hear what is happening."

"She is strong," Jonah said. "If anyone can beat this, she can."

"I believe you. God would not give you a weak wife. You need someone strong."

"Why do you say that?"

"From what I remember, you're a strong person," Catherine said. "You need someone of equal strength."

Jonah looked downcast. Her memories of him were incorrect. "I am anything but strong."

"We are often our own worst critics," she said.

Jonah was desperate to change the subject. "What have you been up to, Catherine? Did you take a *rumspringa* while I was away?"

"Yes, but not like yours," she said. "I did a volleyball youth group. That's how I met Josiah."

"This is your fiancé, who is away visiting his family."

"That's correct," she said. "I think you would like him."

"Really? Why do you say that?"

"He reminds me of you," Catherine admitted. "That's probably why I fell in love with him." She blushed scarlet. "I'm sorry, I shouldn't be telling you that." But she couldn't help herself. Looking coy, she made eye contact with him, then cast her eyes downward, and continued. "When I was younger—before you left— I was certain that you were the man I was supposed to marry."

The cat had Jonah's tongue. He had no idea that Catherine had felt that way and had no inkling of what to do next. Catherine did not seem to notice his anxiety.

"Not that you would have had any idea," Catherine babbled on. "No, you wouldn't have," she said, shaking her head. "I was just a child; there was no reason for you to notice me. And obviously, I was wrong. I thought God had placed you in front of me, but then you were gone."

"I had to go," Jonah said, hoping to shut her up rather than to inform her. "I had to go because of what happened. I wouldn't be the man I am now if I hadn't left."

"I understand," she said, but the exhilaration of her forbidden confession had made her lightheaded. "I thought about writing to you, but I didn't know where you were." She chuckled and shook her head. "I have no idea what I was going to say, back then. Whatever it was, I'm sure it was silly."

"Perhaps," he said. "If I had written down all of the things I thought about as a child—"

"The list would be larger than your plans for the house?" she teased.

Jonah smirked and nodded his head. "Maybe. I just want to build a big, beautiful house that will impress Mary Lou. I want *her* to be happy." Bringing up his fiancée made him feel like he could wrest control of the conversation back from Catherine and steer it to a more productive conclusion.

"Tell me about her."

Jonah shifted on his feet. *How does one describe one's love?* he wondered. "Mary Lou is…perfect, literally the best person I've ever met. Selfless, optimistic, always looking for a way to do the impossible…" His voice trailed off, but the strain on his face betrayed a yearning for more adjectives. He could not let Catherine win back the upper hand. It was unflattering to hear another's confession of love at a time when his fiancée was bedridden and unresponsive.

"And it's cancer that she has?" Catherine asked.

"Yes, and it's really ravaged her. I cannot wait until she is done with treatment."

"Do the doctors think she will be done soon?"

"Hopefully," Jonah said. "I mean, first she has to wake up, but I have faith." He sounded like he was trying to convince himself.

"Indeed," Catherine said. "If God placed her before you as your wife, he would not take her away before you had the chance to marry her."

Is God really like that? Is He held accountable to our desires once He's put them before us? Will Mary Lou truly make it through this ordeal because of their desire to marry? Jonah wondered. He said nothing, choosing instead to return to the task at hand. Deep theological reflection would have to be done another time. "Should we get to measuring?"

"Yes," Catherine said, grabbing her end of the knotted rope.

When Samuel returned, Jonah and Catherine had the necessary measurements. Jonah, however, had other things on his mind when he saw his old friend. "Any calls for me?" he asked.

Samuel shook his head. "Sorry. And the shopkeeper has been off the phone all day, so he didn't miss it."

Heartbreak threatened to interrupt Jonah's preparations. He put on a strong front. "It's okay. I'm sure the doctors will call soon. I'm going to the hospital tomorrow anyway."

"I can make you some sandwiches for your journey," Catherine volunteered. Then she paused to consider Jonah's commitment. "That is such a long journey. You are very dedicated to her," she said wistfully, as though she wished to have someone who would love her that way.

"I don't mind," Jonah said. "It gives me time to think."

"Hopefully, you'll think about this number," Samuel said, holding up a sheet of paper for Jonah to see. "This is what your supplies will cost. And this is at a discounted rate."

Jonah's heart sank. Gloomily, he said, "Really?"

"That's a lot of money," Catherine said. "But I'm certain we can raise enough funds."

Jonah turned to her. "Raise it? No, this my responsibility. I'll figure it out."

Catherine smiled, patiently. "Jonah, you are now part of this community again. We will help you raise money."

Jonah readied his objection, but Catherine continued before he could utter a sound.

"Jonah, are we doctors?" Catherine asked.

Jonah wondered if she meant it rhetorically. When she raised an eyebrow, he figured that he ought to answer. "No," he said.

"So, we can't help Mary Lou," Catherine said. "And we can't go to the hospital and perform a miracle, besides with prayer."

"Where are you going with this?" Samuel asked, feebly masking his impatience with his little sister's statements of the obvious.

"If we can't help her, let us help you."

Jonah was at a loss. He humbly nodded and uttered, "*Danki.*"

"*Wunderbaar,*" Catherine declared, then turned to her brother. "We could do a spaghetti dinner."

"We could," Samuel said, "but maybe you should ask Jonah what he wants."

Catherine turned to her pre-teen crush.

"I know this sounds silly," Jonah said, "but Mary Lou's favorite food is soup. It didn't matter what time of year it was, she wanted soup every day."

"Well, then that's what we'll do," Catherine said. "Soup it is. I can make several different kinds."

"*Danki,*" Jonah repeated.

Catherine smiled a dazzling smile, and Jonah noticed it. "Not at all. God placed us together, didn't he? This is what we are supposed to do."

Jonah nodded, then turned away, unsure with himself and the warmth Catherine's smile had stirred in his soul. He felt uncomfortable, yet dizzy, almost pleased with himself for having her attention. Then again, only Mary Lou's smile was supposed to warm his soul. She had better awake soon.

CHAPTER 4

Day 23: *I could barely sleep last night. I prayed, but it didn't work. This evening is the fundraising dinner for which I feel embarrassed to ask for help. I cannot focus on work until Mary Lou awakes.*

Jonah hated his brutal honesty, his reckoning with the fear of death, the prospect of being alone—for who could love a man whose loved ones all ended up dying? Nothing seemed to help. His gratitude was superficial. His plans kept him distracted rather than optimistic. No activity he had enjoyed doing brought him joy anymore. An Englishman would have recognized this as depression and sought help accordingly, but the Amish were not fond of the English ways, choosing to ignore their diagnoses as well as their remedies. Theirs was more of a profound grieving whilst still couched in the joy of life in Christ. It was an involved process that required drawing from the deep well of the soul in order to find the Lord's living waters. The Amish understood the paradox that the hand of God is large enough to weigh the waters of the ocean whilst small enough to mend one broken heart.

Jonah was caught between the two worlds, thus unable to live in either. He had not properly grieved Jennie's and, later, Mary Lou's sister Naomi's passing, so he carried them along with his grief for Mary Lou, although he did not wish to use the word *grief* regarding the latter since she had not yet passed. Still, as the days strung into weeks, he could only wonder if he would have to thrice mourn. On the other hand, he was unable to grasp the Amish hope and joy in the Lord since he would not seek it. Every prayer was prayed as though it would never be answered, or as though, if it were answered, Jonah would remain disbelieving. The Almighty is not known for His miracles to the self-loathing, only to the faithful. Jonah was looking forward to the soup dinner that evening, if only for the change in scenery. The community was supportive. He hoped that it would keep him going.

Eventually, Jonah dragged himself out of bed and down the stairs. Exhausted from the sleepless night, he felt as though the day ahead of him were a marathon. This had become the usual start to his days, and his gloom now grew to foreboding.

"Jonah, are you going to the hospital today?" Theresa asked him the moment she heard him on the stairs.

"No," he sullenly replied. "I went yesterday, and I just don't know if I can manage it today. Does that make me a bad person?"

His mother was not expecting that line of reasoning. "No." She paused, then felt the need to add, "No, of course it doesn't."

"It feels like it. It feels like I should be spending every waking moment with her just in case it's her last."

"That is impossible," she said. "And that is not what Mary Lou would want, is it?"

"No," Jonah conceded. He sighed deeply before announcing: "I wrote to her parents last night."

"You did?" Theresa replied in surprise.

"Yes. I figured that they should know what's going on."

"That was very brave of you," his mother said, trying to encourage him. "Do you want me to put it in the post this morning?"

Jonah paused, almost freezing in place. He held his breath, afraid of what to say next. Finally, he admitted, "I'm not sure that I am brave enough to send it."

"I know that they are angry with you," Theresa said, "but as a mother, no matter how angry I was, I would want to see my child. Especially if…" she could not bring herself to finish the sentence. Her compassion for these strangers had brought flashbacks of a lifeless Jennie, so she halted the image for fear of crying. Theresa knew what it felt like to have a child die. Thus, her empathy for Mary Lou's parents brought back the raw emotion she felt when learning that she would outlive one of her own.

Jonah knew that his mother was speaking out of her own pain. His sister was gone, and she had not gotten a chance to say goodbye. He was paralyzed from sheer helplessness.

"Why don't you give it to me, and I'll make sure it goes in the post today?" Theresa suggested.

Jonah nodded. Anything to help his mother feel better. He sat down at the table to have breakfast with his mother. His father had been in the barn since before dawn, instructing Jonah to forego the chores in favor of building his house. Jonah was grateful, for he had not the energy to do chores. He ate his toast, drank his coffee, and then headed to the worksite, where he'd hoped to do a bit of work before turning his attention to the fundraiser.

Catherine was there, at the front of the house, digging into a rectangular patch Jonah could only assume she'd marked. This was unexpected, not only because it hadn't been in his plans, but also because neither the girl nor her brother had been asked to work that day. Indeed, Catherine was supposed to be organizing the fundraiser, so Jonah approached her cautiously, afraid that her presence on the construction site portended disaster. "What are you doing?" he asked her.

"I thought I could put in a small garden for you," said Catherine innocently. "I thought if I started a small one now, it would grow quickly since it's the right time of year."

Jonah hadn't thought of that. Now he imagined Mary Lou coming home to a front yard with a small patch of blooming flowers, and he could see her beaming with delight! She'd appreciate the garden, then lay her head on his shoulder as a sign of gratitude and affection. It would certainly set the mood.

"It's what I would want," Catherine continued. "What kind of flowers does Mary Lou like?"

Jonah opened his mouth before he realized that he hadn't the slightest idea. Embarrassed, he acted like he had forgotten. Catherine let him save face. "Why don't I just fill it with my favorites, then?" she asked. "I like a lot of color and variety, so I'm sure that there will be something in there that she likes."

Relieved, Jonah agreed. "*Danki.*"

"Of course," Catherine said with a shrug.

"When is your fiancé coming back?" Jonah asked.

"Another month or two," she replied.

"A month or two? That's a pretty long time."

"I know," she said, "but he wanted to get a few projects done for his family."

"Oh, I see. Do you miss him?"

The girl hesitated, then cocked her head and pretended to strain with the shovel. "I do," Catherine said. "But I am finding plenty of ways to keep busy. Besides, we will have the rest of our lives to be together."

Jonah chuckled. She glanced up at him. Suddenly feeling guilty, he offered to take the shovel. "Why don't you let me help you with that?"

"It's all right," she fibbed. He moved for the shovel, just to show her an easier way to do it, when their hands brushed together. That mere touch exhilarated the young man. He looked up and met Catherine's gaze. She slowly looked away but remained still. Jonah knew something wasn't right, yet the sensation of connecting with someone, he welcomed.

"Sorry," Catherine said, coquettishly. She handed over the shovel. "Show me."

"It's just if you hold it like this…" and then Jonah demonstrated the correct way to hold the shovel.

Catherine's face lit up. "Wow, I was doing it wrong. Where

did you learn that?" It was difficult to tell if she was pleased for having been corrected or for having the strapping man's undivided attention.

"In the city," Jonah said. "I worked in construction for a while, and they taught us all sorts of tricks."

"I didn't know that you did that. What did you build?" Her doe eyes mesmerized him, to the point where he was lost in their flattery.

"We did landscaping, actually," he said, hoping the disappointment of having no stories to tell of erecting edifices would throw her off the scent.

Catherine blushed. "And here I am, digging a garden and talking about flowers like I'm an expert. Oh! I've made a fool of myself."

"No, no, no," Jonah said. "We did trees mostly, and shrubs. I don't know the first thing about flowers."

Catherine could feel him like putty in her hands. "What else did you do?" she asked him. "Did you just do the landscaping job the entire time you were there?"

"I also worked for a delivery company. The truth is, the landscaping made me feel too much like I was here."

"Oh," she said, leaning in as though she were fascinated. "I understand that. Being a delivery man is less Amish."

"Mostly," he said. "I liked to deliver things that had nothing to do with Amish life, like computers and cell phones. I would hang around those shops."

"When I go to the market, I see people with cell phones," Catherine said. "They always have their heads buried in them. They look so distracting."

Jonah got serious. "Well, if you live a life from which you want to be distracted, I understand exactly why they would want such a thing."

"Did you have one?" Catherine asked, trying to reel him back in.

Jonah nodded, feeling safer now that his reminiscence of the city had brought his reasons for fleeing there, and the woman he'd met there, back to the forefront of his mind. Catherine was beginning to seem as she had before their hands had touched. Things, he felt, could return to normal. He ignored her question and answered what he had hoped was asked. "I wish that I had one the night that Mary Lou collapsed. I could have called an ambulance, and she may not be unconscious right now."

"Oh, well, maybe it was God's will."

"How was that God's will?" Jonah asked.

Catherine smiled and her eyes bulged like she had swallowed a parakeet. "Ours is not to question that," was all that she could manage. She was unprepared for the challenge; anyone else in the community would have nodded solemnly and agreed with her. Never had she reflected on what it meant. When Jonah sighed, she quickly changed the subject. "Are you excited for the soup tonight?"

"What kind of soup have you made?"

"Carrot ginger," she replied.

Jonah's face lit up. "That's my favorite."

Catherine giggled and covered her mouth. "I know. I asked around. You told me that Mary Lou's favorite thing was soup, but I wanted you to be happy, too."

Jonah thanked her, then moved into the frame of the house to do some more construction. The girl stayed in the yard to finish the garden, then went home for lunch. With his stomach rumbling, Jonah headed home, too, hoping for carrot ginger soup. His mother welcomed him back, glad to see that he was in higher spirits than when he left in the morning. The two caught up on the morning's events, and Jonah told Theresa about the soup. "And she made my favorite," he told his mother. "I can't believe it."

"Well, Catherine has always been a kind girl," his mother said. "To be honest, Jonah, I always thought that she was sweet on you."

"Oh, she was," Jonah said. "We laughed about it. I had no idea."

"Oh," Theresa replied.

Jonah could see that she suspected something, so he gave her a funny look to draw it out of her. "What's the problem?"

"There is no problem," Theresa replied, too quickly for her son's liking. "Catherine is a good girl with a kind heart."

"But…" he prompted her.

Theresa sighed. "I hate to imply this, but I see the same look on her face now as before you left."

"So, what are you saying?"

Theresa stopped what she was doing and turned to her son. "Just be careful."

"What are you suggesting, *Maem*? Don't you know that she's engaged and that her fiancé is returning soon?"

"I understand," his mother said, "but your fiancée is away, too, and loneliness loves company. Past feelings don't just disappear." She paused and let her words sink in.

"Even if it were true, it wouldn't matter," Jonah finally uttered.

"No, of course not," Theresa retreated. "The two of you are on very different paths in life."

"We are," Jonah said. "So, I'm sure everything will be fine." He excused himself to wash up for the fundraiser.

Jonah was unprepared for what Catherine had put together that evening. The barn was filled with Amish from all over the community. They showered him with kindness and empathy, encouraged him in his sorrow, and wished the fledgling couple well. There were too many tubs of boiling soup; he didn't know what to choose. This community supported each other in any way they could, though it was usually with time, possessions, or service. Still, they were willing to part ways with the little currency that they had in order to support the community's prodigal son. It was as though each one of them approached Jonah like the cheerful father in the story, each willing to hand him their finest clothes and golden ring (if they had such things), then to kill the fatted calf, for the one who was once lost had been found. Jonah, who was dead, stood alive before them. If only the latter could be said for Mary Lou.

Everyone paid generously, sometimes twice the asking price. Jonah was presented with the pot of cash at the end of the night. He gripped it tightly, as though it held the power necessary for him to start anew in life.

"Hopefully, that's enough to build the house of your dreams," his father said with a smile, whilst the community stood 'round.

"*Danki*," Jonah said in a reverent whisper. One might have thought he was addressing them in a cathedral rather than a barn. "I don't know how I can ever thank you all."

"Be a godly husband and a Christ-like father," someone said. "That'll repay us just fine."

Jonah looked around to see from whence the voice came, but he could not find who had said it.

"We are just glad you are back, Jonah," Catherine said.

"Catherine, I want to thank you," Jonah said. "Specifically, all the things you have done for the house, including this fundraiser. I was blessed the day we re-met."

"I am blessed to help you," Catherine said, smiling coyly. Jonah clutched the donation pot. Overwhelmed by their Christian love, Jonah stood to bask in the moment, terrified of moving and causing it to end. Mary Lou was not on his mind, and neither was his curse. He looked around the room, first to his left, then his right, then back again, each time stopping to contemplate Catherine's smile. What a strange sensation it was to feel connected to the living, especially those around him. He had forgotten the two dead girls. Instead, his best friend's sister's smile filled his head. It wasn't until he lay in bed that night that he noticed he had not once thought of Mary Lou since he took possession of the pot. Instead, Catherine's kindness and disarming smile ruled his thoughts.

What was happening? pondered Jonah.

CHAPTER 5

“**A**re you going to the hospital today?” Theresa asked Jonah as soon as she heard him descend from his room. She was beginning to sound like a broken record, but it had been four days since the fundraiser, and he had not yet returned to his beloved's side.

“Actually, I'm going to go work on the house,” he said. He noticed his mother's raised eyebrow.

“Oh,” she said. Her tone irritated him.

“What does that mean?”

“Nothing. It's just, you haven't been there in quite some time.”

“I'm aware of that, *Maem*. I just don't want to keep going and wearing down the horses if there is no change.”

“Do you think that Mary Lou doesn't know you are there?”

“No, *Maem*, Mary Lou does *not* know I'm there,” Jonah snapped. “Mary Lou cannot speak, she is not awake, and it makes no difference to her whether I'm there or not.”

“JONAH!” Theresa shouted, incredulous at her son's naiveté and callousness.

He shrugged. “What? I'm just being honest.” Unable to tolerate his dumbstruck mother, Jonah stormed out of the house without breakfast. Walking briskly, he replayed the discussion in his head, then defended himself whenever he felt remorse for having been heartless. The goal was to be desensitized to his guilt by the time he arrived at the construction site. It didn't work. He concluded that he was unable to begin working with his mind afoul, so he continued, at first unsure as to where he was heading, then realizing that his feet had decided to take him where he had not yet trod: Jennie's grave.

His sister's passing had forever changed Jonah's life. He was unable to fend for her when the creek's current snatched her away from her family whilst his back was turned to rescue her friend. The subsequent nightmares, about which he had told no one, distorted his memories and disfigured her face in his mind. Truth be told, Jonah could not remember what she looked like and was unsure of her hair color, her build, or the sound of her voice. It is said that a lack of sleep can distort one's memories and even corrupt them. Jennie was but a name to him. He had not mourned her; instead, his guilt pushed him to the city where his wallowing made almost every memory of Jennie disappear. Everything had become about him and his curse. The incident caused him to shun himself from his community and to meet Mary Lou.

Jonah was of two minds about this. On the one hand, Mary Lou was a ray of hope in his despair. On the other, God had a wicked sense of humor given her circumstance. Jonah had to live like she was dying. It was taxing on the nerves, but he was learning to cherish every moment with her.

As pleased as Jonah was to have met Mary Lou, he knew that he needed closure regarding his sister's death. Jonah felt disconnected from his kid sister as he approached her modest tombstone. *The whole place feels dead,* he thought without a hint of irony. He shifted on his feet and looked around for where he belonged—for where he could feel Jennie and trigger their shared past in his mind. Again, his feet decided where they were going before his mind had a chance to decide. He was headed to the creek.

Jonah liked to think that Jennie was playing safely in the creek of heaven with Jesus watching over her. It would be her best chance not to drown again. The poor girl's life had been cut short; she would know nothing beyond childhood. Pain and guilt were the first things to reconnect Jonah's memory to Jennie's life. The creek was bringing her back to life.

"Hi, Jennie," Jonah said when he got there. "I miss you." Standing there was painful and exhilarating. The wind was blowing through the trees, and the birds were chirping. It was a beautiful day—the type of day that Jennie would have loved. Jonah's guilt and regret were flushed out in his tears, and the creek washed them away. Someone was there. He could feel it.

"I know I haven't been around," Jonah continued, "and I'm really sorry about that. It's been hard. But what am I talking about? You're the one who died." He paused. "I wish that you were still here because you were the distraction I needed when everything got too hard. You could always make me smile." The birds sang. Jonah sobbed.

"Jennie, is Mary Lou up there with you?" he asked. "Is she already gone? Because if she is, I just need to know," he said. "I just need to know so I can..." He sniffled.

There was, of course, no answer. Even if there were, Jonah didn't want to hear it. The doctors mentioned that the longer Mary Lou stayed comatose, the less of a chance there was that she would wake up. Jonah stared at the spring waters, their current strong like the day they took his sister. Henceforth, he was led, and all he could do was follow. He felt his own hands take off his shoes and socks and then roll up his pant legs like a parent would do for a child. Then he walked into the water as though he were being held by the hand.

The water was cold. Jonah winced. Whoever was leading him to the water let him stand there. He felt the current's strength. No one should have let two small girls play in such waters. What could he have been thinking?

"Is Naomi there?" Jonah heard himself ask. "You would really like her. She's Mary Lou's sister, and she's up there with you—" he snapped out of it— "because I am cursed," he screeched. "Because every family I come close to experiences darkness." He turned to face downstream. His legs stung in the cold, melted snowy waters, but he forced them to walk where Jennie, his beloved sister, had been carried. He was in control now. His rage allowed him to regain his senses. Jonah knew the general vicinity where Jennie washed ashore, drowned, and he headed toward it as though led by a rope. He had to see it, for in doing so, he could feel her pain. Maybe it would kill him. *Oh! How the world would be a better place for it!* he reasoned. As he neared, his vision blurred. *Rage is blinding me,* he figured. *This is good.* Alas! It was sorrow that was blinding him, but he was unaware of her presence despite her salty taste. He kept going. *If I can feel her pain, feel her fear, feel her betrayal, we'll be even, and then God will let Mary Lou live,* he bargained.

Jonah's legs were bright red and numb. No one was at the creek because it was too early in the year. The weather hadn't yet turned for the better. He felt alone. He could die if his feet failed him. *I must press on.* Guilt is a powerful manipulator, but coupled with rage, it is a tyrannical mistress. Jonah wanted to see where Jennie had washed ashore in all its gloom and desolation. He expected to see rapids littered with large rocks where her body would have been flung, tortured, and ripped apart by the speedy current against them. He figured that in seeing her final resting place, he would hear her screams for help, be racked with guilt, collapse, and square the books with the Almighty. Then, for sure, Mary Lou would awake to a better world without him in it.

Jonah reached the place, but sorrow still held a firm grip on his eyes. He scratched at them in the hopes of seeing clearly; he washed his face with the icy current, then wiped them with his sleeves. It was to no avail. He would have to use the little vision he had and his other senses to make sense of his surroundings. He listened. The current did not sound as violent nor as rushed, though it was fast. The rocks beneath his feet were smaller, and the pool was deeper, up to his knees. He sniffed, but his sinuses were still clogged from all his sobbing. Slowly, he began to make sense of the shapes through blurry vision. There seemed to be trees all along the right bank, but the left bank, the same side from which he and Jennie had entered the creek, had an opening. The sun shone brightly where there was no canopy. Jonah blew his nose down into the water as any farm boy would. He sniffed. It smelled wild, with traces of bark, manure, and perfume. He turned back toward his left and made out colors: bright yellows, purples, pinks, and reds. He blinked, his vision slowly returning to him. Before him grew the last thing he had expected: flowers. There was a whole flower bed, full of all sorts of wildflowers. They formed a garden of rainbows. It was the most colorful and beautiful final resting place for a little girl he had ever seen. If Jennie had died there, and that was the last thing she saw, then she would have been at peace. She loved flowers.

Jonah plucked half a dozen flowers, each of a different color, then headed for her grave. He had hoped to consummate his anger where Jennie had come to rest. Now, he was half sulking for the relief from his rage. When he'd reached the cemetery, he placed the flowers before her tombstone and sank down next to it. For all the cold he'd suffered in the creek, the pain he felt was in his soul. His heart was heavy, and his breathing labored, though not from exertion but from sheer grief and turmoil. He had wanted to be angry at God, to blame Him for her drowning, yet it felt as though He had assured her a most wonderful place to be found. When Jonah had turned his back to Jennie, God had, indeed, been watching her. He seemed...caring. Jonah felt dizzy and nauseated by his reckoning. He would not—could not—conclude that his anger since Jennie's death was in vain. He would not relinquish it so easily, for, after all, his sister had died, flowery resting place notwithstanding. Holy Spirit called, yet Jonah pulled away with force. He was at a breaking point. If he were to get through this, he needed to feel less. He had to numb the pain.

"God, forgive me," Jonah said, as he arose. He would never normally consider what he was about to do, but in his circumstance, he was desperate to give it a try. He headed home, as his morning came full circle. Just his luck, it was lunchtime, so everyone was indoors at the table. His stomach rumbled. Nevertheless, a determined Jonah headed to the barn and saddled up a horse. Deep down, he knew he ought to visit his fiancée in the hospital, but he couldn't face her. *She'll talk me out of it, but I don't want to be,* he confessed in a moment of truth.

"JONAH!" Theresa suddenly burst out of the house. "Are you going to the hospital?"

Afraid to face his mother's wrath anew, he lied: "Yes." He mounted the horse and turned it towards the road.

"Come inside and have some lunch first," she said. "We should talk."

"I can't. I have to do something for Mary Lou." More lies.

"Has something changed?" his mother asked. "Did they call?"

Not wanting to pile on his fibs, Jonah spurred the horse and ignored his mother's inquiries. He headed to the one shop in town that sold exactly what he wanted. It was on the edge of town, and some of his former colleagues had praised the shop for curing their perceived ills. God's presence had exposed his sin, and His light had scorched the weed of transgression, but sin is not so easily defeated. Its death grip is sure, and Jonah was headed to fetch water-of-life that it might live again.

On the fastest horse at breakneck speed, the town was a good hour away. Jonah's myopia was causing him to spend the horse without consideration for its condition on the journey home. He just wanted to get there. Normally, he rationalized that those who stared at the Amish visiting the town had nothing better to do with their lives. On this visit, however, he practically snarled at them. He didn't want them to look at him, to raise an eyebrow, nor to turn their heads to notice him. He begrudged all those who did not do as he pleased.

When Jonah got to the shop, he jumped off the horse, tied it up to a lamppost, and marched in like a lion ready for a fight. He did not think twice about the horse, its thirst, or to cover it up from the cold after such an arduous journey. The money from the soup fundraiser was burning a hole in his pocket.

"Hello," said the clerk. Then he cocked his head and added, "I don't see your kind in here too much."

"I didn't realize there was a type of person who could come in here," Jonah retorted. "Aside from being over 21."

"There's not," the man said. "As long as you are over 21, you are welcome to buy whatever you want."

"I am," Jonah lied. "Do you want my ID?"

"No, it's fine," the clerk replied as he looked him up and down. "Do you know what you want?"

"I don't," Jonah admitted. He hated himself for being honest because he found that it cooled his anger. He did not want to lose his anger. His sister died and God had not stopped it. This shop was fuel for the furnace of his rage.

"Well, what do you want it for?"

"Just for myself." More honesty. If this continued, Jonah would leave that place like a lamb.

"To experiment with?"

Jonah shook his head. "I'm not going to experiment. I don't want to feel anything."

"Ah, well, I have just the thing," the clerk said. He presented Jonah with a bottle of what looked like water. It was a beautiful thing! Dark blue paper sealed its cap. On the label was a drawing of a lake before mountains with birds flying over the waters. "Grey Goose" was written beneath it. The image of nature called to him, but the water theme uniting Jennie and the geese unsettled Jonah. "This is vodka. Have you ever given it a go?"

"Nope," Jonah replied. "Is it good?"

"It burns on the way down, but it will do the trick. You looking to forget something?"

"Many things," Jonah replied. "How many bottles do I need?"

"You just need the one," the man chuckled. "Trust me."

"Fine," Jonah said and took out the wad of cash. At this, the clerk shifted tactics.

"You know, perhaps you want something a little more top shelf," he suggested, "if you are willing to spend the money, of course."

"Will it get the job done faster?" Jonah asked.

The clerk nodded. "It will. Come with me down the whiskey aisle." The men then discussed the virtues and distinctions of bourbon, Scotch, and single malt, and the clerk lost himself in his descriptions of barrel age and kind, peatiness, and which notes the palate might prefer. Jonah stopped him to ask if any of these features would improve the drink's effect.

"No. It's the proof that counts." The clerk blushed since he had forgotten to whom he was speaking and had treated Jonah as though he were a discerning drinker. With this correction, he would be able to close the sale. Indeed, once Jonah could read the proof counts on the bourbons, he was easily talked out of a $13 bottle of Grey Goose and into a $99 bottle of Elijah Craig Barrel Proof Bourbon. Jonah smiled to himself when he read "136 Proof: 68% ABV" on the label. *This'll do the trick!* Little did he know the effect such a drink would have on his empty stomach!

"I would suggest drinking it slowly," the clerk said, as he rang him up, "at least until you get to a safe place."

"I have an hour's ride back," Jonah replied.

"Slowly then, until you get home. And don't let anyone see you. You aren't supposed to be drinking in the streets, anywhere."

Jonah did not like being told what to do, and he further resented the clerk becoming a mother hen, telling him how to drink. "That's a stupid rule," Jonah said. "People should be allowed to do whatever they want."

The clerk smiled. "I like you. Come back anytime."

CHAPTER 6

"**A**re you sure you don't want me to stay any longer?" Samuel asked Catherine. The two of them had been working on Jonah's house, but they had no idea where Jonah was. It was supper time.

"No, it's fine," Catherine replied. "I just want to finish the flower bed, and then I'm going to go home."

"Okay," Samuel said. He then squinted into the distance. "Is that Jonah?"

Catherine looked up and then laughed. "Perhaps you need your eyesight checked, Samuel. That's the mail carrier."

Samuel blushed. "Oh, he doesn't normally come searching for us out in the field. It must be a slow day."

"Indeed," Catherine replied. "Maybe there will be a letter from Josiah."

"It's been a long time since you've heard from him."

Catherine's face changed. "I know. He's very busy. He's helping his father build a barn."

"A barn?" Samuel said in surprise. "This whole time?"

Catherine said nothing. She busied herself with the garden.

Samuel was suspicious. Barn raising was a day-long affair that involved as many as 70 men in an Amish settlement. Surely, Josiah had been delayed by other things. Or Catherine was hiding something. "Do you know where you two are going to live once you are married?"

"To tell you the truth, we haven't really discussed it," Catherine said. "I was sort of hoping to wait until he came back and we could figure all of that out."

Samuel wanted to pry about the barn, but he was afraid to upset her. He suspected that Josiah had left her and that she knew. Pretending that he was busy working on a barn in a faraway settlement was likely her going through the denial stage of grief. "But you are going to get married here?" He didn't care for the answer to his inquiry but listened politely since he had only himself to blame for the line of questioning. How he wished he could talk sense into her!

Catherine nodded. "Oh yes. I could never get married in another community, without all my friends and family around."

"I know exactly what you mean. I am glad that my wife and I are both from here."

"Yes, you are lucky," Catherine said. "I have often thought about what Josiah and I will do at Christmas time and how we will split them."

"Maybe you should get married first and worry about the rest later."

The mail carrier approached.

"Hello, Joseph."

"Hello, Catherine," Joseph said. "I have come all this way to look for you." Joseph had been the mail carrier in the community since Catherine was a little girl, but she had never seen him come out this far for a delivery. He handed her a large parcel. "I was told this was the top priority, so I thought that I would put it into your hands directly."

It was from Josiah. Catherine beamed! *"Danki."*

"My pleasure," Joseph said, then he turned and left.

"Perhaps he's sent me a present," Catherine hoped.

Samuel scoffed. "It looks like someone's whole life is in that box."

"Well, he did say that if we got any gifts for the wedding, he would send them here. Maybe he got many from his family?" Catherine smiled, shook the box, then ran her hands over the label.

Samuel could only pity the girl. "Are you not going to open it?"

"I want to try and guess what's in it," she said. "It could be anything."

"Aye, it could be," he said. "But why not open it?"

"You can't expect me to open it in front of you," she said.

Her sibling looked appalled. "Why not?" he asked.

"Because he is my fiancé," she said.

Samuel's face turned to stone. "Catherine, if he is sending you inappropriate gifts—"

"No!" she cried. "Of course, he isn't. But would you want every present that was sent to you from your wife opened in front of me?"

She had a point. "Very well," Samuel said. "How about I head over to the far side of the house? Then you can open it and decide to show me if you like. I have to collect my tools, anyway."

It was a fair proposition, and Catherine agreed to it. Samuel went around the house, picked up his tools, and secured them in his toolbox. It would have been easier to leave his tools there since he came to work on the house daily, and he trusted those in his community, but it was an open field where some English boys might dare to sneak away from their parents to drink. Once all had been sorted, Samuel returned to Catherine. She sat on the front stoop with her back to him. "Are you willing to show me what was in the parcel?

It was then that Samuel realized Catherine's shoulders were shaking in a muted sob. He walked around to face her. "Catherine?" She clutched a letter, now drenched in tears pouring from her face like rain off an unguttered roof. "Catherine! What happened? What's the matter?" He peered into the box hoping it would give him a clue.

It was filled with her things; things that she had packed and taken to Josiah's when she visited his family so that she might have some personal items when she visited with his sister and stayed the night. He lived a half a day's ride away. Some were gifts she'd given him or his family.

"Catherine?"

"He's decided he does not want to marry me. When he went back to his village, his parents persuaded him that he was better off marrying someone else."

Samuel stood, mouth agape, unable to speak.

Catherine held out the letter for Samuel, who grabbed it and scanned it over quickly. "I'm going to kill him. I'm going to *kill* him!"

Catherine had never seen her big brother react this way. She feared for Josiah's life, so she shook her head and said, "No, Samuel, it's fine. I'll be fine."

"It's not fine. He made you cry. He strung you along. You waited for him! This is not the way to treat my little *schweschder*."

Catherine cried, then pleaded with him some more. "Please, don't hurt him. This has happened because it's God's will. We cannot question it."

Moved by her innocence, Samuel calmed himself down and sat beside her. "Catherine, I can understand how you feel right now, that you can excuse his terrible behavior like God wills it, but you have to remember that we have free will, and God can be disappointed in us—disappointed in Josiah."

"He's already married," Catherine said. "There's nothing else we can do."

Samuel picked up the letter to read it again. "What a—"

"Please don't call him names. He's a good man. He's a good man. This has happened for a reason." She folded up the letter and tucked it away. "Can you take my things back to my house?"

"Yes, but what are you going to do?"

"I'm going to stay here for a bit. I'd rather be alone right now."

"I'd rather you not be alone," Samuel asserted.

"I will be fine," she said. "And I won't do anything drastic. I promise."

Samuel looked hard at his sister, trying to discern if there was a hint of dishonesty in her countenance. Once satisfied, he nodded.

"*Dank, Bruder*," Catherine said. She lay her hand on his forearm.

"Anything for my little *schweschder*. Do you want me to tell our parents?"

"Please," she said.

"Okay." He picked up her box of things and added it to his tools. "I'll see you soon."

Catherine sat on the stoop with her hands over her face, trying not to cry. Heartbroken, she tried to console herself with God's sovereignty. *God makes everything happen for a reason; God has a bigger plan,* she told herself. *Perhaps this is a blessing in disguise.* Then, despite herself, as though she were coming to her senses, she blurted out, "Well it seems to be quite effectively disguised!" Her *faux* theological pep talk was not having the desired effect. She wanted to die. Did God not know that this was the worst thing that could have happened to her? That she was humiliated? How could she grieve if her inner dialogue conspired to stymy her pain?

With that, Catherine had had enough. She arose and decided to take a long walk home. She felt the letter's corner press against her from her apron pocket. Suddenly, she was distracted. In the distance, a horse approached, one who's silhouette was unmistakably from Timothy and Theresa's farm. She squinted to see who rode it, and when her heart leaped, she knew that it had discerned Jonah approaching. Even though she had told Samuel that she wanted to be alone, at that moment, she thought Jonah's presence would comfort her.

Catherine waited patiently as Jonah approached. With every step, her heart warmed as though radiant heat emanated from her girlhood crush. Her tears were now forgotten.

"Catherine?" asked Jonah when he stopped the horse. "Just the girl I wanted to see." He slid off the horse and almost slipped, catching himself from the fall by grabbing the stirrup. Catherine had bolted forward to catch him, though it was of little use since he was a beast of a man compared to her frail frame. He lost his balance, and they both fell to the ground. The horse snorted and moved away, unimpressed.

"Whoops," Jonah said, then giggled. "Let me help you up."

"Are you all right?" Catherine inquired, concerned. "I think you need a hand more than I do." Jonah looked half asleep and was acting ridiculously. Had he gotten bad news in town? Had Mary Lou taken a turn for the worse?

"Of course, I'm all right," he said. "I feel great."

Catherine noticed a bottle in his hands that she did not recognize. With disgust she asked, "Jonah are you drunk?"

"Just a little bit," he said, and he put the bottle in her face. "Want to try?"

Catherine pulled away. "No thank you. I don't want a drink!" she said louder than what Jonah thought was appropriate.

"Ssh, Catherine. I'm allowed."

"Why are you allowed?"

"Because I don't want to feel anything," Jonah said. "Just for once. Don't you ever want to just feel nothing?"

Catherine's stomach lurched. "I do not want to feel anything *right now*, but I wouldn't resort to drinking."

"What happened?"

"Josiah broke up with me," she said as she pulled the letter out. "He went home and got married."

"He did *what*?" Jonah squinted at the letter. "Oh my God."

"Jonah!" she cried, "don't use the Lord's name in vain!"

"It's okay, He doesn't mind," Jonah replied. He looked up at her, then held her gaze. With eyes locked, Jonah leaned forward. "Catherine," was all he managed before their lips met.

Out of nowhere, a voice from behind him asked, "Jonah? What

is going on?"

It was Mary Lou's mother!

Jonah fell over. He was doomed.

BOOK 5

CHAPTER 1

Being good with words had been Jonah's specialty. No matter the situation, he was used to being able to talk his way out of it. Recently, that skill had soured and had been used sarcastically, but he could still make use of his charm from time to time. However, he was normally sober, chaste, and well-behaved before his future in-laws. None of that applied at present. Jonah's sinning had reached a new level. However, he didn't blame himself. It wasn't his fault that his fiancée, Mary Lou was in a coma. It wasn't his fault that he had prayed for her recovery, and God had ignored him. It wasn't his fault that his soul had been scarred years ago when his sister had drowned right in front of him. It wasn't his fault that he had to leave the community in order to survive, only to find the courage to return when Mary Lou needed a quiet, peaceful place to heal in between chemo treatments. Coming back to the community was supposed to be for her, yet she wasn't there. Surely, anyone could see that it was all too much, that no one could have handled his situation any differently.

So, Jonah had gone out to buy whiskey to numb the pain, an idea that seemed good at the time. He hadn't expected his best friend's sister, Catherine, to be waiting for him at the house he was building for Mary Lou upon his return. He hadn't expected Catherine to announce, with teary eyes, that her fiancé had left her.

He hadn't expected to want to heal her pain with a kiss. *Didn't I just lose my balance and fall into her lips?* he reasoned. Yet, there he was, kissing her, blurry-eyed, and feeling good, until he heard the voice of Mary Lou's parents, standing behind him, watching.

Jonah had written to Mary Lou's parents, begging them to visit their daughter *in the hospital.* The poor girl had not seen her parents throughout her chemotherapy, and they were unaware of her latest stay in the hospital. Jonah thought it was a good idea to let them know about Mary Lou's situation, though he didn't expect them to visit at all, or if they did, he expected them to be by her side, not behind him in a field.

For the first time in a while, Jonah was unable to talk his way out of a dilemma. His brain was foggy, and he giggled uncontrollably, yet he was terrified of Leah.

"This isn't what it looks like," Jonah finally managed in a moment of sobriety.

Mary Lou's mother raised an eyebrow and looked at him and Catherine, utterly unimpressed. "Really? What is it then?"

Jonah giggled again, despite the seriousness of the situation.

Joshua shook his head. "This is exactly why we told her not to marry you." He then pulled his wife away from the sorry spectacle. "Come on."

"This is the house," Jonah bellowed. "This is the house I built for her." He gestured to the frame of their future home.

Mary Lou's mother softened for a brief second, then returned to her stone-cold self upon seeing Catherine again. "Who are you?" She made no effort to hide her disdain.

"I'm Catherine," she answered. "Jonah is my brother's best friend, and I didn't mean for this to happen. My fiancé just broke up with me, and I was sad and...." Her voice trailed off when her insecurity overcame her. She was unsure if she was making matters worse.

"A likely story," Mary Lou's mother said.

"No, it's true." Catherine reached into her apron and thrust

Josiah's letter forward. "See?"

Jonah was trying very hard to pay attention, but nature's call, as well as his condition, made it like listening to a sermon delivered by an uninspired preacher the morning after a sleepless night.

Neither of Mary Lou's parents wanted to read the letter, but her mother glanced at it. "Well, that's still no excuse for what we just witnessed."

"Shame on you," Joshua said. "Shame on you both."

"You should stay away from Mary Lou," her mother said to Jonah, then stormed off.

Although the incident had sobered the drunk Amish boy, he was still under the influence. Jonah felt helpless, then discouraged, then enraged. He couldn't breathe.

Catherine turned to him. "Jonah, I'm so sorry."

Jonah looked at her, blamed her, wanted her, then turned away as though that would make up his mind. What had he done? If Mary Lou had been there, things may have been different. He shook his head. If Mary Lou were there, he might manage to pull himself out of this slump. *No, no, no! If Mary Lou were here, I wouldn't be in this mess! None of this would have happened!* Jonah scolded himself.

To Catherine, an innocent girl who'd never seen a drunkard, the whole scene looked evil. Jonah seemed to be speaking to himself in mumbled tones, shaking his head, then jerking it, only to grab his hair with both hands to pull, exhale, then repeat. She feared that he may have been possessed by a demon.

"Go," Jonah muttered menacingly. It was all Catherine needed to hear before eagerly heading home.

Breathless, Jonah clutched his chest. His pulse pounded at his temples mercilessly. He was warm. He feared death. He opened his mouth to cry for help, but it was then he realized that he wasn't dying; he had gone berserk. Rage welled up within him, an unadulterated hatred for the On High, so that from his mouth came a primal wail from the abyss of his defeated soul. Catherine, now half a mile away, heard it and shivered, certain her fear had been warranted. She quickened her pace to get more distance between them.

Jonah thrashed his head, clenched his fist and jaw, and flexed every sinew and ligament in an effort to evacuate his anger through his cry. Rather than calming him, his actions exhausted him. Unable to speak, yet incapable of cursing, Jonah wailed more, only to descend further into his tantrum. Desperation galloped toward him, and he punched the frame of the house in the hopes of crashing the edifice to serve as a barricade before her horses, unaware that they made haste from within. Despair consumed him, so he climbed to the peak of the two-story frame to throw himself off. Bracing himself with one leg up higher on the roof truss than the other, Jonah's silhouette resembled an *h* in the night sky. *Hell*, he thought, and he took a swig of whiskey before addressing the sky.

"WHY?!?" Jonah shrieked. He said it again, holding it longer. A third time, then a fourth, his voice climbed the scale and cracked as his rage drove the note to his question ever higher. A fifth time was blood-curdling, held for his entire breath before a *decrescendo* into the evening air, leaving him bent at the core, head hung low, breathless and unsure he wished to inhale the crisp evening air. He would rather it have been his last breath, allowing himself to topple over and die. Yet the sky beckoned. It called to him. He raised his gaze to look at it in curious contemplation, the picture of a defeated man submitting to the authority above.

It was dusk, the almost indigo heavens streaked with orange hues peppered with thin, gray clouds. Then it all disappeared. Though the sun had not yet set, one could be forgiven to assume it was the dead of night. So quickly had the rain clouds come that Jonah did not perceive them. He thought he'd gone blind! No wind had brought them, no leaf rustled, no hint remained from whence they'd come. The air, however, did not signal rain. It was not yet humid enough. The Amish drunk was now fully attuned to this change in circumstance, anticipating the Almighty to act with vengeance.

Lightning flashed. Jonah ducked, then turned his head this way and that, much like a boy raised by wolves would try to make sense of his environment. He leaned into his knee, then shivered, awaiting God's next lightning bolt, sure that He would eventually find His mark. Another flash, then another. All were above him, but none were directed at him. The fourth caught Jonah's eye, which followed it across the sky, illuminating everything in its path. The bolt showed him his front door, his front yard, further still through the trees, and into a clearing with flowers—his sister Jennie's flowers.

When God's faithfulness meets man's stubbornness in full force, it pushes him in one of two ways: denial or surrender. Twice in one day, Jennie's flowers had had a soothing effect upon Jonah. Yet, in the morning, he was unaware of their proximity to his and Mary Lou's house. Now it was clear. The Lord had been working on Jonah's heart all day long, and not even a stomach full of whiskey could make him miss it. Jonah was feeling. He was no longer numb, but alive! Jennie had come to rest in a peaceful place, likely her favorite part of the creek, and now Jonah and Mary Lou could watch over that portion of the waterway in loving memory of her dear soul. He who had once been blind could now see. Where there had once been death, now there was life.

"Oh! My God!" Jonah cried in surrender. "Glory be to God! You are my Savior; my spirit rejoices. You have kept me humble, and now I will be blessed for You have done great things for me, and mighty is Your name. You have shown me mercy, You have shown me Your strength, You have kept my paths straight, delivered me from harm, and returned me to my sister's side, where I shall live with the wife You have set before me. You have given new life, and You restore my soul." Then Jonah did the only thing a broken man could do to be made whole: he cried, his sobs purging his rage, his every breath, now, a life-giving breath of God.

The skies opened and the rains came, as though baptizing

Jonah into his renewed faith in the Lord. His sins were washed away. From the waters came a new man. He dropped the whiskey, for it was now the Spirit of the Lord who lived within him.

CHAPTER 2

"JONAH!"

Were the heavens calling his name? Alas! Standing below Jonah, in the pouring rain, was Samuel, his childhood friend.

"JONAH!" Samuel cried again. "Don't do this. Please don't do this."

"Samuel!" Jonah said.

"Jonah, it's Mary Lou! She's awake."

Jonah almost fell off the roof. "What?" he asked.

"SHE'S AWAKE!" Samuel screamed up to him. "Please come down from there, safely."

Carefully, Jonah climbed down into Samuel's waiting arms. "She's really awake?" he asked him. "Really?"

"Yes," Samuel said. "The call just came to the general store. You have to go. Now!"

Jonah stumbled forward, then looked at Samuel. "I'm unwell," he said, euphemistically.

"Catherine told me. Hopefully, you can sober up by the time you get there."

"Her parents saw everything," Jonah confessed.

"Catherine also told me that," Samuel said. "Don't worry. They were stressed out too."

"I'm not sure *stressed out* are the words I would use," Jonah replied.

"Focus, Jonah. Don't let this opportunity to see Mary Lou go to waste."

"Right. I'm not going to throw away my chance to see her, maybe one last time."

"One last time?" Samuel asked, over the rain. "Jonah, you just came down from the roof. I'm not letting you climb back up there."

"That's not what I mean. Her parents aren't going to let me near her now," Jonah said.

Samuel shook his head. "None of that matters. Do you want to go home first? Maybe change your clothes?"

"No," Jonah said. "I want to see her. Samuel, I need to see her. I've been dying to see her."

"So, let's go. I'll drive you in my carriage."

"What about my horse?"

Samuel turned to look at the horse that Jonah had just ridden into town and back. "Have you seen your horse?" He didn't wait for Jonah's reply. "Come on, buddy." Both men headed to the buggy.

"Did the doctor say whether she is, you know, more than just awake? Is she talking? Does she remember me? Is she the same?"

"The message just came that she is awake," Samuel said. "I don't know the rest. I'm sorry."

They boarded Samuel's buggy. Samuel snapped the reins, and the horses pulled forward. The rain had become a mere drizzle, and the full moon pierced through the clouds. Each could see the other in the pale moonlight. Jonah was pensive, calmly taking stock of all that had happened, and trying to cipher how he had missed noticing that Jennie's flowery end was but a stone's throw from where he and Mary Lou would spend their lives.

Samuel glanced at his friend. He wondered what had happened to him, whether Jonah would have leaped from the roof truss, and why he had not been at all what Catherine had described. "What happened to you up there?"

"I met with God. I was going to kill myself, but God

intervened." Jonah said nothing more.

Slightly vexed, Samuel could not help his sarcastic tone. "Well, then, just another quiet evening in Jonah's life. Care to give me some more details?"

Jonah didn't feel like there was anything to add. "What do you want to know?"

Incredulous, Samuel enumerated his curiosities. "First of all, why were you drunk? Second of all, how did you get up there? I've seen English drunkards who can barely walk straight, let alone climb. And then, you know, the whole God thing."

"I went to see Jennie's final resting place this morning," Jonah began.

"The place near your new house?"

"Yes, but I didn't know that," Jonah said. He continued. "I felt angry at God for Mary Lou, for Jennie, and for Naomi, Mary Lou's sister. I hoped to find peace, but I felt nothing. So, I went to the creek, walked into the water all the way to the flowers—"

"At this time of year? Are you crazy? It's freezing in there!"

Jonah continued to tell his friend about the peace he felt at the sight of the flowers, the resentment towards God's overwatch, the whiskey, but sidestepping Catherine and what Samuel already knew, then the bout with the lightning, and how he felt that his new beginning started with Jennie and Mary Lou in it.

"The flowers on your property don't bother you?"

"No," Jonah replied. "It gave me the sense that God watched her until the end, and now He's watching over me, too. Because of that, I'm sure Mary Lou will be fine. What I can't figure out is why I didn't know where I was when I discovered it. How could I have missed it?"

"Truly," Samuel said, "it had to have been kept hidden from you for God to reveal it at the right time. Too early, and you would not have been prepared to receive it. Only the tilled soil receives the seed. Otherwise, nothing grows."

Jonah pondered Samuel's words. God had revealed much

about His character and the great lengths to which He'd go to find His lost sheep. Samuel was correct: had Jonah noticed where he was in the morning, he would have resented the Lord entirely and would not have been able to accept it. Indeed, that was why he had gone into town and why he'd climbed up on the roof truss. Thus, all had to be revealed to him piecemeal until he was ready to see the whole thing. Mary Lou's influence was key to his re-opening up to the Lord. Now, he was free from his anger, released from his curse, and a new man. Unfortunately, now he had a different worry. "I'm afraid her parents are going to turn me away at the hospital. Do her parents know she's awake?"

"I didn't tell them," Samuel said. "And I don't know where they would have gone."

"Well, they said they were going to the hospital," Jonah recalled. "So, they have probably already arrived there and are likely to bar my entrance."

"Jonah, her parents were scared. I can't imagine they are spiteful people, especially given Mary Lou's fragile state."

"I think they are," Jonah said. "They never listened to Mary Lou long enough for her to tell them her diagnosis. They made no effort to stay in touch with her. They said that she had made her choice, being with me, and that they disowned her. And up until now, they kept their promise. When I finally sent a letter telling them about her cancer, they didn't rush to her side; they came to mine! They can hate, Samuel. They can hate."

"But they came. And they came because you wrote to them. Something has changed."

"Yeah, they thought she was dying," Jonah said. "They wanted to say goodbye."

"And the only reason they had that opportunity was because you put your pride aside to write to them," Samuel said, hoping to reassure him. "They won't forget that."

Jonah shook his head and swallowed the lump in his throat. "I understand why they made their decision. I feel guilty about it every day that she chooses to be with me."

"But she made the choice for herself," Samuel said. "That has to mean something."

"I wish she didn't have to choose at all. No doubt that made her sicker."

"I wish, I wish," Samuel parroted. "Deal with reality, will you? No one made her choose. She's strong. She chose this herself. Now she's awake from an I-don't-know-how-long coma, and you're her answer to prayer."

Jonah admired his friend. "When did you become so wise?"

Samuel shrugged. "I guess while you were away because we certainly weren't smart when we were kids."

"We were not," Jonah agreed, "but most of our ideas seemed like good ones at the time."

Samuel scoffed. "Yes, until we were late for supper. Then, they never seemed worth it."

The two men arrived in the city. The moon was bright, their spirits were lifted, and Mary Lou beckoned.

Once at the hospital, Jonah hesitated. "I was happy until we got here. I mean, I want to see Mary Lou but—"

"It's complicated," Samuel interrupted, hoping to hasten his friend's reunion with his fiancée.

Jonah nodded. "I don't have it in me to fight with her parents."

"Look, from what you've told me, you make her happy. She wouldn't have chosen you if you didn't. So, don't fight her parents; fight *for her*."

Inspired, Jonah disembarked and headed into the hospital without looking back. He was headed to take his place by Mary Lou's side to be at her service. *God, give me strength,* he prayed as he walked through the sliding doors and headed down the familiar path to the elevator. Today was the first time he was there for good reason. His guilt no longer owned him. Living in service of another is the only way to discover one's purpose. Mary Lou would be loved and cherished for the rest of her life.

Jonah reached Mary Lou's floor, headed to her room, and, to his dismay, her parents were there, with her dad blocking the door. When Joshua heard footsteps, he turned around.

"Jonah? You have a lot of nerve, coming in here."

"Please, I just want to see her."

"She doesn't want to see you."

Jonah took a deep breath. "I think she does. And if she doesn't, she'll have to tell me herself." He pushed by his elder and presented himself to his fiancée. Mary Lou was sat in bed, pale, eyes downcast, her complexion unflattering under the fluorescent lights. Jonah put his arm around her before she acknowledged him, yet she was stiff and disengaged, disinterested in seeing him this time.

"What's wrong?" asked Jonah.

Mary Lou seemed not to have heard him.

"Mary Lou? What's the matter?"

Still no response.

Jonah looked to her mother and asked, "What's wrong with her?"

"Nothing's wrong with her," replied Leah. "You're the problem."

All at once, Jonah understood that Mary Lou's parents had informed her of the incident with Catherine, perhaps even delighted in it, imagining themselves putting the last nail in the coffin of their relationship.

Leah continued. "We told her that while she lay here fighting for her life, you were out boozing and kissing other women." It seemed as though Leah relished in repeating the story, assured of her assessment of Jonah's character, and affirming to her daughter that disowning her for being with him had been the right choice.

"I can explain," Jonah said. The wordsmith returned. He was certain that if he held Mary Lou's ear captive, he would be able to talk himself back into her heart where he longed to stay.

"Can you?" Mary Lou asked, staring directly before her.

"Yes, I can."

Mary Lou looked up at Jonah, incredulous, a bewildered look that was as near to condescension as she could manage. But there must have been something in his gaze that changed her mind because she looked at each of her parents and declared, "I would like to be alone with Jonah so that he can explain."

"He doesn't need to be alone with you," her mother snapped. "And he doesn't need to explain anything. I already told you—"

"*Maem*," Mary Lou said, "I have just been to the edge of death and back. I would like to hear Jonah's side of the story now that I have returned to the world of the living."

Leah looked like a steaming teapot. She gazed upward, wide-eyed, jaw locked, and fists clenched, holding back a scream, for she could see victory slipping away. There was no reasoning with a girl in love. "Five minutes," Leah managed towards Jonah in vexed politeness, "is all you get. And that's far more than you deserve."

"I understand," Jonah said. "*Danki.*"

Leah glared at Jonah as she made her way around her daughter's bed to join her spouse's side. They exited, and Jonah turned to Mary Lou. He was exhilarated. God had met with him and changed his very soul. Now was his chance to share it with the one who would love to hear it most. Mary Lou's patient gaze, which he'd not seen in over a month, calmed his mind whilst simultaneously making his heart leap. He was about to commit his life to loving her.

"I don't deserve you. You deserve all the kindness and happiness in the world," he began.

Mary Lou sat quietly, giving him rope as though waiting for him to hang himself. Jonah, however, was using it to weave a silken cocoon around them. The girl did not see it coming, but, goodness, was it ever smooth!

"I was dying inside," Jonah continued. "I couldn't eat, I couldn't sleep, and I was begging God daily to heal you. He wouldn't answer me; He wouldn't talk to me. Still, in faith, I decided to build us a house. I got Samuel and his sister, Catherine, to help me. There was even a fundraiser with the entire settlement pitching in what they could to help us buy the building supplies. It was as though I was the prodigal son coming home. But, once I had the cash in hand, ready to begin our life together, you weren't there. Despair consumed me, and my hope in the Lord soured. I was angry because you were not restored to me. So, yesterday morning, I felt led to the part of the creek where Jennie had been found. It was beautiful, covered with flowers. She would have loved it. Maybe that's where she was trying to go that day—" Mary Lou felt a lump in her throat whilst Jonah spoke valiantly through tears. He let the sentence trail off and chose, instead, to get to the point. "God's spirit worked within me, but I resisted. I didn't want Him to change my attitude because I felt safe in my anger. It was my shield. With it, I never had to let anyone near me ever again. Still, I could not deny the Almighty's handiwork, so I fled to drown His redemptive work in my soul. I needed to be numb."

"So, you drank?" Mary Lou asked, tearfully.

Jonah nodded. "I went back to our building site, afraid to go home in my inebriated state. Little did I know that Catherine would be there, brokenhearted because her fiancé had informed her that he had married another while she waited for him. I leaned in to tell her that her fiancé was a scoundrel, but our lips met, instead. That's about the time your parents showed up. Everyone left, and I wanted to die, so I climbed up the roof trusses to throw myself off when God showed me the flowers but 100 yards from our front door. That's when I got the news that you were awake."

Jonah sat down onto her bed, held Mary Lou's frail hands in his paws, looked her straight in the eyes, and said, "I love you. When we met, I was at the lowest point of my life. I couldn't forgive myself for Jennie's death. You brought me out of the darkness, out of my self-loathing. When Naomi died, I ran out on you as you were grieving the loss of a sister. I was convinced that I was cursed and that I would bring harm to anyone who loved me, but you never gave up on me or on us. I thought that by taking care of you during your cancer treatment, I was finally doing something right, but when you fell into a coma, I couldn't handle it. It seemed like every time we were about to get our happy ending, something else would knock us down. I held on for as long as I could and tried to focus on the future. I channeled my energy towards building our home. Having Samuel back in my life was a big help, too. But all it took was the reminder of Jennie's death to push me toward the one thing I knew would numb the pain. That was the dumbest mistake I've ever made. Mary Lou, please believe me when I say that I have never had any feelings towards Catherine. She's my best friend's little sister. You've already forgiven me more times in the short while that we've known each other than any woman should have to in a lifetime, but God has made me a new man. He has put you before me as my wife. If you'll have me, I shall love you and cherish you in obedience to Him for the rest of my life."

They sat silently together, appreciating the moment. Then Mary Lou smiled and asked, "You built me a house?"

"Yes," Jonah replied, slightly taken aback. "At least, I'm building you one now. I wanted it to be ready for when you awoke. It's mostly done. The frame is up on the foundations, there's a chimney, some siding, and trusses. We just need to add a roof, some shingles, and the finishing touches for the interior, like cabinets, and then we'll be ready."

"I can't believe you built me a house. You're serious about this. This is really happening?"

"Indeed. I want to be your man. Will you forgive me and be my wife?"

Mary Lou sighed. After stealing a quick glance at Jonah, she then looked away. This Amish boy in a white shirt that contrasted with his olive complexion, that accentuated his broad shoulders, and caressed his firm biceps, was enough to make her forget the whole thing and lose herself in his barrel chest. He stroked her hair as her head rested on his torso. Jonah's eyes mesmerized, so Mary Lou avoided looking into them. Instead, she looked straight ahead to gather her thoughts.

"Jonah, I am disappointed in you. You are a better man than that." *Frankly, I thought Porsche would have been the one to lead you astray*, she thought. "I cannot express how much it hurt to hear what you had done with Catherine upon my waking from a coma—" she paused to lick her lips, mindful of her sense of betrayal and the venom it could cause her to spew. She said to herself all of the hurtful things that she wanted to say, everything that could have destroyed Jonah's confidence and made him feel worse than she did, and then it passed. In its place resurfaced every memory of their time together, his diligence in getting her to her appointments, him carrying her in his arms to the house they shared with the actors, and she was moved. She inhaled, turned to her fiancé, and said, "I forgive you. This one incident cannot erase your faithfulness to me in my time of need." Mary Lou bowed her head, almost ashamed to admit what she was about to say. "I think my mother was keen to get here first out of spite. She didn't raise me to behave the way she has treated you."

Mary Lou and Jonah sat in silence, the former, pensive, the latter, observant. Jonah held his tongue, confident that he had made his case. He needed only to wait for Mary Lou to fall into his arms, and all would be well. But the girl was still coming to grips with having been unconscious for a month, taking stock of what she had missed, and replaying Jonah's words in her mind. She sat upright, no longer leaning into Jonah, so he waited. It was only a matter of time. Suddenly, her countenance changed. She smiled, turned to her fiancé, leaned back, and asked again, "So you built me a house?"

Pleased, Jonah nodded, his smile melting Mary Lou's heart. "I designed it and drew up the plans myself. It has a central node with everything that we need, and it can be expanded upon as our family grows. I wanted it to be perfect."

Mary Lou pondered their life together as parents, picturing her brawny fiancé as a father with an infant dwarfed in his mighty hands. She would grow flowers in the front yard with their daughters, and he would work the garden in the back with their boys. They would grow old together in a home filled with laughter and love. He had built her a home while she was at death's door; he would make a good husband. Mary Lou was confident in her choice to forgive him. "Let's get married," she suggested.

"Yes, let's," Jonah said, kissing her on the forehead. "What do we do about your parents? I'm sure they aren't going to agree."

Mary Lou shrugged. Jonah was surprised at how lightly she took it. "I know," she said, "but I'm on *rumspringa*."

Jonah chuckled and shook his head. "I think your *rumspringa* is over."

"Plus," Mary Lou continued, "I'm not sure how my parents are going to look having disowned their daughter simply because she wanted to live with a nice Amish boy in his *wunderbaar* community in the house that he built for her."

Jonah shot her a look. *How shrewd*, he thought, *she's a snake and a dove!* "I think that it's more complicated than that. It's about other things for them."

"I know," Mary Lou said, "but that's how it's going to look. Committing a sin is bad, but confessing it, repenting, and being granted forgiveness is Christlike. You're a diamond, Jonah, and diamonds are valuable, even the ones with flaws."

Jonah's nerves tingled with delight, his limbs longing to pull her to him to squeeze her lovingly, his heart quietly anticipating their wedding night when they would be permitted to share in each other's love. There is a violence to a man's love, one that makes him want to seize the object of his affection and gather her up, but, once he contemplates his love in her fragility, warm tenderness relaxes each muscle, allowing him to melt in her hands. Such was the effect Mary Lou had on the strapping farmer's son. The wonder of love is that the one party never truly understands what is happening in the other's heart, for words can hardly express a feeling, let alone the plethora that possess young lovers in their quest to bond for life. One can only marvel at the Lord's creation and stay determined to remain in His ways as assurance of the good life. Indeed, the Amish pair was secretly planning in their own hearts how to expedite their wedding, for, as the Scriptures say, "It is better to wed than to burn with passion."

"Call my parents back in."

Jonah looked uncertain, fearful that their presence would ruin the mood.

"Just leave them to me," Mary Lou said with sparkling eyes. "I have a plan."

Placing his trust in Mary Lou, Jonah arose to head to the door, taking one last longing gaze at his betrothed, memorizing the most beautiful face in the world. *Life is short*, he thought. *Please, Lord, give us the second chance we so desperately need.* He prayed, now, as though it were second nature to him, almost unaware that he had neglected this gift since he was three, the last time he was in the presence of the dying. The Lord was working within him in the most tender and subtle ways. Jonah's redemption had begun.

CHAPTER 3

"**I**'m not going to lie to you, *Soh*; you've made a mess of things," Theresa said, half annoyed, half exasperated that her son could not get out of his own way. "Why didn't you come to us? We could have taken your mind off of things." Theresa was pouting, irritated at having her son return to her in body, though he remained estranged in mind. "You don't have to be alone, you know." Jonah had barely walked in the door before his mother, dressed for bed, laid into him.

"I know, *Maem*," Jonah said in an even tone that gave the impression he was struggling to control his temper, though he was really worried about the conversation Mary Lou and her parents were having without him regarding their wedding. "However, I've done what I can. I've confessed, I've apologized, I've been forgiven, and now I'm waiting for her parents' reaction. It's all in God's hands, now."

Theresa shook her head and sighed. "I suppose that you can't undo the past, so your course of action was a sound one. Trusting in the Lord is all we have to do." But it is difficult to wait when there is no clear course of action. At least Abraham had a journey to take while he waited on the Lord. Theresa looked into her son's eyes and smiled like a cat who'd been caught eating a canary. She slapped her hands onto her thighs, then crossed her arms.

Jonah inspected the pathetic display that was his mother. "Do you trust me?"

Theresa looked uncertain.

"Do you trust that I want Mary Lou as my wife and not Catherine?"

"Of course, I trust you," Theresa finally said. "You're my son. Do you trust yourself?"

Her question hit hard. The Amishman had not taken stock of his own vulnerabilities. Should Catherine return, would he still be distracted by her flattery and beauty? Mary Lou was his strength; he was weak without her. One month apart and he had sinned more than he had during his entire shunning. *I desperately need her back by my side*, he thought. "I suppose. I don't know what else to do."

Theresa turned to the fireplace and searched the flames for answers. Perhaps they reminded her of Leah's fiery temperament, for in a moment of inspiration she asked, "Do you want your father and me to talk to Mary Lou's parents?"

"No," Jonah said. "As much as I would appreciate it, I think this is a battle that Mary Lou and I have to fight alone."

"That has been your attitude for too long," Theresa said. "It needs to change."

Though he saw truth to his mother's insight, Jonah did not wish to ask for help, stubbornly believing that he and Mary Lou could handle it. "I know that you will be there if I need you. For that, I am grateful."

Mother approached son and put her hands on his forearms and looked into his eyes. The pair looked like a squirrel dancing with a moose. "I appreciate hearing those words from you, *Soh*," Theresa said, "because I think there was a time when you didn't believe that." Her tears moved the boy so that he looked away to hide his.

"After Jennie died," Jonah said, carefully, "I thought no one was there for me, not even the Lord himself. How wrong I was!" God's faithfulness to him since Jennie's passing flashed before him in his mind's eye, and he was comforted. He had never been alone.

"And that is why the good Lord put Mary Lou in your path," Theresa said. She smiled as though the Almighty had been faithful to her by being faithful to Jonah. "It was to help you realize that someone was there for you all along."

"I suppose," Jonah said. He then held his mother's hands to change the subject. "I should go to bed. I have no idea what tomorrow is going to be like."

"You're right; everyone needs a good night's sleep."

"*Gut nacht, Maem. Danki.*"

"For what?" Theresa asked.

"For always telling me the truth," Jonah replied. "Even if I don't always want to hear it."

"That's what mothers are for. *Gut nacht, Soh.*"

Once in his room, Jonah collapsed in bed and went to sleep. It was a fitful sleep, a worried slumber in which he chain-dreamed of Mary Lou disappearing, of her never seeing the house he'd built for her, and of him praying for her safe return into his arms. His desperate pleading with the Lord aloud in his sleep was what roused him on the morrow. Although he awoke to a lovely, bright, bird-chirping morning, he felt as though he needed a nap to recover from his night's sleep. Dragging himself out of bed, he lumbered downstairs to fetch a morning coffee.

The kitchen was empty. Jonah's father was likely in the barn, occupied with chores, but where were his mother and the rest of his siblings? A note had been left for him on the table.

Call came to store at 5 a.m. Go to hospital.

Jonah re-read the note twice, unable to make sense of it. Who had written it? What did it mean? Was Mary Lou in danger? He bolted out of the door to grab the fastest horse and galloped towards town. The mystery that awaited vexed him. *Were my dreams an omen? Were they a sign? Is Mary Lou well? Will I be married to her? Oh, God, please don't let her die! Please don't give her to me just to take her away. Spare her. Please take me instead.* As the horse neared the hospital, Jonah had exhausted all of his prayers. He would have had to pray in tongues to say anything new.

The elevator ride gave Jonah time to convince himself that Mary Lou was not dead. But by the time he got to her room, he was sure that she had passed. So certain was he that he cried in surprise when he found her sitting up in bed. She smiled as he entered.

"What are you doing here?" Jonah exclaimed, his mouth having a delayed response to what his eyes had witnessed. "I mean, are you all right? Is everything okay?"

"I'm fine," Mary Lou said. "I just woke up early, and I wanted to see you."

Jonah moaned in perplexed excitement, disappointed that he had worried for nothing yet delighted to see her alive. He struggled to calm his conflicting emotions. "Where are your parents?" he asked, hoping that the sound of her voice would pacify his shock.

"They went down to the cafeteria," Mary Lou replied. "This is actually the perfect time for us to talk."

"Talk about what?"

"About our wedding."

Jonah squinted as though he were trying to discern whether her last words were a mirage. "You managed to convince them?"

"Jonah, I don't have to convince them of anything," Mary Lou answered. "But yes, I spoke to them."

His heart rate was still fast. "So, what did they say?" He hoped that a longer answer might give him the time to focus on her voice, thus soothing his soul.

"They said if I am fit enough to walk down the aisle with you before they return home, then I can marry you. And while I don't think that I must agree to their condition, it would be nice to have them there."

"Of course," Jonah replied. "Wait a minute! You can't walk?"

"Not yet, but I am sure that I will be able to, soon."

Jonah cocked his head.

"The doctors said that it often happens, after a coma. Sometimes, parts of your body just don't work."

Frustrated with the abstract, Jonah preferred practical things. Like every man, he sought a course of action to fix a situation. "Is there anything I can do to help?"

Mary Lou shrugged. "I don't think so. I know everything is going to be all right, but I just don't know what else to do besides pray. The doctors seem to be vague with their prognosis." For the first time, Jonah witnessed Mary Lou scared.

"What did they say they would do for you?" Jonah asked.

"Nothing, really. They said that I should take it slowly, and that I should walk a few steps at a time, rest, and start over until it all comes back to me."

"So, they want you to work at it," he said. "I can do that. I can help you."

"This will take a while, Jonah. I don't think that you can dedicate that amount of time to me."

"Why not? I'm ready to dedicate my whole life to you. What else could be more important?"

"Well, you know, you're busy."

Jonah looked her straight in the eye. "Mary Lou, maybe I wasn't clear because I made a horrible mistake, but you are my priority—my only priority. Nothing else matters. I love you."

"I love you too," she said, "but I'd love a roof over my head when we get married." She paused to let her words take effect. "I think you should finish the house. Let my parents help me walk."

"I see," Jonah said. He could not deny her logic, but he was gutted at having his offer to help rejected. He desperately wanted to be by her side to avoid any more mishaps with alcohol and women.

Sensing Jonah's distress, Mary Lou made him this offer: "But if you give me your arm, I'd love to walk you to the door."

Beaming, Jonah placed his hand on his belly and offered his betrothed his services. "Let's get you out of bed and walking."

Mary Lou was determined and stubborn in the days that followed. She had read somewhere that the only way to climb a mountain was to look ten feet ahead of you, make it to that spot, then look ten more feet ahead of you until you've reached the top. So, for her to relearn how to walk, she set a goal of two steps, then five, then ten, then reaching the door, then reaching the nurses' station until she could walk to the elevator and back unassisted.

Joshua helped Mary Lou initially, but his daughter's dogged determination soon wore him out. "I'll wear out these shoes more quickly with you, here, than when plowing the fields!" he lamented. Part of him blamed Jonah for this mess, yet he knew that Mary Lou had been ill *before* she had left for *rumspringa*.

"Pretend like you're walking me down the aisle, *Daed*," Mary Lou coaxed.

Joshua shook his head. His girl had English ideas.

One of the nurses chimed in. "Imagine fresh rose petals on the floor in front of you."

"Amish weddings don't have flowers," Joshua said matter-of-factly. It decidedly killed the mood, yet Mary Lou's progress could not be denied: she would be home in no time.

CHAPTER 4

J onah, Samuel, and Timothy busied themselves with the house's finishing touches so that it was ready to be lived in after the wedding. With the roof complete, the men laid the hardwood floor. Its echoes underfoot finally made it sound like a home. When the walls were insulated and painted, the men installed cabinets, then the shelves for the pantry. Jonah imagined it filled with canned green beans, pickles, strawberry jelly, and all of his other favorites. He envisaged Mary Lou and Theresa initiating their daughters into the time-honored tradition of preparing for winter by canning all that Jonah and his sons had grown in the garden, and his heart rejoiced. Though women imagine their wedding and their married life from childhood, men come to terms with it much later, which was what Jonah was doing. He reckoned with his forthcoming life, and he looked forward to what was to come.

The men installed a wood stove for heating and cooking. The groom could imagine Mary Lou preparing hearty meals for the couple and their strapping boys. A large, hand-crafted wooden dining table large enough to seat the entire family would be where family memories would be made, and the word of the Lord would be discussed. Memory verses would be recited, and the Lord's prayer memorized upon full stomachs. One of the boys may even have the hiccups as he recited the 23rd Psalm! Jonah sat on one of the dining chairs. For their lack of modern conveniences, an Amish dinner table is never wanting, neither for food nor fraternity. The evening meal is the highlight of an Amish day, and Jonah would soon enjoy a lifetime of pleasant memories with Mary Lou made just where he was sat. It was all coming together for him now.

Once the kitchen and dining area were done, Jonah moved on to the master bedroom. In the center was a four-post bed, something Jonah had seen in the English world and sought to incorporate into his new life. He blushed to think of what it would be like for him and his bride in there. Suffice it to say that he hoped it would serve as a playroom first, and a sleeping chamber, second.

As much as Jonah wanted to begin his life with Mary Lou, of course, they could not live together until they were married, so his fiancée left the hospital and returned to her future in-law's guest room.

"Oh, my goodness," Mary Lou said upon seeing the guest room. "When did this happen? There're so many things in here. When did you get this?" she asked, pointing to the enormous doll.

"The day after you were admitted to hospital," Jonah admitted, sheepishly. "After that, I would find trinkets and things that reminded me of you, and I wanted you to have them. Take this clock, for instance. I wanted to have it so that we could count every minute that we have together."

Mary Lou's blushing smile was all Jonah needed to see to assure him that his sappy gesture had worked. The girl stood shaking her head and smiling, disbelieving the effect she'd had on her beloved while unconscious. "You're *wunderbaar*, Jonah." A picture of delicate, elegant joy, Mary Lou's reaction warmed Jonah's heart so that he gazed at her, then looked away, partly embarrassed at the collection of gifts, yet wholly fighting the urge to embrace her and twirl her around. Jonah was discovering that a man in love fights many urges. Self-control is a gift of the Spirit.

"You're *wunderbaar*," he argued. "I cannot believe that you are home. I cannot believe that we are finally getting married."

Mary Lou was not quite as taken in the moment as Jonah was. She slowly moved about the room. "Wow, Jonah."

"I can get rid of some of the things, if you like."

"No, don't. I want to save them to share with my *kinner* and with their *kinner*. I want to tell them this story when I do."

"Our *kinner*," Jonah said, as he leaned in the doorway. "I thought that this moment would never happen."

"What? Me seeing this doll?"

Jonah ignored her. "I thought that we'd never talk about our *kinner*. I thought we'd never get married. I thought that I was at the end of my rope. I thought that I was going to lose you, Mary Lou."

The mood in the room froze. A cloud covered the sun, and the room darkened. "There were times when I thought that I wouldn't find my way back," Mary Lou said, "times when everything was dark and cold, times when I was lost."

Jonah shifted on his feet.

"Do you know what got me through it? Your voice."

"You could hear me?"

"Uh-huh."

"I didn't think you could. That's why I just told you silly things."

"But you told me things," Mary Lou said. "And I could hear you. Knowing that you were there, that you were waiting for me, made me fight my way back."

"Were you in heaven?" Jonah asked, feeling stupid as soon as he said it.

"I don't think so. I wasn't dead." Mary Lou shrugged. "It was this strange in-between space where there was neither life nor death."

"Could you feel the presence of God?" Jonah hit a nerve; Mary Lou bit her knuckle. Jonah retreated. "I'm sorry, I shouldn't have said anything."

"No, it's fine."

"I didn't mean to upset you," Jonah said. "Maybe I should let you rest."

"You shouldn't. It's good for me to talk about it. I want to tell you what I saw, what I heard. I want you to know that you weren't the only one who wavered in the faith."

Jonah's jaw dropped slightly, and he squinted, again, trying to decipher whether the words he'd heard were real.

"I wasn't awake," Mary Lou continued, "but I was there. My mind was active."

"If I had known, I would have talked to you more. I would have visited every day. I would have done more."

"I believe you, Jonah." She sucked her bottom lip to keep herself from crying. "Most of the time, it was just me, lying there, lost in my own thoughts. I thought God had abandoned me."

"Not you," Jonah objected. "God would never abandon you."

"It's hard to remember that when you are somewhere between this world and the next." A tear escaped down Mary Lou's cheek.

Mary Lou had had a crisis of faith! She was the strongest person Jonah knew, and certainly the most pious. Unwilling to take advantage of her pain yet pleased to know that he was not alone in his spiritual meanderings, he felt comforted by the fact that one so firm was nevertheless shaken.

"Anyway, it wasn't the Lord who brought me back; it was you. When I hadn't heard you in a while, I willed myself to wake up." She paused.

"Go on," Jonah said.

"I felt that something was wrong, that you needed me, so I came back." Mary Lou pressed her tongue to the roof of her mouth and tilted her head back, but her tears overflowed anyway. "Since I couldn't walk, I suppose that I wouldn't have been much help."

Jonah rushed to her and held her feeble frame against his burly one, where she could cry her grief away. Thunderous sobs came from the girl, convulsing her body to evacuate every weep and every tear onto her beloved. She pressed hard against his barrel chest, and Jonah braced himself to keep his balance, such was the weight of her sorrow. Any outsider would have sworn someone had just died. There they were stood, the pair of them who had sought to die when separated, now alive once rejoined.

When Mary Lou's cries spaced themselves out, she relaxed, secure in her man's arms. Jonah rubbed her back until her breathing evened, then he kissed her forehead. Inspired, he did not make any promises to her, nor did he offer words of comfort. Instead, Jonah could feel His presence. "Sometimes, in our darkest hour, that's when God is there the most."

"That's what my mother said," Mary Lou retorted. She wiped her tears on the back of her hand. "Mind you, she wasn't talking about the same thing."

"What was she talking about?"

"Loving you."

Jonah shook his head.

"But you're making an impression."

"I've done nothing," Jonah said.

"You changed their hearts by coming back to me."

Jonah found little comfort in her words. Instead, he foresaw infinite tension between him and his in-law's. He had to ask her one more time. "Mary Lou, are you sure this is what you want?"

"What do you mean?"

"Us getting married," Jonah answered. "I am far from perfect, and I don't know that your parents will accept me."

"Do you think I expect you to be perfect?" Mary Lou asked.

"No."

"Then why are you asking me to expect that of you? I know who you are. I know what you have been through."

"I don't deserve you," Jonah said.

"Well, you've got me no matter what."

"No matter what," Jonah repeated. "So, I'm stuck with you?"

"I'd say," Mary Lou replied, sniffling, "unless you have other ideas."

"Sleep!" Jonah said. "I can't believe how tired I am."

Mary Lou yawned. "This must be what it's like to get old."

"To get old?" he asked. "This isn't old. We aren't old yet." He expected her to smile, but she was serious.

"What if this is all we get though?" Mary Lou wondered.

"What do you mean?"

"I mean that if this is all the time we get, will it be enough? You know the prognosis for cancer."

"Mary Lou, let's not talk like this."

"I need to," she said. "The doctors said that talking like this is healthy, and it helps us come to terms with whatever we need to."

"But it's not all we are going to get," Jonah said. "We are going to get years and years."

"That's not what I asked, is it?"

Jonah sighed, his shoulders drooped, and he raised his palms in surrender. "Yes, *mei lieb*, yes. Of course, it will be enough. I would be blessed to get even one more day with you."

"And if something happens to me?" Mary Lou asked him.

"Nothing is going to happen you," Jonah tried to assure her.

"If something happens to me, will you be fine?"

Jonah shook his head once more. "I don't want to talk about this."

"I need to talk about this," Mary Lou insisted.

"Yes, I will be fine."

"Good," she said, "because I will be looking down from heaven, and if you aren't fine, I'll convince God to make it rain. That way, you'll remember what you said."

"Couldn't you throw me butterflies or something?" Jonah asked. "Something a little less cold?"

"You're lucky I'm not making it snow," she chuckled. "Anyway, rain is good for the crops. Rain is about growth and washing away pain."

And yet water has been the source of much pain for us, Jonah thought. "Will you watch out for Jennie up there?" he asked. "If you get there before me?"

"Of course," Mary Lou said. "I'm sure she and Naomi are great friends, now."

"If they aren't, you'll have to organize sleepovers."

"I will," Mary Lou promised. "And when you get there, the four of us will be happy."

"But that is not going to happen for a long time," Jonah said. "For now, you and I are going to get a good night's sleep."

Mary Lou giggled her consent.

"*Gut nacht, mei lieb*," Jonah said to Mary Lou, then headed into his room. Once he had closed the door, he sank onto his knees to look up at the sky. "Please, dear God, please don't take her away from me so soon," he prayed through parched lips. His tongue stuck to the roof of his mouth. "Please give us a life together." God's answer was an overwhelming sense of peace that settled his spirit, rested his soul, and eased his mind. God was watching over them and would care for them.

A knock at the door interrupted Jonah's meditation. He opened the door to a giant doll. Mary Lou peeked out from behind it and smiled.

"I'm sorry," she said, "but I've moved it around the room three times, and there's just not enough space. Do you think that you could keep her here for me?"

"I'll take care of her," he said, "until we can all be in a room together."

Mary Lou giggled and handed the doll over. "*Gut nacht, Jonah*," she said.

"Sweet dreams, *mei lieb*," he said. *Everything is going to be fine*, he thought, *one way or another.*

CHAPTER 5

Jonah and Mary Lou still had to be baptized. Proud to have returned to a faith that valued God and family, Jonah was looking forward to publicly professing his faith. It would cement his return as a prodigal. Also, no Amish could be married unless both the bride and groom were initiated into the faith. Normally, there was an 18-week training with the church leadership prior to baptism. However, given Mary Lou's dire circumstances, Jonah's parents had called in the favor the bishop owed them to expedite the process to have her marry in case she did not have 18 weeks left.

The bespectacled bishop appreciated the political diffusion handed to him on a silver platter. As he sat in his study, he rested his second chin on his chest and stroked his beard whilst he rehearsed his explanation to anyone who might object. A knock at the door interrupted his daydream. He stood quickly, tugging his pants back over his potbelly, then reached for the door. His pants settled back below his belly.

"Good day, Bishop. I am Jonah, and this is my fiancée, Mary Lou."

"Yes, of course, come in, come in," the bishop said, then stepped aside to allow them to enter. "*Willkumm*. Congratulations. I trust you are well."

"Yes, indeed," Mary Lou said, beaming.

"Thank you for seeing us. We appreciate you accommodating us," Jonah said.

"Of course! I am delighted to help given the present circumstances." He did not introduce himself. Rather, he took his seat and began his inquiry. "So, you wish to be baptized into the faith. Is that correct?"

"Yes," the couple said in unison.

"Well, we are pleased to welcome you into the faith," said the bishop.

"We are pleased to join," Jonah declared. He was sat on the edge of his chair, ready to declare his faith to the world.

"*Gut*. Now, I understand that Mary Lou, you've been on *rumspringa*," the bishop said.

"Yes."

"Tell me about your adventure."

Mary Lou proceeded to explain her job at the seamstress shop, how she met Jonah, their trip to her community, Jonah's proposal, and the incident with Naomi. That's where the bishop stopped her. "Jonah, how did you feel when this happened?"

The groom-to-be shifted in his chair, looked down at his feet, then to his fiancée. The bishop leaned onto his elbows on the desk before him and crossed his fingers, watching the young man intently, though his smile diffused any tension. Mary Lou sat upright in her chair with her hands on her lap, pursing her lips, and waited for Jonah to answer.

"I am ashamed to say that I ran away," Jonah admitted, without elaboration.

The bishop did not press him. "Please, continue," he instructed Mary Lou.

It seemed as though the bishop had an idea of all that had befallen the couple, and that he was merely listening as a formality. Still, Mary Lou thought it wise to tell the truth, so she opened up about her grief, her need to return on *rumspringa*, her tenacious hunt for her fiancé, and their reunion.

"Jonah," the bishop said, "what was it like for you to see your love in the hospital?"

"I hated it. I blamed myself." Jonah licked his lips, unsure whether he wanted to continue. Since all eyes were on him, he felt compelled to say something more. "I didn't want Mary Lou to love me because I thought that she would die. Look, I get the feeling that you already know all of this stuff, so can we move on to the training?"

"Patience, Jonah. All will occur in good time," the bishop said. "Why did you feel that you were cursed?"

"Because my sister died on my watch, then Mary Lou's sister; Mary Lou got hit by a car, then she got sick and hospitalized twice. I thought that God hated me."

"Do you still believe that now?" asked the bishop.

"No. I am certain that He is with me. He lives within my heart."

"*Gut*! And what about you, young lady?"

"I can say the same," asserted Mary Lou. "I felt His presence most when I suffered. He is my rock."

"Excellent! Now, what happened next?" the bishop asked, though not specifying whom he expected to answer. The couple looked at each other, unsure of what to do next. Jonah pushed his hand forward as though signaling for his fiancée to resume.

"Jonah helped me tremendously with my hospital treatments, but I'm afraid that I was in a coma for the last month. I've no idea what happened." Mary Lou was keen to pass the storytelling onto Jonah. After all, they were meeting with his bishop, and there was far more concern for his soul than for hers.

All eyes turned to Jonah. He shifted in his chair, straightened up, and began calmly. "It was tough to see her suffer, and it was difficult to get into town to see her, so, I decided to busy myself with building us a house. I hoped she and I could live in it once we were married."

"I see. So, Mary Lou, was it your treatments that prompted

your coma?" the bishop asked, back on the scent.

"No. At least, I don't think so. No, we'd come here to rest—well I did. Jonah came to reconcile with his family. Jonah, why don't you explain?"

"Yes, well, I heard God's voice telling me to 'go home,' so I obeyed. Mary Lou obliged me and returned with me, too."

"Where were you living before?" the bishop asked.

It was this question that made the couple nervous. Mary Lou looked down at her hands, then over to her fiancé. He raised his upper lip and shrugged. "We didn't sin," he said to her, then looked to the bishop. "We lived together with many others, sharing a house but not a bed. I was the caretaker of the premises, whilst the others were colleagues of Mary Lou."

"Why didn't you live with your parents?" the bishop asked the girl.

Mary Lou sought desperately to avoid any mention of her having been disowned lest it jeopardize their wedding. Seeing her distress, Jonah intervened. "Her parents lived too far away from the hospital for the commute. It was better for her to live in town, so I took it upon myself to care for her, ferrying her to and from the doctor." The rosy retelling of the past is a stalwart of the human experience. Perhaps it was because Jonah was ready to assume his responsibilities towards Mary Lou that he spoke as though he were always prepared to do so, or perhaps it was because he was eager to tell of the transformative power of the Lord. In any event, he spoke with conviction of his glossy retelling without a hint of guilt.

"What did your parents think of that arrangement?" the bishop asked.

Mary Lou glanced at Jonah to gauge whether he was anxious. The bishop seemed not to hide that he knew their story. So, then, for what was this inquisition?

"My parents didn't know about it, and her parents did not want to know about it. So, we pretty much looked after ourselves."

The bishop leaned back in his chair, as though he had not

expected Jonah's answer. He stroked his beard, his head now glistening from the spring sun shining on him through the window behind him. He looked up as though he were going to say something, but Jonah spoke up, first.

"Can we just get to the part where I found God?" Jonah was eager to cut to the chase. "I want to tell you how I was lost, but now am found. I want to get to the reasons why I wish to assert my faith in public and begin—with haste—life with the one the Lord has put before me to be my wife. For I know, now, that I need the Lord. Christ is my all. In Him, I am free from sin, and it is He who redeems. The Father has been good to me and has called me to be His son. I will answer the call, and by His Spirit, I will serve the Lord with Mary Lou all of the days of my life. I want to be baptized into my Amish faith, and so does my fiancée. Will you do it, sir?"

"Well, I'm pleased with your enthusiasm for the gospel! It is *wunderbaar* to see youthful exuberance. Praise be to God!" The bishop was used to seeing young men joining the faith as a matter of course; they chose the life that they had known best, afraid of what they did not know. Jonah, however, was different. His joy and enthusiasm for the gospel betrayed a man who had met with the living God and was so moved by it that he could not contain his excitement. The bishop had heard of such people but never had he the pleasure of seeing one before him. He knew Jonah and had seen him grow up in the faith of his parents, so it was unlikely that his enthusiasm was for the novel, the main reason, it would appear, that *Englischers* sought to join Amish ranks. The bishop had had to be careful about allowing such individuals in lest the novelty wears off and they become frustrated with the faith. But he had to test the Spirit and make sure that the couple was joining the faith—and getting married—for the right reasons and not out of pity for the dying girl.

Jonah and Mary Lou were relieved to have skipped the episode of the drunken kiss, about which the bishop seemed none the wiser. Mary Lou played along with the 'dying girl' act only to get Jonah in the bag. She, herself, was unconvinced that she would die soon. Alas! the folly of youth who believe that they shall live forever.

"We are delighted that you are no longer lost, for Our Father wishes not to leave His lost sheep as they are but will go to the ends of the earth to return them to the fold. We praise Him for your testimony. Nevertheless," the bishop continued, "I want to make sure that this is for real, that you understand what you are getting yourselves into. Normally, I'd do a months-long training with you both about the faith before you'd be baptized, but I understand you have extenuating circumstances."

The couple nodded.

The bishop continued. "Christ is our only hope. We are the furthest thing from the image of God for we have all sinned. As a result, we shall die, because, without the Spirit of life, we cannot live. The human heart, when left to its own pursuits, cannot find its God-given purpose, and thus leaves one empty, alone, and destitute. When we try to find that purpose without God, we end up in the vain act of rebuilding a bridge to Him that only He can rebuild. Filled with pride, we realize our impossible task but are unwilling to admit defeat, and so we seek the most ungodly thing that there is to seek: death. Humanity's plight is that we have all sinned and are destined to die; our worst outcome is not that we get there, but that we *want* to get there. Left destitute, a man will seek to end his own life rather than to admit that he needs God." The bishop turned to look Jonah in the eye. "I am pleased to hear that you have not been so proud."

An uneasy silence followed. Jonah felt no compulsion to speak, yet his mind would not shut up. Mary Lou's eyes widened at the thought of their secret being revealed; then she smiled when she remembered that Jonah was now returned to the Shepherd's fold.

"Life with God Almighty, the creator of heaven and earth, is our purpose," the bishop declared. "Without Him, we are lost. Did you know, *Kinner*, that the word *sin* means 'missing the mark'?"

The pair shook their heads, astounded to learn this. Usually, sin was synonymous with *evil, wicked,* or *bad.* To hear it put this way made it seem trivial.

"Do you realize that, if a ship were to leave New York and head for Ireland in a straight line, yet begin its journey across the ocean a mere two degrees south of where it intended to go, it would end up in Spain? Like a ship aimed in the wrong direction, when we miss the mark, we are lost. And because we are, the Father has sent His Son to find us and to give us life. Make no mistake, young ones; Christ did not come to make bad people good, but to make the dead live again." The bishop paused to let his words take effect.

Mary Lou had never heard it said that way before, but she could see the point. The Amish believed that Christ would return and give all those who were faithful to Him eternal life. Indeed, Christ's sacrifice would wipe away all sin for those who believed. Jonah, however, was deep in thought. The bishop's words were profound because he had wanted to die, because his sister had died, his would-be sister-in-law had as well, and Mary Lou had been on the cusp. *Christ came to make the dead live again*, Jonah repeated to himself. *That is why I feel alive again. I didn't feel as though I were good after God spoke to me, but I wanted to live. God has given me life— new life—and I will live with Him.* He smiled, and the bishop resumed, as though it were his cue.

"God will give us life in Christ Jesus, both now and in eternity. When we obey Him, we find the freedom to do as we were meant, which is to freely abide with Him. Goodness comes from Him. We are not good, but when we act like Christ, we are made whole. He is good, and in Him, you will find all good things. Will you both abide by the faith of the Amish and abide by our *Ordnung* so long as you both shall live?"

"Yes," they answered in unison.

"Then I will agree to baptize you, given the circumstances, under one condition: that you meet with me regularly to learn the *Dordrecht Confession of Faith*, as is our custom, for as long as is required, after you have been married."

This pleased them both, and they exhaled, smiling, and

246

ecstatic that all was falling into place for their beleaguered selves. The bishop called in a deacon, who held a pitcher of water. Then the couple's parents entered to join in the ceremony, much to their delight. The bishop's wife was the last to enter into the study. Jonah and Mary Lou knelt before the bishop, reiterated their commitment to Christ in renunciation of the devil and his worldly things, agreed to obey the *Ordnung*, and Jonah promised to be involved in ministry should the opportunity arise. The bishop held out his hands over Mary Lou's head, and the deacon poured water through them and onto her. She arose, was kissed by the bishop's wife, and joined her parents, who were somber in light of the occasion. The same act of pouring was repeated over Jonah, who was kissed by the bishop when he arose, and he joined his parents who could hardly contain their joy. Theresa was teary-eyed, whilst Timothy gave his son a bear hug. "Welcome to the community," the bishop said, and Jonah clapped. "Hallelujah!"

As they made their way out, Joshua put his hand on Jonah. "A word, please," he said, signaling away from the group with his head. Jonah agreed. Both men made their way to the other side of the building.

"Listen, *Soh*," Joshua said, "you've come a long way. Now you're one of us. Don't screw this up."

CHAPTER 6

T he day after they were baptized, Jonah and Mary Lou were to be wed. Amish weddings are not like English weddings. They take place after the harvest, usually in November and the early part of December, yet with upwards of 600 people involved in a wedding, and with multiple weddings happening on the same day, some youth opt for wedding dates as late as March. Two days were necessary for prep and clean-up, so Tuesdays and Thursdays were preferred wedding days. Wedding ceremonies happened after a normal church service and were celebrated by the whole community, usually in the same building or at a large house within the community.

Jonah's wedding day began at 4 a.m. Timothy had chores to do regardless of the festivities. Theresa had kept her promise to Mary Lou and had made the dresses, whilst some of Jonah's relatives hosted Mary Lou and her parents and offered their kitchen for the wedding meal preparation. It had been a generous compromise that allowed the bride's family to save face whilst hastening the wedding date. As untraditional as it was for the bride to be married in the groom's settlement, Mary Lou's frail health and the assumption of her imminent passing caused the Amish to gather 'round Mary Lou and Jonah to give their prodigal son a chance at love. Fortunately, all witnesses to the Catherine kiss had kept the incident to themselves, quelling any rumors. The Lord had blessed Jonah in that regard since the bishop would not have been so cooperative, and neither would have the community.

Jonah had decided to set out to the wedding by himself. A brisk morning walk would rid him of the butterflies in his stomach. He stopped dead when he saw Catherine in his path. He had forgotten about her. Since the garden she had started in the front of the house had been finished, he assumed that she had done so when he, Samuel, and Timothy had left the building site. Thus, they had not seen each other since the incident. Jonah could not decide whether to be frightened or relaxed. He kept his distance.

"Catherine, are you all right?"

"I just wanted to talk to you," she said, "before you went into the church."

"Why?" he asked, cautiously. "What's happened?"

"Are you sure this is what you want?"

Jonah cocked his head, figuring he had solved the riddle of her presence. "Yes," he said, mustering all of his confidence so as to sound convincing. "Yes, this is what I want. I have wanted to marry Mary Lou for as long as I have known her."

"You've said that," said the wench, "but this is your last chance to see if you want to change your mind."

Jonah grimaced. "Why would I change my mind?" he asked, stepping right into her trap, looking like he'd stepped on a thorn.

"Because…I could change mine," Catherine confessed.

Jonah raised an eyebrow. "Are you feeling okay, Catherine? You're talking—"

"Josiah came around last night to ask me to marry him again."

Jonah said nothing, only exhaling like he was trying to blow out candles on his 80th birthday.

"I know," Catherine continued, "I know, I'd be stupid to marry him. But I love him. And I can't help thinking that God has placed him in my path to be my husband."

"He's already married," Jonah said.

"Funny thing: he lied. He was scared of being a husband, afraid that he couldn't take care of me."

"Then you should marry him," Jonah said, desperate to be on his way. He took a step to walk past her, but she blocked his way. Now, they were both standing but a breath away.

Catherine's lip trembled. In such close proximity, she seemed vulnerable and submissive when looking up at him. Her eyes could melt stone. Jonah felt light-headed, his appearance of dominance over her making him drunk with power. "But, what about us?" she asked.

Jonah grimaced again, which brought him back to his senses. "There is no us." It was important for him to keep Mary Lou at the forefront of his mind, lest he fall for Catherine anew.

"There could be. This is our last chance to change our minds. Who knows how much longer Mary Lou has? I'm healthy. We could have a long, happy life together. Our *kinner* could grow up playing with their cousins. Samuel would love that."

Jonah looked into her eyes and felt drawn into her spell. For a brief moment, he let himself imagine what it would be like to marry Catherine. They were from the same community. Their parents were friends, and he wouldn't have to deal with the ire of Mary Lou's parents. He pictured himself as her savior, a knight rescuing a damsel in distress. It felt surprisingly like the whiskey. A quick shake of the head brought him back to reality. Exasperated, he raised his voice. "Why now?"

"Well, what will people say if I marry Josiah after he ended our engagement?"

"How many people know?"

Now she was on the back foot.

Jonah continued. "It doesn't matter what they say. What matters is what your heart tells you."

Silence. Catherine pondered. Then, a soft breeze blew, and she looked at Jonah as though transformed.

Jonah spoke first in the hopes it would be the final word. "If you trust God, and you believe He has put Josiah in your path, then you need to marry him."

Catherine held his gaze, then lowered hers. "I do love him," she said.

"Then that's enough," Jonah said, sounding like a gavel pounded against a desk. "If I can leave any legacy behind, Catherine, it's that you need to follow your heart."

"Very well. I trust your advice, Jonah."

"I wouldn't trust everything I say, but in my case, I can say I've been in Josiah's shoes, and I would want nothing more than the woman I love to marry me. I'll see you at my wedding?"

"You will, watching and smiling from the sidelines."

"I am glad that you will be there," Jonah said and continued his walk down the road.

"God bless you today," Catherine called after him.

A year ago, Jonah would not have been able to give advice like that. Today, though, he felt at peace. He was the happiest person in the world.

Jonah arrived at the wedding place in time. The bride and groom had their customary meeting with the bishop prior to heading down the aisle together and taking their seats. The church sang beautifully, and the wedding took place without delay or drama. The bishop then stood to preach.

The sermons at an Amish wedding are excessively long, perhaps to give the ladies ample time to prepare the meal, or, just as likely, to allow those in attendance to build up their appetite. The bishop's sermon for Jonah and Mary Lou focused almost exclusively on what a spouse owes to the other *in sickness*. Indeed, the sermon was directed more at Jonah, who had taken a years-long leave of absence from the Amish faith. It was clear to the groom that Mary Lou was assumed to be the stronger of the pair in the faith, so any marital advice directed at her was encouragement to continue in what she had been doing. Nevertheless, as the bride and groom sat through the sermon, their hearts were lifted for they were on the threshold of the rest of their lives together.

The bishop was emphatic about the place of Christ in married life. He described the condition of the world as diseased due to the devil's work. He continued: "The sickness of sin keeps us from finding the Father. Indeed, we are lost in our sin. The sickness of pride inoculates us from any desire to reconcile ourselves to Him, to accept His invitation to repair the breach that sin opened up between us, separating us from the Lord's presence. The sickness of the devil surrounds us. It distracts us, seeks to have us work for ourselves rather than for the things of God. Idle hands are the sign of its infection. For this, Christ is our only hope. He alone can heal us. He alone is our salvation.

Our love may transform our partner, as Christ's love has made us a new creation. However, we must not seek to reform the other's heart, because that is to be done by the hand of God. Indeed, that is idolatry. For it is in His image that we are made, and it is like Christ that we are to behave. Do not be tempted to make your spouse into an image that you would prefer but treasure the one whom God has put before you. Likewise, love your children and ensure that you are not impeding the handiwork of God on their souls by making your children into who you wish them to be. Let the hand of God guide you both. Love one another as He has loved you, serve one another as He has served you, and you will be satisfied with what the Lord has done. The Amish home is the kernel-sized Kingdom of God, where love and forgiveness are shared daily between spouses to teach the next generation what it is to be in Christ. Jonah, Mary Lou, it is not in each other that you shall find fulfillment, rather it is in the fulfillment of your obligations to Christ. Do not rely on one another for meaning; that is only found in obedience to the Lord."

Mary Lou seemed to gain color and strength as the ceremony went on. Wifely status suited her, and it marked an important milestone in a feeble life. Motherhood would soon follow, and she hoped to have a daughter to replace the one her mother had lost. If only she could live so long as to see them into adulthood, she would be grateful. It is a peculiar thing with Amish women that they dream of finding a husband, so they cocoon themselves from other males to ensure purity before their kin and the Almighty. Yet, on their wedding day, when a husband is almost at hand, their desire, hardly satisfied, metamorphoses into one for motherhood. The groom, on the other hand, is focused on his new wife for the foreseeable future. And, so, bride and groom begin their journey together with varying ideas and divergent expectations for their matrimony. Compounded on the present situation was a sickly wife whose prospects were hopeful only by the grace of God. However, if the couple were only to take heed of the bishop's sermon, they would have wisdom from a deep well upon which to draw when the mismatched expectations lead them to conflict. Their vows would keep them on the straight and narrow, for their pledge was to look to the Lord as to how best to love one another.

When the bishop had finished, he questioned Jonah and Mary Lou on their marriage-to-be. The Amish wedding questions, which serve as vows, have the dual purpose of reminding all of the married couples in attendance of their vows from their wedding day. Such is the purpose of tradition, for, in it, one finds themselves in their past in preparation for what is demanded of them in the present. Once the bride and groom were blessed by the bishop, it was the turn of other married couples to testify to the goodness of the institution. And so, they did. Perhaps it was the spring air, or perhaps it was the uniqueness of the situation between Jonah and Mary Lou, but the Amish present spoke of their marriages in earnest. The parents of the groom, particularly, lauded the most important commitment they'd made in their lives. Theresa beamed that her son had found his way back to the faith thanks to the Lord's vessel, a jar of clay. "Precious treasures are stored in jars of clay, so handle her gently, my *Soh*," she told Jonah. As for the parents of the bride, Leah contented herself with letting Joshua speak for the family, and he merely welcomed Jonah to the family before hastily returning to his seat. He avoided Mary Lou's gaze.

When the ceremony was over, the congregation clapped as the pair walked down the aisle and into the sunlight. Neither minded the chill of an early spring day for they had been dealing with Leah all week. The midday nip in the air was a welcome change from the biting cold Jonah had to suffer from his mother-in-law in the days preceding the nuptials. The bride and groom could now hold hands and lock lips freely. And, so, they obliged one another as they walked to their wedding feast.

"I can't believe we made it," Jonah said to Mary Lou. Whatever he planned to say next escaped him as he lost himself in his bride's loving gaze.

"You doubted us?" Mary Lou asked.

"Never," Jonah said. "I mean, it wasn't you that I doubted. It was me."

"You were tested in so many ways," Mary Lou said, "and the fact that you still drew breath at the end of it was a miracle in and of itself. I think you have paid the price for whatever sins you feel you have committed. The rest of your life should be filled only with happiness."

Jonah chuckled. "I will be happy if you are happy until the end of your days." Jonah was thinking of the wedding night.

Mary Lou was ahead of him. "I was thinking about names for our *boplin*; for a girl, I know that we are supposed to give her a biblical name, but for her middle name, what do you think of 'Rayne'?"

"Rayne?" Jonah asked. "How did you come up with that?"

His bride smiled. "Like the rain I will send you when I am watching from above."

"Maybe it is I who will send you rain if I go before you. Or maybe we will be lucky and spend every moment together until we are both nothing more than rain."

"We can pray for that," Mary Lou said. "Either way, the rain won't be a sign of sadness. It will be a sign of happiness."

"Yes," Jonah said, and a drop of rain bounced off his nose! He burst out laughing. "I think God agrees!"

The rain was warm, and it was beautiful in the sunlight. The couple delighted in the sun shower, and the Lord delighted in them. A rainbow appeared.

"*Ich liebe dich, mei Alt.*"

"*Ich liebe dich auch, mei Aldi.*"

"We should probably go inside," Mary Lou said.

"Probably," Jonah concurred. "Everyone will think we are crazy, being out here in the rain."

"Let them," she said, "I know the truth," and she leaned in for a kiss. They then headed into the feast.

Thank you, God, Jonah said, as he touched the wooden beam of the barn. *Thank you.*

EPILOGUE

"Y ou're still out here?"

Jonah turned to see from whence the voice came. It was Samuel, who had likely come to borrow some tools from the barn he had helped Jonah build. Since returning to Amish life, Jonah had routinely worked hard in the barn from the crack of dawn until supper time, a task for which he was grateful because he felt alive again. Rarely was he in the barn after supper, so the sleuth Samuel surprised him.

"Yeah," Jonah said. "I just was doing some thinking."

"Uh oh," Samuel said with a grin.

"Uh oh?" Jonah asked. "You don't like it when I think?"

"I don't mind it. Just don't think too hard, or you might hurt yourself."

Jonah smiled, but he didn't give Samuel the normal wide grin he had these days. Marriage had been good to him, and the newlywed was usually beaming as a result of his new life. Samuel sensed that something bothered his best friend.

"What's wrong?"

Jonah paused, eyes downcast. Taking a deep breath, he ventured, "Mary Lou has her follow-up tomorrow morning."

"For the cancer?"

"Yeah, for the cancer," Jonah confirmed. "Apparently, we

have to see if it has come back."

"I'm sure everything will be fine," Samuel said with genuine optimism. His faith in the Lord was unshakeable.

Jonah looked off into the sky. "I'm not so sure," he said.

"Hey, trust in God. He got her through a miracle once before."

Jonah grimaced and looked upward, searching for something upon which to fix his gaze. Dropping his gaze to his hands, he confessed, "I know, but this time, it feels different."

"Talk to me," Samuel prompted, then leaned against the workbench to signal his undivided attention. Since reuniting after years apart, the two had not missed a beat, picking up where they had left off in adolescence. Jonah trusted him with his life. He was willing to share his heart with Samuel, but he couldn't quite find the words. It unnerved Jonah lest his closest mate think he was stonewalling.

"She's been acting differently for about a month now," Jonah finally managed after hemming and hawing.

"Different how?"

"Just...off," Jonah said, eyes wide, thrusting his hands forward as though trying to say that it was all he could offer. He remained unwilling to look Samuel in the eye. His tongue touched his teeth before he continued, "I can't go through that again." His eyes watered.

"You won't," Samuel assured him, "because God will take care of her. He did last time."

"I know," Jonah said. "Still, I don't think I can go through that again. Mentally."

"Are you afraid that she will fall into a coma again?"

"I don't know what I'm afraid of." Upon reflection, Jonah corrected himself. "I suppose I'm afraid of seeing her like that again." The image of Mary Lou in her wired and tubed cage returned to him, and he closed his eyes to chase it away. Samuel had not seen the Amish girl in her worst state, so he held his tongue.

"Frankly," Jonah continued, "the doctors said that if the cancer comes back, it can do anything."

"I will pray for you," Samuel said. "Why didn't you ask us to pray last week in church?"

Jonah smiled sheepishly. "I was in denial, I guess."

"Jonah," Samuel said, giving Jonah a disapproving look, "you're not having another..." His voice trailed off, hoping Jonah would finish the sentence.

"No, I'm fine," Jonah reassured him. "No crisis of faith this time, I promise."

"Go see your wife," Samuel said, after a few moments. "I'm sure she has a nice bedtime snack prepared for you."

"Yes," Jonah said. "She probably does, along with some hot tea. And I'm out here. That's not very kind."

"It's not about kindness," Samuel said. "Mary Lou will understand if you are having a difficult time. Talk to her about it."

"I'm sure that she will be understanding, but that does not mean that I shouldn't be strong for her."

"Go," Samuel said, gesturing towards the house with his chin. "Talk to her."

Jonah complied. It wasn't that he was afraid of talking to Mary Lou; he was afraid of heading into the doctor in town. He'd grown sick of hospitals while he cared for Mary Lou, for they were cold, industrial things devoid of joy, of singing, of God.

Mary Lou greeted her beau with his bedtime snack, as he'd expected, served with hot tea. Married life suited her, and she enjoyed her new home, built in love by the man whom God had put in her path to be her husband. By candlelight, however, she looked ghostly pale. Jonah's apprehension at the morrow's journey was spat all over his face. Knowing her husband's mind, the malignant bride looked down, forced a smile, and tucked her hair behind her ear. Rare, indeed, was the sight of an Amish woman without her prayer covering. Such a sight was the special privilege of her groom.

"I've prepared a little snack for you, *mei Alt*."

Jonah did not seem to hear her. "We can always reschedule

this for another day."

"It's fine," Mary Lou tried to assure him, with a smile. "Really. I'm just a little bit tired."

"You don't look tired," Jonah said, bluntly. "You look ill."

She looked away from him. He grunted.

"Mary Lou," he said. "You have to tell me the truth. What is happening?"

"I just felt a little nauseated," she said.

"Did you vomit?" Jonah questioned, now agitated. Mary Lou nodded. Jonah felt his stomach turn. "When?"

"Just this morning," Mary Lou said, softly. "And yesterday morning. And this afternoon." She could have gone on.

"*Mei lieb*," Jonah said, reaching for his sweetheart's hand, "you are supposed to tell me these things." He was remarkably composed given his internal state.

"I'm sure it's nothing," Mary Lou said. Then, rousing her last energies to sound more convincing, she leaned into Jonah's grasp, placed her opposite hand over his, smiled, and said, "I'm sure I'm just nervous about the doctors. It'll all be fine." But then, a cough betrayed her best acting!

"Mary Lou," Jonah said, tilting his head to the side. His agitation was harder to control, so he inhaled, though it only served to stoke the fire within him. He was afraid, and his fear conflicted with his chauvinistic display of strength for the weaker sex. He was in danger of feeling just like her. Collecting himself, he stood straight with his shoulders back and asked, firmly but gently, "Is that likely?"

"I don't know," Mary Lou said. Her eyes remained downcast so as to hide her terror. She did not believe her own words.

Jonah squeezed her hand. "Look at me."

Her gaze was pitiful.

"No matter what happens, I'm here for you."

"What if it's back?" Mary Lou exclaimed much louder than she had expected.

"If it's back, then we will take care of it." Though Jonah had not calmed his anxieties, it did not show in his gaze or in his voice. His short breaths would have been his tell, but Mary Lou was unaware, preoccupied with the sirens of worry ringing in her own mind.

"Jonah, you know the chances of beating it twice…"

"It doesn't matter. We will beat it."

Standing across from him, Mary Lou seemed feeble and frail, like one unable to keep up with her own shadow.

"Have you been feeling sick in other ways?"

Mary Lou paused, decidedly to choose her words carefully, for worry could rob them both of a good night's sleep. Sensing her husband's impatience, she nodded but said nothing more. He would have to pry the specifics out of her.

"How so?" Jonah asked, trying as best as he could to sound strong and in control.

"Just weak and tired."

Jonah exhaled slowly through pursed lips. His eyes shouted, *The cancer's back!* though he did not dare say it. He leaned back, but there was no wall to hold him, so he fell plumb on his bottom.

"Jonah!" Mary Lou exclaimed. She bent towards him, but that made her dizzy, so she stood up straight once more and put her hair back behind her ear. Her hands stayed on her locks, twirling them like she had as a child, for it soothed her.

Jonah decided to remain seated, folding his knees up to rest his elbows upon them. He hung his head and gazed at his navel. He was spent after a full day's work and his wife's confession. Would he have the energy to help her through the night? An Amish day is a taxing one, leaving every man, woman, and child sapped of energy in the evening, enticing one to sleep, which is good for a lifestyle geared to avoid sin.

Mary Lou had regained her composure. With head held high to avoid another dizzy spell, she bent her knees and settled on the floor next to her spouse. She was sat as a mermaid, then arranged her nightgown so as to assure her modesty. "I wanted to talk to you," she said. "In case it is back."

"What do you mean?" Jonah asked. "We're just going to do whatever the doctor says."

"No," Mary Lou said, then she corrected herself, "I mean, of course we will. But what if things don't go so well?"

"What are you implying? Of course, they will. God will protect you." Jonah feigned certainty.

"Jonah, look me in the eye. Protecting me doesn't necessarily mean saving me."

Jonah turned away, feeling like he was about to cry. It was not right to do it in front of her since he was to be the strong one. "What do you want to talk about?" he asked.

"In case the treatment does not work a second time," Mary Lou said.

Jonah steeled himself for the conversation he never wanted to have. They had never gotten a chance at a life together, and now they had to face the prospect of life apart.

"If the treatment doesn't work," Mary Lou's voice shook, "I want you to take care of yourself."

Perplexed, Jonah squinted one eye by raising the corner of his mouth. "What do you mean?"

"If the treatment doesn't work, I have to know that you are going to be okay."

"I'm not going to be okay, Mary Lou. If you leave me—"

"Do you think it's a choice, Jonah? Do you think I want to leave you?"

Jonah gave her the same squinty eye, only this time with a scoff. "No, I don't think that you want to leave me."

"Then please don't accuse me of such things."

Jonah closed his eyes and exhaled. He'd hoped it would dislodge the lump in his throat. His show of strength had served only to upset his beloved. After a moment, he asked, softly, "What do you mean, *take care of myself?*"

"I want you to marry again," Mary Lou declared, "and find happiness."

"That will never happen! You are the love of my life. You are my everything."

"I know that," Mary Lou said, "and I feel the same way about you."

"Then why are we talking about it?" he asked. "You know that I won't find happiness again."

"When I met you," she said, quietly "You were so sad. You were so broken."

Jonah was near tears. His voice quivered. "And you saved me." Choking back his tears had the effect of silencing him.

Mary Lou smiled. Usually, her face shone when she did, but her monochromatic complexion muted its effect, rendering her grin pitiful.

"You did," Jonah cried. "You were the difference between life and death."

"You are my soulmate, Jonah. God put us together."

Jonah brought his fist up to his eyes to wipe away tears and simultaneously nodded his agreement to his wife's last statement. His fist rose so quickly, and he nodded his approval so violently, that he nearly knocked himself out. Embarrassed, he buried his head in his arms, which were crossed on his raised knees.

Mary Lou continued, unperturbed. "God put us together because He does not want you to be upset or to be broken anymore."

"Well, then if that's what He wants, He won't take you away from me," Jonah said into his navel.

"We're not going to be able to have a conversation about this tonight, are we?" she asked.

Jonah used his sleeves to wipe his face. "I refuse to accept that you could be taken away from me."

Mary Lou sighed. When men are afraid, they need a mother, not a wife. His stubborn machismo was preventing her from a necessary conversation. Those who are near death do well to discuss their impending doom with honest terms. She tried a different tack, seeking first to console him so that rational conversation might occur. "So, why are we going to the doctor at all then?"

Jonah said nothing, his sniffles telling her that he was preoccupied with his own wallowing. When he finally looked up at Mary Lou, she merely raised her eyebrows to prompt a response.

"When you met me," Jonah said, "I had lost my faith in God. Today, because you are here, it is restored. I will pray before we go."

"I will pray as well," she said. "Do not think for a moment that I don't want to be here. I have great plans for our life."

"And we are going to conquer all of them," Jonah said, halfheartedly, then hurriedly tacked on, "with God's help."

"With God's help." They both closed their eyes and bowed their heads. Jonah led them in prayer, inspired by Mary Lou.

"Our Father," Jonah began with a trembling voice, "we come before You, this day, to glorify Your name. You are Almighty and wise. You know all things and can do all things. We humbly approach Your throne to ask that Mary Lou be spared more suffering, that our lives together may thrive, that no disease put asunder what You have brought together."

"Please keep me with Jonah," Mary Lou whispered. "Amen." They squeezed each other's hands, then leaned in to kiss each other.

"Every moment with you is a delight," Jonah said.

Still upset at the prospect of dying, Mary Lou failed to acknowledge the compliment. "Your tea is getting cold."

"The food looks delicious," Jonah said, unable to tell her that he had lost his appetite. The road beckoned, and Jonah was bent to answer the call. An entire night lay before them before they would get the answers they sought. The couple rose and made their way to bed, Mary Lou having decided that the opportune time to discuss her concerns with Jonah would come only after having the test results. Neither fell asleep until just before it was time to get up.

Jonah dressed and went to fetch the horse and buggy. Mary Lou prepared a small continental breakfast and some coffee. The night's fast did nothing to build their appetite. When Jonah returned, he ate a bit, but he desperately wanted to leave. The longer they were delayed, the worse he felt. Jonah returned to the buggy to wait for his beloved to finish up indoors before she joined him. Mary Lou went upstairs to vomit, then made haste to prepare herself.

Having spotted her standing still through the kitchen window, Jonah called out to her, "Are you ready?"

"Yes," Mary Lou said. She exited the house carrying a small travel bag.

Mary Lou sometimes carried a small purse, but she never brought a duffle bag. "What's that?"

"It's an overnight bag."

"Why?"

"In case it's back, and I have to stay the night," Mary Lou said, then she climbed into the buggy.

Jonah turned to see her, incredulous at her preparedness. Hadn't they prayed? Wouldn't God answer? Surely, they would live a long life together. "You won't," he said. "Put it back."

"Jonah, we should still pack the bag," Mary Lou objected.

Her beloved glanced at the bag, then at her, then back at the bag, before looking forward.

"It's a bad omen. It's a sign that we lack faith."

"There may still be a chance that I have to stay overnight in the city hospital, and I don't want to be stuck without the things that make me comfortable," Mary Lou protested.

Jonah sighed, then snapped the reins. The sky was blue, the birds chirped, the air was fresh and pleasant, enough to encourage any optimist that it would be a fine day. He couldn't bring himself to accept that God would pick such a day to deliver terrible news.

And so, Jonah and Mary Lou were off to the city that neither of them had visited for months. There was a time when they couldn't fathom leaving the city. Nowadays, the Amish lifestyle was all they could imagine for themselves.

"Did you write to your mother?" Jonah asked. "Did you tell

her that you are worried?"

"She knows the appointment is today, and she said that she would pray for me."

"We'll need the whole community to be praying for you."

They rode in silence, Mary Lou preoccupied with her nausea, and Jonah thinking that her eyes were closed because she was praying. Soon, the city lay before them. A sense of dread overcame Jonah. He struck up a conversation to distract himself from the fear. "Do you remember when we used to live here?" He pointed to the street that they used to take to their large house.

Mary Lou smiled, albeit pitifully, like she awoke from a nightmare to find breakfast in bed. "I have such fond memories of living there."

"The actors were fun," Jonah remembered. He managed a smile, remembering how Porsche and Johanna would tease him about having an Amish girlfriend. "We were in love and unsure of what to make of it."

Mary Lou smiled, though, in her current state, one could be forgiven for concluding that she had grimaced. "We're still in love," she said, softly.

"Yes," Jonah agreed, taking his eyes off the road to gaze at her, "we are."

The confession of love was the last Mary Lou and Jonah were able to hear of each other, for the city's noise overtook their senses, deafening them to reason, empathy, and logic, leaving in their place fear, mistrust, and a growing sense that all others on the road were blithering idiots who did not watch where they were going. Indeed, Jonah could see eyes directed only to the palms before them, as though led by a luminescent Pied Piper.

The couple eventually made it to the hospital, a place of dark memories of Mary Lou in a coma, unable to wake, enveloped in tubes and wires, flanked by bleeping screens and lights, the picture of a girl who had not quite lived, yet was not quite dead. Jonah shivered. *Lord, may it not be so this time,* he prayed. The buggy stopped, and Mary Lou's beau disembarked first to assist her down and to escort her in.

What a gentleman! she thought.

The place was bustling; the hurried traffic exiting to get on with their lives collided with the moderate pace of the sickly who sought care, creating a bottleneck at the entrance. "Wow," Jonah said, "it seems that the whole city is here today."

Mary Lou was preoccupied with the mass that swirled around them. "Or maybe we are just used to our quiet community?"

The sea of people made the hospital loom impossibly large. The task of merely checking in seemed overwhelming. Then there was the wait for the elevator ride with nowhere to sit. Mary Lou felt faint. Jonah held her tightly around the waist.

"Mary Lou!" said one of the nurses, "How are you today?"

"I'm doing well," Mary Lou lied. The Amish girl could not recognize the face. "I am nervous though."

"Don't be nervous, sweetie. It's just a follow-up. Anything bothering you?"

"I feel weak," Mary Lou confessed.

"Here, come with me." The nurse led them to the front of the line for the elevator, and they embarked together.

"Thank you," Mary Lou said, squeezing Jonah's hand with her right and covering her mouth with the other.

"What room are we going into?" Jonah asked.

"Room number six," the nurse responded. "The doctor will be in shortly."

Jonah escorted his wife into the room and then sat on the chair opposite the hospital bed.

"Did you finish your chores this morning?" Mary Lou asked.

"Yes," Jonah replied. "Of course, there will be the normal afternoon chores when we get back, but I'll be fine."

"If we get back," she said.

Jonah gave her a look, like a father telling his child to keep quiet in church. "I'd rather you didn't say such things. We must believe."

"I do believe. I've always believed. I've always trusted that, whatever path God is taking us on, He knows best."

Jonah was inspired by her faith, for his own had been a mere façade, for his own sake, to prevent him from unraveling. When the doctor entered, Jonah was beside himself with nerves.

"How are you, Mary Lou?" the doctor asked.

Jonah couldn't help but answer for his wife. "Don't let her say good. She's not been well."

The doctor looked surprised, then turned to Mary Lou. "Is that true?"

Mary Lou nodded, pitifully, as though a child caught in a lie. "It's just been small things, maybe nothing to worry about."

"Tell me what's been bothering you."

Looking torn, Mary Lou began her narrative truthfully, adding detail when prompted, avoiding her husband's gaze. Jonah soon realized that she had not told him everything. It was obvious why she would not look at him.

"You fainted?" Jonah exclaimed.

"Just a little," Mary Lou said.

"What do you mean, *just a little*? How do you faint *just a little*?"

Neither Mary Lou nor the doctor ventured an answer.

"I'd like to run some additional tests, Mary Lou. Would that be fine with you? You'll have the results today."

Mary Lou nodded. A nurse escorted her to the lab, where she was instructed to roll up her sleeve and to make a fist. Mary Lou obeyed. She shivered and seemed frail. Her skin was translucent. Her twig-like arms seemed as though they would break under the weight of the needle and vial. Then came the urine sample, and the couple was then off waiting for the results.

"We should pray," Jonah said, reaching for Mary Lou's hand. There was nothing else to do, nothing with which he might help, nothing to control. There was only waiting. Mary Lou took his hand

and lowered her head. Jonah prayed aloud for ten minutes, sometimes forgetting their place in a waiting area, stopping only for a drink for his parched throat. It was when he paused that Mary Lou noted how their spirits lifted. They were no longer afraid, but, rather, secure in their Heavenly Father's might and guiding hand.

"Thy will be done," Mary Lou concluded.

"Maybe this is working," Jonah pondered. "Maybe this is what God wants us to do, to pray more. Maybe we don't pray enough."

"I do feel like we have been busy lately," Mary Lou concurred. "And we have not been praying as much as we could."

"Maybe we should offer to host a Bible study of our own?" Jonah asked.

"That would be lovely," Mary Lou said. "I would love that."

The two became so enthralled with their plans to host a small group, losing themselves in what to serve for refreshments, when to have it, at what time, and what would be the first book studied that they did not hear their names called. What broke the spell was the nurse screaming Mary Lou's name out a third time.

"Here," Jonah said, waving his hand. Mary Lou braced herself using Jonah's bent arm and arose. They were led to an office where the doctor awaited.

"Mary Lou, Jonah, I have the test results from earlier."

The couple held each other's hands, keeping their eyes on the doctor and refusing so much as to blink.

"The symptoms you gave me prompted me to order these tests. Given your medical history, I think that it is appropriate to take all of the necessary precautions. In this case, I am glad you are both sitting down."

Jonah could feel his heart sink into his stomach. Mary Lou sniffed. They each looked gloomy.

"Did you find something?" Jonah ventured. *Is she going to die?* is what he really wanted to ask.

"We did," the doctor said. He shifted his gaze to the downcast Amish girl. Mary Lou had her hand on her lap and fiddled with her dress. "Is the cancer back?" she asked, though she did not want to hear the answer.

"No," replied the doctor said.

The couple sighed, relieved, and the tension lifted but for a hair's breadth. Then Jonah spoke up. "Then, what did you find?"

"Is it worse?" Mary Lou chimed.

"The tests today showed something else. It was as I had predicted when you enumerated your symptoms earlier, but I wanted to be sure. I can now tell you why you've been sick." He then paused.

Mary Lou, eyes wide and fixed on the doctor's every word, urged him on. "Please, continue."

"Mary Lou," the doctor began, slowly, "the tests today showed that the reason why you are sick is…" and he paused.

Jonah and Mary Lou both leaned in from their seats.

"…you're going to be a mother." And the doctor broke into a wide grin.

"I'm going to…what?" Mary Lou stammered.

Jonah turned to look at her, and with bated breath managed to say, "You're going to be a mother! I'm going to be a dad!" He shrieked his last words and slapped his thighs, the sound of which triggered tears of joy from Mary Lou. The poor creature washed away her tension and fear with saltwater, placing her hand over her belly to acknowledge the life inside her.

Then Jonah was pale. Ever the practical one, he had to know: "Is it safe?"

"Yes. I'd like to keep a close eye on her, but she should be fine."

"So that would explain everything?" Jonah asked. "The way she's been feeling and everything?"

"Yes," the doctor replied. "We Englishmen call it *morning sickness*. It ought to pass a little later on.

"I can't believe this," Jonah replied. "I can't believe this."

"Is this a happy occasion?" the doctor asked.

Jonah and Mary Lou looked at each other and nodded, unable to speak for the joy within them.

"This is fantastic!" Jonah beamed with pride. "I can't believe it. We prayed to God to give us life, and He gave us another one! He giveth abundantly more!"

"We have been blessed," Mary Lou said, as she looked up at Jonah. "We've been blessed by a miracle."

"It is a miracle!" Jonah said, then turned to the doctor. "Are you sure that it's okay?"

"It's okay," the doctor assured the nervous father-to-be. "It is my understanding that most Amish women do not seek prenatal care, but given Mary Lou's medical history, I recommend that she gets regular check-ups. We're going to take care of her every step of the way."

Jonah hugged Mary Lou, then pulled her away to gaze into her eyes as though they would tell them whether this were true, that he could believe in what had just transpired. *"Ich liebe dich,"* he said, "and I can't wait to start this journey with you."

"Ich liebe dich auch," Mary Lou said. "You are going to be the best father who has ever existed!"

They embraced again, though this time, they let in linger. Eyes closed, Jonah prayed silently in his heart. *Thank You, God for always being there, for Your generosity, for Your kindness, and thank You for Mary Lou. Thank you for returning my wife to me along with a miracle.*

ABOUT THE AUTHOR

Sylvia Price first met Mennonite missionaries in Montréal when she was 13 years old. She was captivated by their faithfulness to Christ, their politeness, their calm lifestyle—especially in comparison to the bustle of a major city—and how they could enjoy the simplest things to the fullest. When they opened their home for her to stay with them for three weeks, she was made to feel like family. Their enduring legacy in her life was to get her a library card and to encourage her to start reading to cope with the loss of television and radio. With a new-found appreciation for books, Sylvia set her sights on Bible college and then seminary, in service of the Lord. She now spends her time writing, hoping to inspire the next generation to read more stories.

Subscribe to Sylvia's newsletter at newsletter.sylviaprice.com to stay in the loop about new releases, freebies, promos, and more.

Learn more about Sylvia at amazon.com/author/sylviaprice and goodreads.com/author/show/1134593.Sylvia_Price.

Follow Sylvia on Facebook at facebook.com/sylviapriceauthor for updates.

Join Sylvia's Advanced Reader Copies (ARC) team at arcteam.sylviaprice.com to get her books for free before they are released in exchange for honest reviews.